I0636317

JEX BLACKWELL SAVES THE WORLD

P. WILLIAM GRIMM

Jex Blackwell Saves the World by P. William Grimm

ISBN: 978-1-938349-77-5

eISBN: 978-1-938349-82-9

Library of Congress Control Number: 2017957285

Copyright © 2018 P. William Grimm

This work is licensed under the Creative Commons Attribution-NonCommercial-NoDerivatives 4.0 International License. To view a copy of this license, visit http://creativecommons.org/licenses/by-nc-nd/4.0/.

Cover art by Emily Timm

Heart and Stethoscope illustration by Cardiac Cat

Layout and book design by Mark Givens

Excerpt from GREAT MISTAKE MAKER by Spoonboy. Written by David Combs and used by permission of the artist. All rights reserved.

Excerpt(s) from ONE FLEW OVER THE CUCKOO'S NEST: A NOVEL by Ken Kesey, copyright © 1976 by Ken Kesey. Used by permission of Penguin Random House LLC. All rights reserved.

Excerpt from CRICKETS IN THE RAIN by Allo Darlin'. Written by Allo Darlin'. Published by Angular Publishing, Ltd and used by permission. All rights reserved.

First Pelekinesis Printing 2018

For information:

Pelekinesis, 112 Harvard Ave #65, Claremont, CA 91711 USA

www.pelekinesis.com

JEX BLACKWELL SAVES THE WORLD

P. WILLIAM GRIMM

CONTENTS

For Emily

FREE-STYLING

JEX BLACKWELL IS NOT A FRIGHTENED GIRL. The alley is dark. It is raining lightly. The streetlights stream through the fog, soaking the alley in a faint glow. The scene is reminiscent of a Sherlock Holmes book or Dashiell Hammett novel. Jex has read them all, from *A Study in Scarlet* to *The Thin Man*, and so she is confident of two things: the hero always gets it right and the hero never dies. The problem, Jex thinks to herself, is that she is no hero. She never gets it right and in her sixteen years, she has come close to dying more than once, with only dumb luck between her and the reaper. Still, she loves the hazy street, the late night, the piercing silence of the downtown evening. Standing precariously on an old oil barrel, she shakes a can of spray paint. The only sound in the cool Los Angeles night is the rhythm of the glacket clacking like a broken Christmas bell.

Jex sometimes stencils when she tags, but tonight she is going free-style. It is a throwie design that is mostly in her head and she didn't have time to cut the stencils, anyways. This project won't take long. In any event, free-style is just that, free. Jex is feeling like she needs some freedom tonight. The day was rough and the sun couldn't set fast enough. The quieting of the angry din of the day came slowly, but finally it came. Cars and people and the inevitable conflict that goes with them bring out things in Jex that she does not like – anger and sadness and rage. So, mostly she hides in the daytime. When the moon rises and spreads its arms around the city, Jex can relax a little bit. The combination of precision and panic that forms the art of free-style tagging is a meditative environment for Jex. The long strokes and quick bursts of spray paint, with the ever-looming possibility of a fast run from the cops or some angry random tagger, somehow calms Jex. It allows her to think. In the moment is the only time she can really think.

Jex never listens to music when she tags. Too many risks out there, and she has to stay sharp. It's too bad because Jex loves music. Her favorite band right now is Mischief Brew, a folk punk band from Philadelphia. They are old school as hell, for sure, but if you ask Jex, she would tell you how rad they are, her Southern California twang popping up and down in a sing-song tone she uses only when discussing subjects that interest her. Those sorts of subjects are few and far between, but Mischief Brew is at the top of the short list. She knows these songs well, old friends each of them. They ring around in her head when she is tagging, an imperfect but sufficient replacement for the music itself.

The song is slightly out of tune in Jex's head, blunt pounding on an acoustic guitar, Eric Peterson screaming out about hopes and dreams and fears. Peterson isn't around anymore, his time ended by his own hand, and so neither is Mischief Brew. But Jex is still here. And Jex still has her dreams.

Jex steps off the barrel and carefully plops three feet to the ground. She has done the same thing a hundred times before and so she moves with grace and purposefulness, almost silently. She peers left and right. Seeing nobody, she takes a moment to appreciate her work. The graffiti is about two feet high and two feet wide - taking up most of the center of the alley wall. It covers up a couple of faded out pieces but not anything by anybody that would give Jex concern. Jex's piece is mostly red with outlines and highlights of black here and there. The tag is simple but bold, the same way she has tagged it all over the city, from Venice to Silver Lake and back.

* * *

Jex looks the piece up and down, and nods her head in approval. Not her worst work, not by a long shot, but it's OK. She looks down at her left hand, which is covered in black paint, and wiggles her now-aching fingers. It is not her first tag of the night. She is dressed in a long sleeve gray sweatshirt and blue jeans with a hole in the knee. Her black Chucks are covered in a splatter swirl of paint – black, gray, white, red and more – and her short dirty blonde hair is pulled back in a small ponytail. She wears the same thing all the time, her look is as simple and punk elegant as her graffiti. No posing. No bullshit. She pulls out a pack of Camel Crushs and lights one up. She puffs out smoke and crushes the filter between her fingers. It brings a weird satisfaction, and Jex disappears into thought.

"Jexie, Jexie!! It's the Pope. Jexie, Jexie. PoPo."

The young girl, she couldn't have been any older than Jex, probably younger, appears out of nowhere and is running as she shouts out her warning. "Jexie, Jexie. It's the Pope." She has dark hair, stands maybe five feet, and is wearing a black backpack, black jeans and a black long sleeve shirt. She disappears as quickly as she appeared.

Jex disappears even faster. By the time the young girl is past her, Jex has already climbed the fire escape ladder and is in the hallway of the building. She blasts through the stairwell, slams open the roof door, and is outside again, five stories up. Blue and red lights illuminate the streets below, but Jex is far enough up that the colors are faded and hollow.

Jex pauses for a moment to listen to her breathing compete with the radios echoing through the alley. After a moment it is clear that the cops aren't looking to harass taggers tonight. Someone shot someone somewhere and the police want to know about it. Jex, having nothing of interest to say on the subject, moves along at a leisurely pace over several buildings before deciding to open a roof door and head down back to the street almost a block past the cops. Even with nothing to hide, Jex is happy to keep her distance. Maybe everybody has something to hide.

Five minutes or so pass before Jex hears the sounds of a skateboard coming up fast behind her. She can tell by the sound of the wheels hitting the concrete who it is, so she doesn't flinch at all. "Thanks for the heads up," she says without bothering to even look up.

"Oh, no problem," says Q. "Fuck the police." Q, the young girl who gave the warning earlier, her chin up as she jumps off the board, kicks its tail and it flies up into her waiting hand. She starts to walk next to Jex but finds she needs to nearly jog to keep up. . "They're nothing but haters," she shrugs.

"That's for sure," Jex mutters quietly, almost silently, as she stares aimlessly down the alleyway. "I"ve got no time for cops."

"Me neither," Q quickly agrees, her head bobbing up and down. "I think it was about that bum down on Grand Street. The one with the big blue hat and yellow pants. You know that one?"

"Yeah," Jex confirms aimlessly. "I think I remember seeing him. I don't know him, though."

"Yeah, I didn't know him, either, but I heard he was dead. Dead as could be after he got beat up by two guys."

It doesn't seem to phase Jex at all. "Where did you hear that from?"

Q just shrugs. "I just heard it," she says.

Jex smiles. "You just heard it?"

"Yeah, I just heard it."

The two walk awhile in silence, onto Broadway. The night is dark and there are few people around. Some of the old lights of Broadway still flicker on and off but mostly it is dead so late at night. Downtown Los Angeles being what it is, it is dead most of the time, late at night or not.

Q seems awkward and she is the first one to break the silence.

"Anyways, I just been walking around tonight, not doing much of anything. I was at the library until closing time and then I just been walking around."

"Yeah, I was working tonight, shelving books until it closed."

"Yeah, I saw you but you looked busy and I thought you looked like you could use some space so I didn't say anything."

Q stops speaking for a moment, that kind of pause you allow when you are hoping someone is going to say something. Jex doesn't say anything and so Q starts up talking again.

"Yeah, anyways, other than that, I haven't been doing too much. Did some dumpster diving behind the Standard. Nothin' there but half a beer, and I didn't want any beer."

"That's good."

"Yeah."

The silence returns for a moment as the two walk down Broadway, heading with determination precisely nowhere. Q's phone breaks the silence, a digital frog's strained ribbit. Q looks down and reads a text. She shrugs again, in the way she does, not quite angry and not quite sad; some kind of twisted frustration she knows too well for someone of this age.

"So hey, Jex, I was meaning to ask you this, but I didn't yet."

"What's that," Jex responds with a sigh, as though she knew the text was not anything good. As though she had heard the same build-up to a request many times before and they were never good.

"So you know that woman, Betsy? The one that used to work at the 7-11?"

"You mean the one with the tattoo on her face?"

Q pauses. "No, that's Jolene. She still works at the 7-11. Betsy is the one with the long fingernails that doesn't work there no more – she has the nose ring like you have."

"Septum ring," Jex specifies.

"Yeah, a septum ring. That's what I said. The one with the long fingernails and the septum ring. You remember her."

"I remember her. She was pregnant, right?"

Q's eyes light up. "Yes! Yes! That's the one," almost hopping. "The pregnant one. She was pregnant. She had the kid like four months ago. It's a boy. His name is Ben."

"Congrats to Betsy. Now she's a mommy," Jex responds, something like sarcasm dripping from her words.

Q continues with a renewed reluctance in her voice. "Well, anyways, yeah, she's a mom now. And the baby has been crying, like, non-stop."

"That's what babies do," Jex interrupted. "They cry like non-stop. It's why they are a pain in the butt and you shouldn't have them when you're, like... what is that girl, twenty?"

Q studies her sneakers as she walks. After a few moments, Jex continues.

"So … the baby cries. What els..."

"The thing is," Q breaks in excitedly, "Ben has this stupid high fever. And it's, like, totally off the charts. And I know you don't know Betsy or nothing, but trust me, Betsy isn't the kind of girl to be taking her baby to a doctor and all that. She's like off the grid, you know?"

Jex shakes her head. "Nice," she whispers with a hint of anger or frustration or something.

"Yeah, well, anyways. She isn't never going to go to a doctor with a sick baby. She just don't trust anybody. But the fever is really bad and when I went there today, I went there after the library closed, when I went there, the baby was like really hot. I tried to pick him up but man that baby wailed. And I have held that baby like ten times before at least and he always loves me. It was like he was in pain or something. Like he was just lying there doing nothing but sobbing and I picked him up and he just squealed. And he was so hot, it was like he was in a microwave or something."

Jex doesn't respond but Q can see that she piqued her interest, however reluctant it might be. There is a long pause and Q, now impatient, begins to talk again. There's not time for Jex to get to the point in her own good time. She knows the point.

"So, anyways, Jex, you know, I was wondering, if you're not doing anything, you know, you're all smart and shit, and I was thinking, maybe Betsy wouldn't see no doctor, but…"

"But maybe she'll let some punk kid play doctor on her," Jex interjects, shaking her head.

Q looks at her with those pleading brown eyes, wide and insidiously innocent. "You know you could Jex. You're almost like a fucking doctor already, with all those books you're reading and that stuff in your bag. You're like Inspector Gadget. If you saw her and you talk the way you do and you check her out, I bet you could tell her what's wrong. I bet you could tell her and get her to go a doctor."

"I volunteer as an intern at the hospital when I'm not working at the library," Jex smiles. "Pulling sheets off beds and shit. Not exactly a medical professional."

"Aw, bullshit, Jex, you know you do all kinds of cray-cray shit at the hospital. Remember that time you helped that guy who thought he had gas and he was really having a stroke and you …"

Jex cuts her off. "And I have no doubt I could tell her to go to a doctor. What I can't get her to do is to listen."

"But you can try," Q protests. "That baby is so hot, Jex. I'm worried. "Q touches Jex's arm and the two stop walking for a moment. "Come on. Do it for Ben. I am asking you, not for Betsy, but for the baby. At least see the baby."

Jex looks down at Q, and then she looks left and right, as if someone or something might be coming down the street that would lift her up and out of this interaction. Having no such luck, she lets out a heavy sigh, the weight of the world on her shoulders. But it doesn't seem to slow her down.

"Shit," utters Jex in a tone of resignation, pulling absently on her ponytail. "OK. We can at least see the baby."

* * *

It is some time after midnight when Jex and Q step into the dirty apartment building, just a couple blocks east of the Mayan Theater. The hallway smells sweet, but not sweet like candy – sweet like something bad. Q doesn't react to it, maybe because she was there earlier in the day and knew what to expect. Jex doesn't react to it, either, maybe because she just doesn't care; maybe something else.

"Knock again," Jex urges. Q resists, saying, "it hasn't been a minute."

"Yeah, but are we going to stand here out in the hallway all friggin' night?" Crap apartment hallways late at night don't scare Jex. But why tempt fate?

"Give it a minute," Q says in a loud whisper.

"Uchhh," Jex groans and raps on the door herself. The suddenness of the knock causes Q to jump. She punches Jex in the arm but the rapping seems to do the trick, as something stirs behind the door of apartment 204. After another moment, the door cracks open. There isn't much light but Jex can see Betsy's face. She seems even younger than Jex remembered, not much older than Jex. It is clear she is agitated.

"What you want, Q? And who the hell you have with you? You know I'm busy. You know I'm distracted."

Betsy moves to close the door but Q is quick, sticking her Doc Marten in between the door and the skirt of the doorway. "Boo, wait a second," Q pleads to Betsy. "This is the girl that I told you about. She can help you." Her voice shifts to a whisper. "She can help Ben."

Betsy's eyes widen in disbelief. "This little punk bitch can help me?" she yelps incredulously. "Q, you gotta stop doing whatever drugs you be doing, or give some of 'em to me, else you crazy as this little white girl if you think she's going anywhere near my baby."

Q squishes up her face in protest. "Boo, don't be like that. I am telling you, if you trust me, you can trust Jex. She …"

Jex interrupts Q in a voice that is suddenly calm and cool. "Betsy, my name is Jex Blackwell. I may not know much, but I know how to figure out if major, basic illnesses or sicknesses are present. Triaging, it's called. I have received training directly from the chief medical officer at County USC, Dr. Catherine Stephens. I have a stethoscope and otoscope and a baby thermometer and everything else I need to get an initial sense of whether your baby is just throwing his first temper tantrum or whether it might be something worse. Your baby is four months old Q tells me, which means the immunoglobulins that you transferred to him in your last twelve weeks of pregnancy — the things that protect him from sickness and bad stuff — have pretty much disappeared from his body, but he is still too young to develop his own immunoglobulins. He is vulnerable right now. That also means he is still too young to be vaccinated against some of the worst stuff he can expect to see in his life. Seriously."

Betsy's expression turned blank as Jex spoke. She responds equally blankly. "She's not getting vaccinated. I don't want her to get autistic."

Jex takes a deep breath before waving the comment off with her hand. "I am not going to address that because it really doesn't matter right now. This is a very risky stage of a baby's life. With just a little bit of care, though, he will be just fine and he probably is." She pauses for just a moment to study Betsy's face, still blank, before she continues. "He probably is. The point is that I can look at him, just for a minute, and maybe, at the very least, I can tell Q to go shut her mouth and stop butting in, because, frankly, I don't really want to be here any more than you want me here."

Betsy stares for a moment more before stepping back from the door: "Come in."

Inside, Jex looks around the dark apartment, lights off with blinds closed shut. It is a small place with a tiny foyer that leads into a series of small rooms. The walls are dirty, but the apartment itself is relatively tidy. "Is it just you and the baby here?" Jex asks Betsy.

"Naw, I have two roommates. They out right now."

Betsy leads Jex and Q into a small bedroom. There is not much more than a bed, a crib and a small closet stuffed with clothes. There is a table and a chair. Not much more than that. The window is covered with a blanket, which seems to Jinx to be pink, but maybe not. The room is dark, no lights other than a Minion nightlight. Jex squints her eyes and shifts her focus quickly to baby Ben. She walks over and peers into the crib. Q and Betsy follow and gather behind her. It is immediately obvious that something is not right.

"Something is not right," Jex mumbles under her breath as she furrows her brow in concentration. The baby is still but his eyes are open, though only narrowly, no more than thin slits.

"Oh, dear lord," Betsy murmurs, her eyes clouding over.

"Don't worry, Betsy. It will be OK." Jex speaks her words with a calmness that is tangible. It eases the pain of the silence just a bit.

"See," Betsy explained. "He don't cry or nothing when he's lying there like that. But if I try to pick him up to feed him or something, he just wails. He just wails away, like the dead is rising up."

Still looking at the baby, Jex says, "I am sure that's not how he normally acts, right?"

"No way, honey. Up until last night, the only thing that would stop him from crying is hugging his mama." Betsy's next words come out with a choke. "Now it just makes him bawl away."

Jex nodded her head up and down. "How's he eating? "

"He doesn't barely eat at all now. Yesterday, I couldn't pull the food away from him… It's a little unsettling. But the fact that he won't let me pick him up without crying … I just can't take that."

Jex nods. "The doctors call it paradoxical pain. Like something hurts when it shouldn't; and doesn't hurt when it does."

Betsy's eyes open wide. "So what does that mean? Is he OK?"

Jex returns her attention to Ben, and looks him carefully in the eye, once with her blind eyes and once with an otoscope. He squints and squirms, squeals at the light of the otoscope. She gingerly places his finger on the baby's head. He is hot to the touch. Jex traces the round circumference of the baby's small head, from the eyebrow all the way to the back of the head. The baby murmurs a bit but does not cry. Jex seems to notice something.

Jex shrugs. "His fontanel seems to be swelled."

"His what?" question both Q and Betsy at the exact same time in unison.

"His fontanel. It's the soft spot on his head that newborns have. It seems a little swelled." She inspects Ben's head again, putting her finger near his skull but not touching it. "Maybe a lot swelled."

"Oh dear lord. But that soft spot is normal for a baby," Betsy objects. "Even I know that. Right?" The last word is said with something resembling doubt, maybe hope.

"Yeah, it's completely normal. The plates in the skull don't fully close until around two years so it's not a big deal. But his seems a little … swelled." There is a short pause. "And I suppose you have all the lights turned out because the light makes him cry?"

Betsy's eyes open wide. "Yeah," she confirms in a disbelieving tone. "How'd you know that?"

"And, uh, well, has anything weird happened to him? Like shaking or something in a weird way for a couple of minutes? You know, like a seizure?"

"No," Q answers. "there hasn't been anything like that. She would have gone to the hospital for sure if something like that happened."

Jex and Q look at Betsy, who suddenly has an odd look on her face. She doesn't say anything and the room suddenly fills with tension.

"There hasn't been nothing like that, right Betsy?" Q asks, the smallest bit of hesitation now in her voice.

Jex takes her turn. "Betsy, it's kind of super important to know if something like that happened."

Flustered and desperate, Betsy breaks down. "It was just once and it only lasted a minute or two. I wasn't even sure it really happened. Still not sure."

"Shit, Boo, that shit happened and you didn't tell me? What the hell?" Q bursts out in an anguished wail.

Betsy breaks down, tears and snot all over her, and drops flaccidly into Q's small body. "No, no, it just happened. An hour ago. It was after you left. I swear. I didn't know what to do. It was so scary. What am I supposed to do? Those doctors scare me to death." Q holds her hard, and then turns to Jex in a panic.

The room tilts and turns; swirling and spiraling. Betsy and Q hold onto one another for dear life, like they are passengers on a sinking ship. The baby wakes up and begins to cry. Outside, a dog begins to bark. The floor beneath them begins to wobble. Chaos is beginning to descend in the small apartment.

"Jex!" Q cries out. "Please, take out your stethoscope and that other stuff from your bag and figure out what is wrong."

Jex stands up and holds her hands firmly on her hips. Her voice is calm and strong, no quivering or doubt to be found. "I don't need any of that stuff to know what's wrong with Ben. I know exactly what's up."

[What's the problem with Ben? Will he be OK? Turn to page 159 to read Jex's diagnosis and the conclusion of the story.]

FREE-STYLING

AFTER LEVIATHAN

JEX BLACKWELL IS DANCING WITH HERSELF. To paraphrase an ancient guitar hero, every single night of the week provides the opportunity for a different band to be the best in the world, depending on the stage and the crowd and the vibe between the two. Tonight, the best band in the world is a Macedonian anarchist punk collective, banging away in a sweaty, sultry basement somewhere in the middle of Echo Park. There is no stage and so the band is eye level with the crowd, which consists of maybe two dozen people. All four band members are consumed with their music, the guitarist particularly animated, dancing up and down with abandon. The female singer twists and turns with the music, wrapping the microphone cord around her body like a cocoon, yelping loudly in Macedonian over the chug of the rhythm section, bass and drums.

Jex Blackwell pogos around the crowd, lost in the music, lost in her mind. Or maybe just lost. She does not understand any of the foreign language lyrics, but they resonate inside her anyways. Maybe it is the vibration of the floor. Maybe it is something else. She smiles to herself, her neck extended up as the music streams over her face.

Despite the torrid heat, Jex is dressed as usual – gray long sleeve sweatshirt, a black v-neck t-shirt underneath, shapeless black pants and black Chucks on her feet. Sweat dripping down her forehead and down her short ponytail, the heat does not seem to bother her or slow her down at all. She has dealt with much worse. She moves back and forth to the hard Macedonian rhythm, somehow connected to the crowd beating around her while still managing to be completely separate from it.

Flailing around is not unusual at punk shows, sweaty bodies coming in contact with one another. Crowd-surfing. Dancing. Small rooms. Low ceilings. If asked, Jex would say that people are mostly cool at shows, trying to avoiding hurting anyone and staying away from people much smaller than them when dancing hard. But every scene has its issues, and bro-punks can be a real issue in the punk scene, Jex knows. She keeps her eyes on her environment, a particularly important task for her, as she mostly goes to shows alone and so can't rely on anyone to have her back. She knows all that stuff about safe spaces and a woman's right to be free from violation and you shouldn't be forced to be cautious. She can't agree more, but she still keeps an eye open and an eye on the exit door, just in case. She knows most of the pain-in-the-ass bros – and some pains-in-the-asses that aren't bros at all. Some people like to start fights; some like to grab an ass or more. Jex knows the usual characters and stays the hell away. She keeps her distance when she can. She fights back when needed.

One of those bro-punks is Archer. A sophomore at USC, Archer is tall and lanky, a lacrosse ace in high school that found the scene in his freshman year. He listens to Against Me! like they are AC/DC. Jex has heard him described as a macktivist: he goes to anarchy fests and vegan bake-ins to meet scenesters to screw, not to get involved with the issues. Said differently, he is a frat boy who listens to Jeffrey Lewis just enough to occasionally seal the deal with some punk girl. Jex doesn't really know if any of that is actually true or just a bad reputation, but she doesn't care much, either.

Regardless of whether he is actually a cad, Archer is on her list of people to watch, which is why she is watching him when he begins to move a little funny. The change is subtle at first, and she barely notices it out of the side of her eye. The music is booming and the room is hot, so everyone is a little exhausted in their exhilaration. A change in movement is not that unusual.

Jex moves on in her thoughts as the band switches from one song to another. The basement is dripping with humidity and the room stinks of perspiration and homemade kombucha. Jex's dance is more jumping up and down then anything else, like a character from a 1973 era New York Dolls audience. She used to feel funny about people watching her dance. Now she just doesn't care. Thoughts of past and present and future flow through her head. She is a thousand miles away.

"Naw, he's not drunk," Jex hears a voice say to her left. "He's not. He went straight-edge like six months ago."

"Damn, he's heavy. And his skin is fucking cold. Shit."

The voices distract Jex from the vibe that is lifting her up and out of the room. Suddenly she is aware of her existence again, sucked straight into reality and plopped back on the bouncing dance floor, surrounded by hot, pulsing bodies, the room sweltering. She looks over to the voices and sees Archer. He is hanging on to one of his bro's shoulder and the bro does not seem pleased about it, his face scrunched into an angry snarl. There is a sorority chick with cut off jeans and a white tank top holding on to his other arm with both hands. He seems about to go down.

Jex does not hesitate. She pushes in front of the sorority chick and grabs Archer under the armpit. He is at least a foot taller than Jex, at least it seems that way to her. "We've got to get him to the back of the room and lay him down," she yells over the music. She has no time for delay. "He's going to fall over otherwise."

"He's fine," the bro protests. "He's just drunk as fuck."

"No, he's not drunk, Jason," pleads the sorority chick. "He's straight-edge like me. We didn't drink at all tonight."

"None of that matters," Jex yelps, slapping her head with one of her hands, while struggling to keep Archer on his wobbly legs with the other. "He is going to fall face first if we don't get him lying down like right now." Archer is murmuring now and his eyes are just slits in his head. He seems to be trying to focus on Jex, and at one point his hand is on her head, but he doesn't seem to be focusing much on anything at all. Jason the bro punk, could be right, maybe he is drunk, Jex calculates. But the sorority chick said he hasn't been drinking and, to Jex's eyes, he doesn't quite seem drunk. She begins to drag him to the back of the room. Jason the bro punk lets out a sigh of frustration but holds on to Archer's other arm and leads him along with Jex. He is so reliant on Jex and Jason that his feet are barely touching the ground.

Somehow, they manage to get Archer to the back of the room before he goes entirely limp. Jex looks up at the stairs and they seem treacherously steep. People seem to be going up and down non-stop, even though the band is still playing. There is a dude sitting at the top of the stairs, holding his head in his hands and blocking a portion of it. Now that guy looks drunk, Jex thinks to herself. She shakes her head back and forth. "There is no way we are going to get him upstairs," she shouts to Jason the bro punk. "We need to put him down right here." she continues. "I'll use my bag as a pillow," she declares and begins to lower Archer down, not waiting for a response from the bro dude.

Archer is non-resistant and, indeed, seems quite ready to completely drop. In a moment, he is lying down completely on the cold floor. Jex pulls her backpack off and uses it as a pillow to prop Archer's feet up. She opens the bag and pulls out a bottle of water, a small towel, a blood pressure monitor and a Snickers bar. She wastes no time and is by Archer's side in a quick moment, kneeling down low. She leans over and speaks quietly but firmly into his ear.

"Archer. Don't worry. You're OK. I think you just got yourself a little overheated. Chill out and relax for a minute. I've raised your feet over your head so there should be blood moving up. Relax. You're going to be OK. Just give it a minute."

Jex drenches the towel in the water and lays it across Archer's forehead. He lets out a relieved groan and lays his head back. He says something that sounds like, "guh." She pulls the blood pressure monitor from her side and wraps the cuff around Archer's upper arm. He looks up at Jex, still not quite focusing. "I think I pissed myself," he whispers, his voice shaky.

Jex locks her eyes into Archer, touching his face gently. It is sweaty and cold. "Don't sweat it, Archer. You had an episode of vasovagal syncope. When that happens, that is totally in line with what to expect."

Archer lifts his head up and scrunches his face, and after a moment, as Jex seems to come slightly into focus for him, just says, "huh?"

Jex smiles slightly. "Don't sweat it," she repeats. "Just relax." She reads the monitor. "Your blood pressure is ninety over sixty. That's pretty low. Just relax and chill out. You'll be fine in a minute." She releases the valve and the cuff loosens around Archer's arm.

He lowers his head to the ground and murmurs something again, but it isn't audible to Jex. He brings his hand to his crotch to feel it. He groans a bit when he confirms the wetness, and then lifts his head up again to look at Jex. "And I have a hard-on," he squeaks.

"Lovely," Jex retorts. "Again, completely normal for this kind of episode. So congratulations on that." A moment passes and Jex begins the process again. Thirty seconds pass. "You're 110 over 70. Getting better. Relax for a minute. Take some water."

He nods his head slowly, filled with shame. Jex hands him the water bottle. He drinks some. Jex pours a bit into her hand and rubs it on his face. After a minute, he rises up to his elbows and looks around. Jex notices for the first time that a crowd has gathered. The set seems to be over. Jex looks Archer in the eye again. "You're feeling better, aren't you," she asks. "The color is coming back into your face."

"What happened to him? Did he have like a spaz attack or something?" bro dude Jason demands over Jex's shoulder. She looks up at him menacingly.

"No, jackass. He didn't have a spaz attack. I think he had a vaso-vagal syncope episode. It's because this room is so hot, I bet. It's a trigger. And he hasn't had enough water." Jex turns to the sorority chick, who has been shocked into silence the entire time.

"Have you had much water to drink?" The girl just shakes her head slightly from side to side, not seeming to know quite what to say.

"Yeah, it's no big deal, really." She looks back at Archer. "Different people get triggered by different stuff you know … differently. Sometimes it's heat, standing up too long, flashing lights, dehydration, all that stuff. Loud music even. When that happens, and you get triggered – your parasympathetic nervous system, which is in charge of your body when it's relaxed, get enhanced; and your sympathetic nervous system, which tells your body when to fight or flee – you know your flight or fight instinct – that gets reduced. So your body is telling itself to relax and lay still so it can correct itself and get the blood flowing again. As soon as you laid down, your body started to fix itself immediately."

"Parasympathetic nervous system?" says Archer. "You mean like in the Andrew Jackson Jihad song?"

Jex smiles. "Yeah, kind of like in the AJJ song."

Jason the bro punk chimes in. "Sounds to me like the bitch had a spaz attack," and he chuckles.

Jex stands up and glares at the bro punk. "Sounds to me, bro," Jex says, "like you're a big friggin' jackass and don't know your ass from your elbow."

Jason the bro punk is instantly defensive. "What the hell do you know anyways? What are you, sixteen years old? Dumb-ass punk girl."

"You can say what you want, motherfucker," Jex counters quickly. "But I know you're a jackass who didn't hesitate to leave his bro behind."

Archer is sitting up now and looks up at Jex and Jason. Jason's face is turning red. "Yeah, whatever. Everyone knows you're a bitch wannabe poseur. And besides, I didn't leave anybody behind. I dragged his faggot ass over her." His voice is getting louder.

"Nice, dude. Well, here's the thing," Jex begins.

"No," Jason interrupts. "I'll tell you what the thing is…"

"Stop," Archer says, now up on his feet and fairly steady. "She helped me out, dude. Leave her alone."

Jason looks Archer up and down. "Did you piss on yourself?" Jason demands in an incredulous tone. The two are suddenly in one another's face.

At this point, a guy in a Mastodon shirt steps in. He seems older than most of the rest of the crowd, maybe in his late twenties, and has one of those presences that would be described as commanding. "Ok, enough. He seems OK now. Let it go."

Jason is not backing down. "I'll say when I will let it go."

Archer immediately shoots back. "No, I will say when it gets let go."

"Uchh," Jex exclaims in exasperation. She pushes a Snickers bar into Archer's hands. "Here, eat this. You shouldn't have gotten up so quickly, but now that you did, go ahead and eat this. And finish up that bottle of water. On the house. I have to pee now, so have a nice night all. I'm going upstairs."

With that, Jex grabs her backpack and heads towards the stairs. The guy in the Mastodon shirt follows her, but does not catch her in time. She closes the bathroom door before he even gets up the stairs.

When Jex gets out of the bathroom, the guy in the Mastodon shirt is waiting for her. "Hey, can you hold on a second?"

"No. move," she says in a derisive tone.

"I'm not hitting on you or anything," the guy in the Mastodon shirt protests. "I was just wondering how you did that. You know, so reflexively? It seems pretty incredible for someone as young as you."

"It's no big deal. Vasovagal syncope is totally common. I have read about it a bunch."

The guy in the Mastodon shirt smiles. "Doesn't seem like that would really be in books someone your age would read."

"Well, it is."

"You know a lot about medicine, huh?"

"Some."

"Well, I was just wondering …"

"Hey," Jex almost shouts, her eyes locked into the eyes of the guy with the Mastodon shirt. "Listen, dude. I just missed most of Bernays Propaganda's set. I have been listening to them for two years and I doubt they will ever tour in the States again and I missed it. That's just the way it is. So be it. But High Dive is up next, and I have no intention of missing them, too. So, please, thanks for the interest. I appreciate it. But, please get out of my way so I can get a spot near the stage before the show starts."

The guy in the Mastodon shirt steps aside, in genuinely surprised that he was blocking Jex's way. She is down the stairs and into the basement just a few seconds before High Dive goes on. In minutes, she is lost in the music again.

* * *

The show is over and the bathroom line is long. Jex is bummed that she has to pee again, but that's the way it goes sometimes. Her old friend Q found her after the show and is now talking her ear off. Jex loves Q and all but can't figure out which grates more on her nerves: the bathroom line or Q's incessant rambling. At fourteen, she is younger than Jex, but every bit as experienced on the streets. That doesn't make her tales or monologues any more interesting. Jex rubs her face.

"See, Jex, the thing I love about High Dive is the bass. It just kind of rumbles in the room. And Ginger's voice, of course. And the lyrics. The lyrics are the best. I mean, not the best. The Mountain Goats' lyrics are better. And probably the Weakerthans, too. And Pat the Bunny. But High Dive's lyrics are really awesome. So right in your face. Telling truth. Don't you like them, too, Jex?"

"Yeah," Jex agreed, nodding absently. "They are incredible. No arguments from me."

"Yeah," Q nodded back eagerly. "They're awesome. I mean, you couldn't ask for better. And Bernays Propaganda. They were out of this world. Don't you think so, Jex? What a set!"

"Yeah, yeah, I didn't really see much of them, though. But it seemed like a great set from what I saw."

"Oh, shit, right Jex. I'm sorry. I forgot you missed it." A pause. "It wasn't so great, though. Really."

"Yeah, Q," Jex shrugs. "Whatever."

There is another pause, a slightly awkward one. Jex could have fixed it all by just saying, "no big deal," or "I can handle it, it was worth it." Or something like that. And Q surely would have returned to her rapid fire observations. Instead, Jex just lets the silence stretch its legs for a moment.

A third voice breaks the silence. It is the guy with the Mastodon t shirt. "Hi ladies – that was a hell of a set by High Dive, right?"

Q is instantly reinvigorated. "Yes! I loved that version of 'These Are Days.' I saw them a while back and they were good but, man, it has gotten so much better."

The guy in the Mastodon shirt smiles. He turns to Jex. "So, what did you think?"

"Yeah," Jex responds dismissively, in a staccato tone that cloaks the lazy California inflection with which she speaks when she is with friends. "What Q said."

The guy in the Mastodon shirt continues. "Hey, I wanted to ask you about that guy that fainted before. . . "

Jex's mouth opens to retort in a way that would be more dismissive than her last comment. Before she gets out a word, though, Q chimes in. "Jex is a total bad ass. She can figure out what's wrong with anyone. And I mean anyone. I have seen the craziest shit and Jex is just cool as balls and totally figures it out – like out of nowhere. She's punk Sherlock Holmes for sure, but for, like, medicine. And she graduated high school when she was fifteen, like, without even really going to high school. All these bad ass colleges want her, and she's like, fuck them. But she's gonna be a doctor in no time. She can fix anybody. There was this one time …"

"Q, come on," Jex interrupts and Q immediately goes silent. After an awkward pause with Jex just wishing the bathroom line would disappear, Q squeaks out, "oh, yeah, and she's very private, too."

The guy in the Mastodon t-shirt chuckles, and speaks this time to Q, not Jex. "Yeah, I understand that. I have the blessing and curse of being a massive extrovert – strictly loud and annoying. These two are introverted weirdos," the guy in the Mastodon t-shirt gestures to two young men standing awkwardly behind him. They are dressed in grubby black from head to toe, and long hair down well past their shoulders. The two were totally invisible until the guy in the Mastodon t-shirt points them out. "Totally private, these two. But me, I'm an open book."

Q squints at him. "if you're so open, why don't I know your name?"

The guy in the Mastodon t-shirt laughs out loud. "Fair enough. I'm Sam. Nice to meet you, Q," extending a hand with a smile that seems genuine; not plastic. She accepts it reluctantly. "I'm the lead singer of Waters of Chaos."

With that, Sam turns to Jex. "An introvert, eh? Well, I won't even try to shake your hand."

"Thanks," Jex replies in a tone that is not shy but every bit as dismissive as her earlier tone.

"And as for that medical stuff," Sam continues, "That's pretty rad. Waters of Chaos could use it actually, cause I'm pretty sure we're all half deaf from so many years on stage. It would be cool for someone to let us know how we could fix that or something."

"You're not half deaf," Jex shoots back, looking the three of them up and down with a thinly held disdain. "You're just a bunch of metal bros who probably can't figure out how to clean the wax out of their ears." Sam pauses and smirks in response, and the two guys behind him let out Beavis and Butthead giggles.

Q is a little wide-eyed from the words "on stage" and interrupts. "So, you guys are in a band?"

"Yeah," Sam replies. "We kind of play a punk and metal hybrid thing."

Jex rolls her eyes. "Of course you do."

"It's cooler than it sounds, but we haven't played out in a few months."

"Why not?" asks Q.

"Long story," Sam responds and then turns to Jex. "And we're not just a bunch of dirty metal kids that don't clean their ears. I'm twenty eight and have been rocking since I was probably younger than you – all those years tear your ears to shit."

Jex looks him up and down again, and shakes her head. "You're just a wax head. Trust me."

Q's eyes light up. "And she can prove it! Right, Jex? Prove it!"

Jex looks at Q in horror. Just as she readies herself for a snotty response, Sam cuts in, wearing a sardonic smile. "Yeah, Jex. Prove whether we're wax head metal douches or not."

Jex pauses and prepares a response. After a moment, with all three of the dudes and Q looking at her expectantly, she just sighs and shrugs.

* * *

Ten minutes later, Jex and Q and the three metal dudes are in a semicircle in the living room of a dirty punk house, which is mostly empty at this point. Jex has her backpack open and digs grumpily through it. After a minute, she pulls out a felt bag, and then another. She pulls out a black device, the one your doctor sticks in your ears and eyes, from one and from the other, she pulls a tuning fork.

"Hey," Sam cheers. "Cool tuning fork."

"Yeah," one of the other guys pipes in. "It's nicer than yours," he declares, awkwardly laughing his Beavis laugh.

Sam ignores him. "What's that black thing? I've seen that before."

"Yeah," Jex confirms impatiently. "It's an otoscope. It lets me look into your ear and see the bones and stuff. And wax…"

Sam shakes his head jokily. "It's not wax. It's metal ear. We're not waxheads. We're metalheads."

"Yeah, ok, whatever," Jex retorts. She has taken dismissiveness to a new level. "Sit down."

Sam sits in a chair and Jex approaches him. "Arms to your sides," she declares.

"I told you, I'm not hitting on you – you're a kid."

"Yeah," Jex says, testily. "A kid that is about to prove you're a waxhead."

Sam chortles. "Doubtful."

Jex takes the tuning fork and taps it firmly against her ulna bone below her elbow. The tuning fork rings out a perfect C note. She holds it about two inches from Sam's ear. "Listen to that, OK?"

Sam confirms, "OK. It's a C, right?"

Jex nods her hair absently. "Yeah, very good. 512 hertz. But that doesn't matter for this test. Just listen."

Jex lets the note hang for just a moment. "OK," Jex continues. "I'm going to place the bottom of the fork on your mastoid bone, behind your ear, and I want you to listen to that, too, OK?"

Sam smiles, and confirms, with a nodding of his head. "Mastoid bone – like Mastodon, right?"

Jex shakes her head with slight annoyance. "Just listen, OK?" Jex places the tuning fork behind Sam's ear and lets the note ring for another moment.

"Which one is louder," Jex asks. "The one in the front or the one in the back?"

Sam pauses for a second and blinks. "Can I hear the two again?"

"Yeah, sure."

Jex repeats the procedure in both the front and back of Sam's ear. Sam pauses for another moment and then responds. "In front. Definitely the front is louder."

Jex nods with clear satisfaction, murmurs "Uh-huh," and then continues. "OK, that's called the Rinne's test. You passed. Now, one more easy test. It seems stupid, but trust me."

Sam just nods. Jax taps the tuning fork on her ulna bone and places the bottom of the vibrating tuning fork in the center of Sam's forehead. He smiles at its touch. "That tickles," he says.

Jex ignores the comment. "Do you hear more in the left or in the right? Or is it about the same?"

"It's in perfect stereo. Right down the middle," Sam responds.

"Uh-huh," Jex declares again, clearly satisfied. "That's the Weber Test. You passed that one, too."

"What does it mean, that I passed?" Sam asks.

"Well, when I say you pass the Rinne's test, the one where I put it next to your ear and behind your ear, what I mean is you have a positive Rinne. The air conduction in your ear is greater than the air conduction through the bone. That means your inner ear is more sensitive to sound transmitted through the bone – that's a good thing. That's how it's supposed to be. If it was the other way, that would indicate sensorineural hearing loss – I don't think anything can be done to fix that, not a good thing. You don't have that."

"That's good to hear," Sam replies, and then pauses. "Excuse the pun."

Jex rolls her eyes. "Not excused," she declares. "The other test, the Weber test, it basically means that your hearing is the same in both ears. Either that, or the hearing loss in both ears is the same – that's called a bilateral equivalent problem. That's pretty unlikely, particularly where you pass the Rinne's test like you did. If one ear hears the tone more than the other, that's called lateralizing – sound lateralizes, or shifts really, to one ear as opposed to the other. That would mean you would have some kind of conductive hearing loss or maybe what's called sensorineural loss. That's bad, too, and can't really be fixed. You don't have that."

"That's good to hear, too," Sam responds, smiling.

Jex ignores him. "I am just going to look into both of your ears OK, with this thingy – it's called an otoscope, like I said, and it magnifies and lights up the ear, so I can see the bones inside."

"You can see the bones inside? No shit? "

"No shit," Jex sighs and grabs Sam's left ear, gently but firmly. "Does that hurt?"

"No," Sam responds, a little taken aback by the move. "A bit of a surprise but doesn't hurt."

Jex shrugs her shoulders. "It's just a tug," she says, but loosens her grasp slightly. "I am just looking at your tympanic membrane. And … it is looking pretty healthy."

"Awesome," Sam responds. Q and the two other guys with Sam are watching intently, and a couple other people from the show have gathered around to watch. "What else can you see in there," Sam asks jokingly.

"A lot, actually," Jex explains testily. "I can see part of your malleus bone, part of your incus bone, and part of your stapes bone, that one is stirrup shaped – those are your ossicles and all are present and regular. I can see other stuff, too, like the tympanic annulus and umbo – but most important, I can see a very clear cone of light reflecting from my otoscope in the anterior-inferior quadrant of your tympanic membrane. That is very good."

"Why is that good," Sam queries.

Still poking around Sam's ear, Jex explains. "The cone of light is like a triangular reflection of light I can see on the tympanic membrane. That light is a very good thing. If the inner ear is bulging because of, like, fluid, or if there is a tear or something, the light reflection will disappear. That's bad. But your cone of light is clear as can be."

"A clear cone of light. My ears are rocking!"

"Well, I say clear as can be, because everything is definitely present and regular, but I admit I am kind of struggling to really see it."

"Ah," Sam replies in satisfaction. "Not quite an expert as you thought?"

"Nope," Jex retorts immediately. "It's just that there is so much friggin' wax build up, the circle I can see is seriously small. Get your ears cleaned, dude."

"What," Sam objects. "Wait a second."

"No, no need to wait," Jex responds and taps his shoulder. "Get up, waxhead. Next dude, please." One of the two guys with Sam sits down next to him and looks expectantly at Jex. Jex starts her exam and Sam, clearly surprised, stands up reluctantly. After about fifteen minutes, Jex is done with Sam and his two friends, as well as three other show-goers. Everyone is normal. Everyone has too much wax in their ears.

"Well," Jex declares. "It has been a blast, but free exam night is over. Would love to stay, but things to do, people to see." She plops the otoscope and tuning fork into their respective bags and stuffs them into her backpack. "Hey, Q. Still want a ride?"

"Sure do," Q yelps and follows Jex as she heads for the door. She stops in front of Sam and says, "you'll be OK, dude. Just get your ears cleaned. It will change your world, for sure."

Still seeming stunned, Sam just responds, "uh, thanks."

Jex turns and points at Sam. "Oh, and by the way, sorry to say it, but Mastodon didn't release a good record after *Leviathan*." Without waiting for a response, she is out the door, Q close on her heels. Halfway out of the yard, she hears Sam calling to her from behind.

"Hey, wait a second. Hold on!"

Jex looks back and it is Sam, closely followed by his two friends. Jex doesn't really hesitate and continues to head for her car.

"Hey, can you just hold on just a second. We just want to ask you one more thing."

"Sorry dudes," Jex responds over her shoulder. "Not interested in partying with some wax head metal heads." She lights a cigarette but does not slow her gait. Q looks back at the three guys but doesn't want to miss her ride so she doesn't really slow down. Jex has her hand on the car door and the key in the lock.

In a tone that is suddenly both desperate and despaired, an underlying layer of helplessness clear within it, Sam speaks out bluntly.

"Our lead guitarist has cancer. And it's bad."

For the first time of the night, Jex is stopped in her tracks.

* * *

"Yeah, it's called a … sarcoma, I guess. It was in his abdomen. That's why we aren't playing out right now. They cut out the tumor and now he is getting all kinds of treatment – Chemotherapy and that kind of stuff, I guess."

Jex and Q are sitting cross-legged with Sam and the two other guys, whose names she still doesn't know, in kind of a rough circle on the lawn. Jex is doing her best to get into the details.

"A sarcoma can mean a lot of things. Do you remember any other names for what he has?"

"No, not really. Just that it wasn't totally carved away in surgery and it's still spreading. The doctor used a lot of words that Joe didn't understand and we didn't, either. Oh, our buddy's name is Joe."

Jex pauses and considers. "Is Joe at Cedars-Sinai," she asks hopefully.

Sam looks up with a sudden optimism in his eyes. "Yes!," he says loudly. "Do you know it?"

"Yes," Jex affirms, trying to keep any sarcasm out of her response. "It's like one of the biggest hospitals with a specialty in cancer treatment."

"One of the biggest in L.A.?" Sam asks hopefully.

"One of the biggest in the world," Jex clarifies. And then pauses. "My father had cancer and was treated there."

"Did they fix him?"

She pauses again. "Well, he's dead."

"Oh, shit. Sorry," Sam responds.

"It's OK. Everybody dies sometime. And to answer your question, they did fix him, kind of. He had a sarcoma too, pretty rare and lethal. So we kind of knew he would be a goner soon enough. But they helped him a lot and his life was longer and better because of their treatment."

Sam pauses and takes in that statement. "So, you mean Joe is a goner?"

Jex kicks herself inside for referring to it like that, the memory of her father causing her to briefly forget Sam has a friend in a battle with his own sarcoma right now. "There are all kind of sarcoma and they are found at all different levels of severity." Trying to sound hopeful, she adds, "Joe's could be very different and have a lot more treatment options." Her attempt at hopefulness does not seem very hopeful to Jex, and she wonders how it sounds to Sam. She makes a note in her head to think through that later. Communication matters, she thinks to herself. You have to remember that.

For the first time, one of the guys that is with Sam speaks. His voice is louder than Jex would have imagined, and is full of distress.

"Yeah, there are treatments, and those doctors explained them to us, but they only used these big words and they don't make any sense to us. And they only give us like five minutes, and are all arrogant and everything."

The third guy now speaks up, agreeing with the second. "They're a bunch of asshats."

Jex nods her head absently, having had many of her own experiences with doctors, some of whom certainly fall within the category described by the third guy. "What about Joe's family? What are they saying about it?"

"We're the only family he has," Sam responds. "His dad disappeared on him before he was born. His mom died a few years ago. It's just us metalheads trying to figure all this bullshit out. We're family."

Both of the other guys nod in agreement. "True dat," one says.

Sam gets to the point. "Look, we know it's not your problem, but with all that medical stuff you have, maybe you could come to the hospital and meet Joe, see what's up with him?"

Jex can't help but laugh just a little out loud. "Dudes, I'm sixteen with a high school degree and no more. I read a lot of books, but I can't cure cancer. Trust me, the doctors at Cedars-Sinai are giving

Joe the best treatment he can get. They can be asshats, but they are the best asshats out there."

Sam shakes his head in mild frustration. "We know you're not a doctor. We know you can't fix him. But, you know, we could really use, like, a translator. If you talk to the doctors and look at all these papers they give us, maybe you could help us understand what all this is about. Maybe you could even offer up something that the doctors didn't think of."

"Trust me, Sam. I can't think of anything the doctors didn't already think up."

"Maybe not," the third guy chimes in. "But like Sam said, maybe you could translate for us. Help us understand."

"Come on, Jex, maybe you could just meet Joe," Q interjects suddenly, hopefully; the story clearly touching her. "It couldn't hurt."

Jex shrugs. "Maybe it won't hurt, and I don't mean to be brutal, but it probably won't help either."

"But maybe it will," the third guy retorts. "We're just living on chances right now, even if they're small ones."

Jex rubs her face and through her hair in frustration. She pauses and then asks, "What's Joe's' doctor's name? Is there one that is more involved than others?"

All three guys nod in unison and say, "Dr. Cohen."

Jex gags involuntarily in response. "Dr. Benjamin Cohen?"

"Yeah" the three guys respond, again together.

"Do you know him," Sam asks.

"Yeah," Jex nods, reluctantly. "I know Dr. Cohen. He was my father's doctor." The three note Jex's reluctance and she senses the instant worry in their eyes. She clarifies. "An amazing doctor, don't worry. He just … ," she shrugs, struggling for the right words. "He just fits very neatly into the asshat category you describe."

* * *

The next day just before ten a.m. at Cedars-Sinai, Jex is outside the hospital, sitting cross-legged in the parking lot on the hood of her car. She is smoking a Camel Crush and sipping a plastic cup of McDonald's coffee. She woke up feeling bad this morning, but the sun feels good on her face as she peers through her cheap sunglasses, neon green frames, out over the parked ambulances and Mercedes Benz. She runs her hands through her hair. She squints, trying not to think. All the things running through her head, ghosts and echoes of yesterdays, she tries to ignore them. She tries to focus on science, or medicine, or some graffiti tag she might break out over in West Hollywood later this week. Tagging gives her an escape, and she quietly thinks to herself that she could use an escape at the moment. She tries to focus on anything but the things that are piercing into her brain.

"Yo, Jex!" The yelp breaks Jex out of her thoughts at one of those times she doesn't mind being interrupting in her thinking. She turns and sees Sam and his two buddies walking towards her, a big smile on Sam's face; reluctant, hopeful looks on the faces of his friends. She waves to them weakly as they approach, but doesn't try to smile.

"What's up, Doctor Jex," Sam inquires. "You look deep in thought."

"I'm not a doctor," Jex reminds Sam. "I'm just some punk kid."

"Yeah, yeah, yeah," Sam responds off-handedly. "You're sure the smartest punk kid I ever met. And the kindest, by the way. Thanks very much for meeting us. We are super stoked you agreed to see Joe."

Jex shrugs testily. "Yeah, I had nothing to do, so I thought I'd say hi and shut you guys up. But, like I told you last night, just because I know how to do some ear exams doesn't mean I can treat or diagnose or even understand cancer. If your friend wants someone else to talk with, I'm happy to talk to him, but if you've got expectations that I can do anything to help him, your hopes are already too high."

Sam's two friends respond somewhere between shocked glum and I-told-you-so frustration. Sam doesn't flinch a bit. He is, perhaps in his heart, somewhat of a salesman. "Understood, understood. Every word completely understood. Like I said last night, we are just looking for a translator for a minute, to try and comprehend some of this medical crap, and maybe a quick brain storm session. I know it will cheer Joe up, and what the hell, never say never as far as ingenious ideas, right?"

"No," Jex retorts, just as testily. "Sometimes you can say never."

Showing an eternal optimism that may have surprised his two friends if they were asked, Sam says, "OK. We'll see."

"Ugh," says Jex, as she begins the walk to the hospital. Sam and his two friends follow close behind. Sam manages to scurry to the front of the small group just in time to open the door and walk into the room. Jex scans the room. It is just like every other hospital room she has ever seen. Well, to be precise, it is Cedars-Sinai, which is a nice goddamn hospital. Jex privately wondered to herself how this straggly crew of waxheads got their buddy admitted here. Freshly painted walls. Flowers everywhere. Nice framed paintings. Hardwood trimmings. Shiny linoleum floor.

Still, it is the same as any other hospital, sterile and clean;

somehow empty in its cleanliness. Despite the moneyed fever inherent in its hallways. Despite the brilliant minds carried around by all these middle-aged pudgy bodies in white coats. Despite the storied history and famed patients, with their household names and overflowing bank accounts. Instant visions of healing people flood Jex's mind, thinking there is a better way. Through all her negativity, these thoughts always make her smile, even if it is not apparent on her face. For a moment, she is lost in her thoughts.

"Jex, this is Joe. Joe, this is Jex."

The introduction breaks Jex out of her momentary daydream. She looks down and sees Joe. He is bald and has no facial hair; no eyebrows, eyelashes. His face is thin, and the thinness of his body is apparent even under the blanket. His blue eyes are drooped and red but he is smiling.

"Hey there, Joseph Foster. Nice to meet you," he says in a quiet voice with a manner that is genuine and instantly disarming.

Jex smiles for the first time since she left her car. "Hello, Joseph Foster. It is nice to meet you, too."

"So, you're the girl everyone is talking about. Dr. Jex."

"It's just Jex," Jex corrects him through her easy smile. "I'm just a kid. Not a doctor."

Joe smiles easily at her. "Sam tells me you can like save lives and shit."

"Not even close," Jex replies, still smiling. Her smile is worth noting for its calm nature. It's one of those things that is natural, not artificial or forced. You either have it or you don't.

"Well, don't bother trying to save mine," Joseph Foster says, still smiling. "It's already gone." There is a slight, tired slur in his tone, but it is otherwise clear and concise. His demeanor is pleasant to the ear, more pleasant than one would expect under the circumstances.

"Dude," Sam exclaims. "Don't say that. Negativity is terrible for you – you heard the doctors."

Joseph Foster shakes his head. "Man, I can hear these doctors all day long but I can't understand a goddamn thing they say. But I heard what those test results were and I know I'm a goner. So be it. I'm not scared of death. Shit," he continues, speaking to Sam but also turning his words to Jex, almost defensively. "We've been singing about it for ten years, it would be pretty lame if I fought against it now."

"Yeah, but still," Sam objected. "That's why Jex came, man. So she can look at your shit and, shit I don't know. Make some sense of it for us before we hold hands and jump into bed with Satan. I mean, you know, any more than we already are." Sam turns to Jex, chuckling. Jex roundly ignores him.

"Sam asked me to come and say hi to you, which I'm happy to do. But you're at the best hospital for cancer, probably in the world, Joseph Foster, I can assure you of that." Jex spoke firmly but with a comforting manner, so her words, though stark, still held a comforting air in them. "There's nothing I can tell you that they haven't already, I am quite sure of that."

"Yeah," Joseph Foster nods. "I'm super appreciative for you to come here. It's OK. I've never been scared to die. I'm not scared now." Joseph Foster looks over at his band. "That's not a negative thing."

Jex nods. "It's OK to be scared. It's OK not to be scared, too."

Joseph Foster smiles in a lazy way. "Thanks, Dr. Jex."

Jex nods firmly, repeating her early words. "It's just Jex. Maybe the best way to just shut our friend Old Sammy up is for me to have a look at your charts. Would you mind that?"

Joseph Foster shrugs. "It doesn't matter to me. Doesn't say much about me that I'm ashamed of. I caught herpes when I was fifteen, but oh well, I got past being embarrassed about anything a long time ago. Full transparency."

Jex smiles her smile, with its comforting waves. "Thank you very much, Joseph Foster. Unlike your friend Sam here, you are a gentleman."

The two other guys in the band laugh their Beavis and Butthead laugh. Sam kind of raises his eyebrows and leans back in a what-the-hell kind of way, throwing devil signs with both hands. Joseph Foster scrunches his face and bangs his head, in an in-your-face kind of way. These guys have chemistry with one another, Jex thinks to herself as she grabs the file next to the bed.

The seconds pass. And then the minutes. Jex reads page after page, her forehead scrunched up. Jex melts away into the pages, as though medical notes, good news or bad, are her only real solace. Lab reports and x-rays and clinical notes. Page after page. The minutes continue to pass. Sam studies his sneaker.

The two other guys just stand there with their hands in their pockets. Joseph Foster picks at his thumbnail, somehow appearing to be the calmest one in the room. A nurse walks in, drops some towels off into the bathroom and walks out. She doesn't say a word. The silence gets louder.

It's easy to see that Sam is the kind of guy who doesn't have a lot of patience. He's the kind of guy that jumps right out of his clothes at the slightest obstacle. He is kicking lightly at the side of the wall, his eyes darting from Jex to Joseph Foster and finally outside the doorway, into the hall of a hospital. A woman in an electric wheelchair speeds by the room, eyes Sam briefly but pays him little mind. Sam closes his eyes and breathes slowly. He's the kind that doesn't wait around, but here he is, waiting around to hear what Jex has to say.

An eternity passes.

After that eternity, Jex turns to Joseph Foster. "Ok, Joe, you want it straight?"

He doesn't even pause. "Of course."

"Ok. Well, what it says here is you went to County Hospital downtown with stomach pains. They sent you out for tests and took an image of your belly. They found a tumor in your abdomen, right?" She is talking straight to Joe, staring him in the eyes. She doesn't refer to any notes.

"Right," Joe confirms.

"Right," Jex agrees. "So they took a biopsy of the tumor. That was your first surgery. They diagnosed you as having a sarcoma, right? Soft tissue sarcoma."

"Yeah," Joe confirms again. "That's what they call it."

"OK, and a really rare sub-type. It's called a Ewing's Sarcoma/ Primitive Neuroectodermal Tumor. They abbreviate it as PNET. They told you that, right?"

"Yeah, like winning the lottery they said."

Jex nods slowly. "Quite a victory," she says, the sarcasm dripping from her lips.

"Yeah," Sam interjects. "That's how I felt."

"And you were classified T3 N1 M1b," Jex says to Joe, ignoring the interjection. "But you know that, right?"

The room is deathly silent. "Yeah," Joe says, almost in a whisper. "I remember the doctor saying that."

She looks at him closely. "Do you know what that means?"

Joe pauses for a minute and just kind of stares in Jex's eyes. After that pause, the reluctance in his voice is apparent as he slowly shrugs and admits, "not really."

"No worries," Jex says in that tone. "Each of the letter stands for something. So, the T stands for how big the tumor is, and yours is pretty big. It's 3 out 3, which is the highest. So…"

"Kinda serious," Joe offers.

"Yes," Jex says frankly. "It is. And so you have the N, which is all about how far the cancer spread. So, cancer originates in an organ, in you it was the abdomen. A cancer spreads by, like, hitching a ride from one organ to the next, kind of piggybacking, you know. Not quite piggy-backing or hitching, but you get the picture."

"Yeah," Joe replies. "That makes sense." Other than that, the room overflows with silence.

"The further a cancer spreads, the less likely it is you will be able to beat it back."

"Makes sense."

"Yeah. So, that's the N1 part."

"Is that a lot?"

Jex doesn't pause and her voice is calm and steady. "It's the highest classification. It spread."

A flicker of despair pokes up from Joe's eyes, and disappears just as quickly. "Yeah," he says with a quiet choke. "I guess I knew that. It just didn't really make sense until now."

Jex pauses for a moment, but just for a moment. Silence hangs like violence in the room. "M just tells you whether the lymph node was able to transport the cancer to other organs. You're M1, so that means it did, like it made the lymph node ride to another organ. Metastasis it's called."

"Yeah," Joe says, his voice finding its courage again.

Jex takes a deep breath. "You OK, Joe," she asks.

"Yeah," Joe confirms. "I got it."

Jex pauses and recognizes the other three guys in the room, all of who stand in stunned silence. "You guys OK," she says, in a whisper that has a tenderness in it completely absent from her earlier communications. They all nod slowly, saying nothing. Jex nods back quietly and returns her gaze to Joe.

"So, after that great news, you went through a treatment, right?"

"Yeah," he agrees. "The night before that treatment we had an awesome gig. Over at Canter's in the back room. We fucking nailed it. You remember that, Sammy?"

Sam looks like he's about to tear up, but he just nods in agreement, his face red, silence speaking all the volumes of the American canon. Joe looks over at the other two guys, who are both ashen, the reality of Joe's condition suddenly seeming to sink in for the first time. Joe doesn't say anything to them, but returns instead to his conversation with Jex. He pauses on his words, almost clawing them back, before he continues. "That was our last gig."

Jex clinches her lips in response to that and says nothing for a moment, judging to herself whether Joe wanted to continue. After another second, he senses it and speaks. "Go ahead, let's talk about the treatment."

"Well, it's tough with soft tissue sarcoma, because what this tumor does, these malignant cells, is they invade tissue nearby, neighboring tissue, you know, get into blood vessels. And so it spreads really quickly, through the lymph node. What they tried to do with you was pretty typical, and included what they call neoadjuvant therapy, ok?"

"Yeah, that sounds familiar."

"So all that means, Joe, is that they assessed it and categorized it using computer imaging. That's it." She gestures to the flip chart, but doesn't have to look at it. It is all already in her head. She only ever has to ready anything once.

"First you had your a dose of chemo, right? To try and shrink the area that needs to be treated. Then, you had your surgery, to try and get rid of the tumor in the abdomen. It's called local excision, but basically it just means they cut it out."

The two other guys turn from ashen to green. Jex continues. "After that, you recovered for a bit. Then they did radiation treatment. The idea of that is make sure that anything around the excision that is cancerous is killed off." She pauses for a moment. "That must have sucked balls. I'm sorry you had to go through that."

Joe just shrugs.

"And then you had additional chemo after the surgery, which was the primary treatment. That second round is called adjuvant chemo, to try and kill any cancer cells that could have spread before the surgery and to keep the tumor from growing back right away at the operation site."

"Yeah," Joe says, starting to look exhausted. "I get it."

Jex holds off for a minute, as Joe seems to be taking things in. "And they found out after all that bullshit, it spread, despite all the treatment. To the lungs and the liver and the stomach. And it reoccurred in the abdomen."

Joe nods slowly. One of the two other guys looks like he is about to pass out.

"And so now the only treatment regime left is to start from scratch, but not just at the abdomen, but also those other places."

Joe nods. The room is silent.

"And they have had to delay it twice because you've been sick."

"Yeah," Joe says, anger in his eyes for the first time. "This fucking cancer makes it easier to get sick. And so I keep getting sick. Fucking fever. Fucking snotting. Everything. But I don't care. I'm not doing it anyways. I'm sick of being sick and I just want to die here." Joe takes a deep breath. "I'm straight edge man, I've lived my whole life being clean. They are not putting another single fucking drug in me. No fucking way." Tears are running down his eyes. "No fucking way."

"Shit," Sam screams, suddenly alive again and animated. The two other guys jump, startled. Even Joe in his bed recoils a bit from the unexpected outburst.

"This is such fucking bullshit," Sam rages. "Total bullshit. This is what we are left with? Either he gets filled with that shit and it makes him lose his hair and puke and shit himself and then he dies, or he just dies in that bed like an old man right now? After all that, those are the only fucking options that we are left with?"

Sam's chest heaves, his face all veins and red. Tears are flowing down his eyes, part sadness, maybe mostly frustration. He coughs and chokes. Jex looks over at Joe and then back to Sam. She puts her hand on Sam's arm. It is not a gesture she often makes. Sam looks at her.

"Are these our only choices? Our only motherfucking choices," his voice full of pain and emptied of hope. "No more fucking songs? No more fucking CDs? No more …" He sniffs, choking back snot. "No more fucking gigs?"

Jex turns to Joe, whose face is scrunched up, tears dripping down his cheeks. Sam looks down at Joe, his friend's pain etched on his own face. Joe watches his best friend mourn his condition, and coughs out tears. In a friendship that has existed over fifteen years, these are the first tears the two have shared. After a moment, Jex raises her chin and straightens her septum ring. She begins to speak.

[Are those Joe's only choices? Can Jex think up other options? Turn to page 169 to read Jex's diagnosis and the conclusion of the story.]

JENNY THE CHICKEN

JEX BLACKWELL IS STONED. She looks between the blinds of her second floor bedroom and stares down out at the driveway. Her eyes are bloodshot and kind of vacant, pained by the sunlight. Q, her good friend and frequent partner-in-crime, has been knocking on the front door for the better part of an hour. Jex can't be bothered to answer. Sitting cross-legged and surrounded by medical textbooks – her headphones jamming the Max Levine Ensemble as loud as it will go – she is perfectly content to be alone; prefers to be alone. Q knows this, Jex thinks to herself, and it makes her vaguely annoyed that she doesn't just go away. After some minutes of watching Q pace back and forth between her bike and the front door, Jex grows bored and returns to her textbook. It is one of those weeks.

Her townhouse in Brentwood is modest, but at least it is hers and hers alone. Years ago, her father kept it for his mistress, but she left him soon after he got sick. And, so, when he finally died, after all that pain, all that torment, all that grief, the townhouse went to Jex. Just thirteen at the time, the Court didn't let her live alone right away. So it lived vacantly on its own for awhile as Jex wiled away the time squatting in her uncle's basement.

Her uncle was OK but Jex had never been the kind of person to live under someone else's roof. She spent much of her time on the streets. For that matter she still does. As soon as she turned fifteen, having already at that point graduated high school two years early, the Court gave her the freedom she wanted so badly. She immediately moved out of her uncle's basement and into the townhouse, embraced by the calm solitude it offered her. She still loves her uncle, visits him occasionally. But today, as a sixteen year old with experience far in excess of her years, she is independent. That's the way she likes it.

The townhouse is two full bedrooms, with quite a bit of space in it, but it is nearly empty. Just a mattress upstairs on the floor of the bedroom, no frame or anything; various pots and pans in the kitchen, mostly unused, some still new in their packaging; and a loveseat with upholstery in the living room that is for some inexplicable reason identical to the rug from the Shining's Overlook Hotel. Whenever Jex sits in it, she thinks of Danny riding his Big Wheel through the hotel. It is strangely comforting. Sparseness suits Jex fine. She has no intention to add much more to the décor.

The dull thumping on the front door continues and eventually turns into a piercing knock, almost shrill. The difference is substantial enough for Jex to take note. In a fit of frustration, she pulls the headphones off one of her ears to investigate further. After a moment, Jex recognizes the sound: Q is rapping on the kitchen sliding glass door in the back of the townhouse. She must have jumped the fence. Jex pauses for a bit and then sighs heavily with resignation. She pulls one more hit off her purple bong with the Pat the Bunny sticker on it and stands up wearily. She looks around and collects herself, thinking for a moment about cleaning up or at least running some hot water over her face. She decides not to bother and heads out of her bedroom and down the stairs to collect Q.

"Boo, what the fuck," Q shouts at her accusingly, storming into the kitchen in a huff as soon as Jex slides open the door. "You been disappeared on me for like three days, yo. I was starting to worry. Don't do that to me."

"Yeah, what's up," is the only response Jex can muster. Dreary. When it's one of those weeks, that's how it goes for Jex.

"Nothing, dude. I was just worried."

"I'm cool."

"Yeah, I know you're cool now, but I didn't know that ten minutes ago. I didn't know that at all."

Jex just shrugs and heads back upstairs to her room, gesturing for Q to follow her. Q stops at the refrigerator for a second to pull out a Yoo-Hoo. She follows Jex up the stairs, shaking the drink.

When Q makes it to Jex's bedroom, Jex is already back on the floor, cross-legged, purple bong with the Pat the Bunny sticker in her hand, sucking down a bong load. The music is playing, Spoonboy. "Linus and Me," the acoustic version. Q sits down next to her and accepts the bong when Jex offers it.

"What's this stuff?"

"Blue Dream, it's called. It's pretty strong."

Q takes a hit, holds it for a second and lets out a hefty cough. She goes on coughing for several seconds and Jex can't help but smile.

"I told you it was strong."

"Yeah," Q chokes out. "Strong," she agrees.

Jex chuckles. When Q stretches out her arm to hand the bong back to Jex, Jex waves her off. "Go ahead and finish that one. I'll make myself a fresh one when you're done with that."

Q shakes her head from left to right and back again, but keeps the bong.

"So," Q continues, catching her breath from the coughing fit, poking around the bowl with the corner of her lighter. "What have you been up to? I thought about calling the cops, almost."

Jex giggles. "Yeah, right. You call the cops."

Q throws her hands up in disgust. "That's what I'm saying, Boo. You get me all fucked up in the head. You got me thinking about calling the cops."

Jex just shrugs again and starts to say something but then stops. "What is it, Jex?" Q urges her on.

"Nah, it's nothing. I'm cool. I'm cool. I'm sorry I got you worried. I was just thinking about stuff."

"What stuff?"

"Don't worry about it. I was mostly reading. I've been reading a new journal article on this crazy ass heart procedure and it just got me distracted."

Q eyes the fat periodical that is lying next to Jex, filled with post-it notes and dog-ears. Q shakes her head and rolls her eyes. "Dude, I don't know how you read all that stuff, 'specially when you're so high."

Jex laughs. "Whatevs. I've been reading that stuff since I was a baby, practically. You get used to it."

Q shakes her head some more and rolls her eyes. "I couldn't never do that. That shit looks nuts."

Jex giggles some more and lies back on the floor, watching the ceiling fan spin lazily around. A sad song plays on her iPhone. "It's no big deal," she says. "What are you up to today," Jex asks, not giving Q any time to push back on what Jex has been up to the last few days. It doesn't matter anyways and Q wouldn't understand.

"Aw nothing," Q responds and takes another hit. "I'm just hanging out. I don't really want to go home. My mom is being crazy again and I just said 'I'm out.'"

Jex nods. "Dig it," she says and nothing more. Jex closes her eyes and listens to "I Have Regrets" by Garrett Walters. Q watches Jex, and listens along.

The song ends and it is the last song in the playlist, maybe, because the room goes silent. Jex picks at her fingers. Q asks, "You mind if I stick around here a while, then? I won't bother you at all."

"Nah, that's cool. You can hang. I'm headed out to the desert in a little bit, though. To see Eugene."

Q knows that Eugene is Jex's weed dealer. He lives out on a reservation a couple hours east of L.A. "Oh, you want some company?" Q asked hesitantly. She knows that Jex can be peculiar about her alone time and particularly time on a road trips. Sometimes she just likes to think. Q doesn't want to be a burden, but she's got nothing to do and nowhere to go. She has the sense that Jex knows how that feels.

"Yeah, you can come along if you want. It will be a few hours, you know it's all the way down there, almost near San Diego?"

"Yeah," Q says eagerly. "I got nothing to do. I won't say much."

Jex giggles. "You can say as much as you want, Q. I don't mind. It's not like I'm some bitch or something."

"No, I know you're not saying that. I'm just saying . . ."

Jex stops her in mid sentence. "Don't sweat it, Q. I dig it. Come and pop a squat next to me." Jex grabs her iPhone and pecks at the screen, fishing for a new playlist. She finds a good one, as reflected in her whispered murmur of, "oh, yeah" as she selects it. "This next song is rad." Q takes one more hit off the bong and lies down next to Jex. She watches the blades of the ceiling fan spin. Radiator Hospital starts to play.

Jex's brow curls a little as she sings along in her head, staring off into nothing; staring off into the past. She remembers her father's eyes and arms. She remembers what she wanted to be then; what she wants to be now. A couple more songs, slower and sad, pass before a single word is spoken. An old Mazzy Star song plays and in the fade away at the end of the song, Q breaks the silence. "Jexy?" she asks quietly, almost in a whisper. Maybe she didn't want to disturb the melancholy atmosphere of the songs.

"Yeah, Q?" Jex responds just as quietly.

"Are you going to go to college in September?"

There is a long silence. Indeed, the pause is so long that Q begins to think that maybe Jex won't answer at all. Just when Q is convinced that she won't, Jex whispers, "I don't know, Q. I really don't know." And then louder, full voiced, shaking her head slightly almost as though she were convincing herself and not Q. "And I really don't care." Jex sits up, gathers her stuff, and prepares to leave. Q follows.

* * *

Eyes still red and the tone still giggly, Jex and Q walk out the front door of the townhouse and head towards Jex's red Ford Focus. Replete with bumper stickers, Q pauses a moment to read one on the side passenger door. She points at it as Jex messes with her keys. "This is a new one?" she asks.

"Which one?" Jex asks back, as she locates the car key and moves to open the driver's door.

"The 'Kill Fascists' one."

"Yeah, I saw that at a house show last week and thought it was pretty rad ..." She pauses before waving absently at the bumper sticker. "With the red letters and all."

"Yeah," Q nods approvingly. "It's totally rad."

The two get into the car. The ride out of L.A. is surprisingly uneventful. They reach the 10 in less than twenty minutes. It is sultry outside. Jex and Q keep the windows open, and the hot wind flows through the car. For some reason, neither of them think to turn on some music. It is quiet for a long time, just the air; the sound of the air.

A dozen mile markers pass by before Jex calls attention to the silence. "You . . uh . . wanna listen to some music?"

Q nods her head. "Yeah," she agrees and picks up Jex's iPhone, which is connected by a wire to her car stereo. "Damn," Q complains. "This setup is janky."

"Whatever," Jex waves off dismissively. "What do you want to hear?"

"I dunno," Q mumbles, flipping through Jex's iTunes catalog. "You got some good shit in here."

"Yeah," Jex agrees pensively, staring out at the tan mountains as she thinks. She shakes her head and says, "I don't think I feel like listening to anything too, you know. . . No Johnny Hobo, OK?"

Q nods. "I get it," she says, tapping through songs. When she gets to the K section, she stops and smirks. "Yo, I got it."

"Oh, yeah? What is it?"

Q smiles. "You'll see in a sec," as she hits play. In just a second, the music begins. Jex recognizes it immediately and begins to giggle. The sound of the wind is loud and the music is louder. Jex and Q sing along and the world falls away as they speed down Interstate 10, laughing and enjoying the ride as the afternoon turns into early evening. Ke$ha blares out of the speakers, and the two make the most of the night like they were gonna die young.

* * *

The two are still singing silly pop songs at the top of their lungs. "Style" by Taylor Swift is on when Route 79 turns off onto Camino San Ignacio, which snakes quickly into the less-than-imposing entrance of Los Coyotes Reservation. The poverty of the area seems immediately apparent. Jex doesn't seem to notice but Q does not hesitate to remark.

"Shit, Jexy. Why do we got to come all the way out here to get smoke? There are ten places we can get it without leaving West Hollywood."

Jex shakes her head. "No, I don't trust anybody in L.A. They treat me like I'm just some dumb kid."

Q laughs. "You are a dumb kid."

"Oh, yeah." Jex smiles. "Well, I don't like being treated like one, anyways. Besides, I like Eugene. I've known him forever and he's cool."

"Yeah," Q agrees. "Eugene is proper."

"And it's a nice ride, you have to agree," Jex says as she turns off the main road and onto a nameless side street. Her car kicks up dust as they drive into what seems like nowhere.

"Yeah," says Q as she sticks her head out the window, greedily taking in the last of the day's sun. "It's a nice ride."

Jex's Ford Focus pulls off the side road onto a side-ier side road and in just a few minutes they pull into a dirt driveway on the side of a mobile home. There is dust everywhere and a laundry line in the back next to a blue above-ground pool that has seen better days. There is a black Chevy Cavalier convertible in the front that seems to be more dust than paint. The sky is clear above, a smear of color that lies between black and blue, smudges of orange and white splattered throughout. The first twinkles of stars appear. Jex pauses and looks all around her, eyes brilliant with wonder.

Q is already halfway to the front door by the time Jex shakes herself from her momentary distraction and closes the car door. "Come on, Jexy," Q urges her. Jex walks over, her ubiquitous backpack thrown lazily over her left shoulder, and joins Q. Just as she gets to Q, the front door of the mobile home opens.

Standing in the doorframe is a young man, maybe nineteen or twenty, with dark hair tied behind his head in a long ponytail. He is well over six feet tall, and perhaps two hundred fifty pounds. His wide yellow-toothed grin cracks through the imposing appearance and his deep, raspy voice is welcoming and immediate. "Jex! Q!! Good to see you, my friends. Please come on in!"

Jex and Q wave merrily. "Hi, Eugene," they yelp out in unison as he gestures them in.

The Grateful Dead plays softly in the background as Eugene, Jex, and Q lounge on the floor, legs stretched out and the three of them positioned roughly in a circle. It sounds to Jex like it might be something from the 1971 tour, maybe 1972 but Jex isn't positive. Definitely pre-Donna. Eugene lights incense. The lights are dim.

"So, how have you been, my brilliant young friend?"

"I'm good," Jex responds enthusiastically. "I'm feeling really good. Happy enough at the time."

Eugene smiles widely as he was wont to do. "That's good, Jexy. That's good. You staying out of that trouble, now?"

Jex nods. "I am, Eugene. I've put enough people through enough problems. I'm being a good girl now. Well," she continued. "Good enough, I guess."

Eugene's forehead furrows deeply as he continues, asking sternly, "You drinking?"

"No, no," Jex confirms quickly, a note of seriousness in her tone. "I'm not drinking anything."

Eugene looks at her severely and stares more deeply into her than before. His eyes look tired and red, while still remaining deadly serious and alert. "Nothing else heavier than smoke?"

"No," Jex states firmly, in a tone of conciliation that she reserved for only her closest and most trusted friends. "I promise. I'm good."

"Boo's good," Q promises, vouching for her friend. "She's green like me, but that's it."

Eugene's stern glare relaxes back into a grin. "That's good, Jex. Green's good. That's OK. That's good. You got a motherfucker of a brain up there and we don't want you messing it up with your childish ways, do we?"

Jex giggles in a familiar way. "Yeah, you're not that much older than me, Eugene – and I will tell you that sometimes I think you act a lot more childish than I do."

Eugene chuckles loudly, and coughs on the chuckle a little bit. "Aw, Jex. You crack me up the way you call me out. And you're right, you're right. But I'm being good, too," Eugene explains with glee. "I ain't been doing any of that bad stuff. Plus, I'm losing weight, almost twenty pounds," he bragged, patting his belly proudly. "Haven't even been trying."

"I thought something about you seemed different," Jex comments. "You are looking good," she says, noticing but not commenting on the dark rings under his eyes.

"Thank you very much!" Eugene exclaims, a glimmer in his eyes. "I don't even know how it happened. Maybe I'm on a hunger strike and I don't even know it." He lets out a loud guffaw and shakes his head left and right at himself with a sense of self-deprecation. "There are lots of things I would do for the cause, but I don't know if I could handle that," he chuckles.

Q and Jex both smile in a charmed way. "I bet you could do up a mean hunger strike if you wanted to, Eugene," Q proclaims. "We have seen you do some crazy shit to get your point across, yo."

Jex nods her head in agreement. Eugene laughs some more. "I am a dedicated advocate, I will give you that. I'm not going to let my people rot on these goddamn reservations forever, you know. I'm not going to be just some weed dealer the rest of my life." He shakes his head in disgust and coughs a little. "Just a bunch of meth heads around these days, anyways. They don't appreciate kind bud." Eugene seems to catch himself mid-rant and perhaps senses discomfort in Jex and Q who, after all, are here at least partially to buy some kind bud.

"Don't get me wrong, loves, my bud is the kindest," Eugene clarifies with a smile. "And I'm proud of it. The green ain't never killed nobody as far as I know. Not like meth does. Not like alcohol does, mind you." He turns abruptly to Jex and confronts her. "Jexy, you sure you're not drinking?" There is accusation in his tone. Jex is immediate and firm in her denial.

"No way, Eugene. I promise. I know what that shit can do to you. I'm green but straight-edge as hell otherwise. No shit."

Q nods her head in agreement. "That's the Bible, Eugene. Same with me, for sure."

Eugene studies them severely. . After a moment he nods his head in muted approval. "Good," he says. "That's good. You know, it's like Chief Bromden said when he was describing his old man. You know, in *One Flew Over the Cuckoo's Nest?*"

Jex and Q both nod silently. They know the book. They know the character.

"Chief Bromden, he said:

'And the last time I see him, he's blind in the cedars from drinking and every time I see him put the bottle to his mouth, he don't suck out of it, it sucks out of him until he's shrunk so wrinkled and yellow even the dogs don't know him."

Jex and Q are enraptured. They nod at Eugene, like a congregation nodding to their pastor.

"You know how many of those wrinkled and yellow dogs have withered to death on this reservation? I've seen it with my own two eyes," Eugene states emphatically, coughing between his words. "It is never-ending. It is a vicious cycle." His eyes bulge a little bit and his cheeks redden ever so. "You hear a lot of talk about the Holocaust? Genocide in the Holocaust? In Germany and the Jews? And you hear about genocide in America? Black genocide? Genocide of the white man over the black man? Or even the Armenian genocide?

Right after World War I, all those years ago? Well, how come we haven't heard about the genocide of the American Indian?" He coughs. "Of the red man?" He coughs again. "You don't hear about it, do you? No. Not really. We get tossed a bone here and again, one that's been picked over three times by the time we get it. And why don't you hear more about this plight? This plight of reservations and drunkards. Drug addicts? Meth heads? People who never worked a day in their life because they never had a chance? And why don't you hear about this?" Eugene demands rhetorically, his voice almost raising to a scream. Jex and Q are transfixed by his every word.

"Because it was the world's only successful genocide. It's the only one that worked. The Jews are OK. . The United States of America had a black President. But what about us, Native Americans? Nothing? No money. No hope. No future."

Eugene pauses and holds his chin in his hand, his elbow on his knee, thinking like a Rodin, a million ideas seeming to flow through him. Neither Jex nor Q dare to interfere with the silence. After some time passes, he continues. His voice is quieter, more in control.

"The future," he continues quietly. He looks from Jex to Q and back again. "What will the future be? Leonard Peltier said 'Only one thing's sadder than remembering that you were once free. And that's forgetting you were once free.'"

Jex and Q nod their heads.

"I will never forget my people were once free. And we can be free again. There is power in knowledge. There is power in commitment. Recently, you know, this struggle, it has really been consuming me. I have trouble sleeping at night sometimes. Like, I wake up and I'm covered in sweat. Shivering. Like my ancestors, like they are calling to me in my sleep. I have dreams, Jex. Terrible dreams. Visions, almost. I can't ignore them. I feel like my skin is burning up sometimes." Eugene stands up and looks out the window. "The last few days it has gotten worse. My body is aching. It's not like I'm sad or something like that. I'm not depressed. Hell, I'm not even mad or angry. But my body, it is telling me there is something for me to do. There's a calling. Like a yearning deep inside of me, you know what I mean?"

The three sit quietly for some time. There is really nothing to say that is worth puncturing the impact of Eugene's words. The trio just sits there, allowing the gravity of Eugene's emotions to linger. It is clear that the silence is there for Eugene to break and no one else. Jex and Q seem to feel this and wait for Eugene to speak and no one moves until he does so. It is a long time before he does so.

"Jex. Jex, your brother was a good man."

The words strike Jex in a way that she does not seem to have anticipated. Her eyelids pop open quickly and then just as quickly resume to normal. Lips suddenly pursed tightly, Jex is silent for a moment and perhaps is hoping that she doesn't have to respond at all. The silence is awkward, though, and it is hers and hers alone to break.

"Thanks, Eugene."

"A very good man," Eugene continues. "He brought me out of a lot of my misery." Eugene pulls a handkerchief from his pocket and coughs into it. He looks briefly at the handkerchief and then stuffs it back into his pocket. "It was very sad when he left us."

"Yeah," Jex responds quietly. "It's still sad."

"Yes," Eugene agrees. "It will always be sad. Particularly for you. Siblings are tough that way. Family," Eugene emphasizes, raising his voice slightly. "Family is tough that way, you know what I mean?"

Jex can only nod in agreement. Eugene shakes his head and looks out the window. "It's good you're clean, Jexy. Really good. You got a good head on your shoulders. You got to keep it clean like that."

"I will," Jex promises. "I will."

"That's good," Eugene responds. "That's good." He walks away from the window and sits on the floor next to Jex. He has a bag of weed with him, and he picks some stems out, flicks them away. He looks out into nothing before continuing.

"I wish you all had gotten here an hour ago. My little cousin was here. She's sixteen I think, can't be no older than that, anyways. Maybe fifteen." He pauses a bit before continuing. "You're sixteen, right Jex?"

Jex nods in confirmation.

"Sixteen, man. Sixteen," Eugene repeats. "So damn young. Molly is her name, my cousin. She all messed up." He sighs. "Molly is her name and Molly is her game. She's sick all the time. Using. And using more than Molly, you know what I mean?"

Jex nods again. "How long has she been using?"

Eugene just shrugs. "Shit if I know. I've only known for a little while, at least. It comes on so quick, you know. First she was like playing with dolls and shit and next thing you know, I'm finding needles at her house and shit, you know what I mean? That's how the shit works, man. I didn't even think she smoked, and then I'm finding … finding fucking needles in her room?"

Jex nods. "That is how this shit works, Eugene. I'm sorry to hear that. It does happen really quickly."

Eugene shakes his head. "I remember when your brother was around and he had his shit together. At the time, he really had his shit together. We would talk about you. You couldn't have been more than twelve back then." He looks Jex up and down. "It seems like a million years ago. You seemed so cute and so young but you had your demons dancing in you already."

"I remember," Jex murmurs distantly, maybe not wanting to remember.

"And here it is now, what, four years later, and here you are, clean as a whistle, and your brother is gone. Shit, I just don't understand it."

Jex shakes her head. "I don't understand, either. It feels like a million years ago to me, too. I feel a thousand years old, not sixteen."

Eugene nods in agreement. "That life ages your soul. Or maybe your soul is already old, and this life is thrust upon you so you can catch up with your soul."

Jex pauses before responding. "I never thought about it like that. That almost seems … right to me."

"I wish you could talk to Molly. I try to talk to her but I'm like her geeky cousin. She just don't listen to me."

"Sometimes people don't listen until they are ready," Jex responds and then continues. "Hell, maybe all the time people don't listen until they are ready."

Eugene nods. "Yeah. Still, she looks horrible. Skinny and pale and looking like an old lady, swear to God. She's been away at her pop's, down below San Diego, came back to the reservation last month. Staying with me, for now. And the change was so damn obvious. She denied the track marks but I saw them, Jex. I saw them with my own two eyes. I never used the needle myself but I've seen it enough."

Eugene is getting more animated and Jex says nothing in response.

"Shit," Eugene sighs after a moment. "I'm sorry, Jexy and Q. I know it's a long ride back to L.A. I don't want to keep you with my melancholy and sad plight. I'm glad you all came to see me. I know there are other ways to score weed that aren't so far away."

Jex smiles and walks over to Eugene. "Everyone in LA is a pecker wood, Eugene," grabbing the large man and hugging him, nuzzling her head into his thick chest. "I am forever loyal to you. We are family, you know that."

Eugene hugs back and laughs. "Aw, Jexy. You are the best. I am so grateful to have you in my life. I am so sorry for rambling on like a bitter wooden indian."

Jex backs up and pokes Eugene playfully. "You are speaking the truth, dude. Don't ever apologize for that," wagging a finger at him.

"Ok, Jexy, ok," Eugene says between laughs and coughs.

Jexy squints hard at him. "And get that cough checked out. You'll catch a death."

Eugene continues to laugh. "Ok, Dr. Jex. I promise. I will. And you know if you ever need anything, I'll be here for you."

"Right back at you, Eugene. For real, you want me to talk to your cuz, let me know. I'll come back out. And though sometimes family is like that, sometimes it's like this, too."

Eugene's eyes seem to well up with tears as he puts his head on top of Jex's head and messes up her hair. His smile is big, from ear to ear. "Ok, Jexy. Are you sure you guys can't stay? You know I'm having a big get together tonight?"

"Oh yeah?" Jex asks. "What's going on?"

"At the VFW down the road. I'm speaking on the lack of diversity in the UC system. Particularly the lack of Native Americans, you know what I mean? I'm hoping to get a hundred people to show, you know? And I bet we will. We are going to talk about entrance requirements, costs, scholarships, historical context , what we can do to help ourselves, you know what I mean?"

"Righteous," Jex responds with intrigue. "We have to get back though, I have to work at the library in the morning, and I hate morning driving."

"Ah-ha-hah," Eugene responds. "I remember your brother telling me what a nightmare you were in the morning."

"Ah-ha-hah, yourself," Jex says with a playful punch to Eugene's shoulder. "I can get up just fine if I want. It's just a … long ride in the morning."

"Understood, Jexy," he responds with a cough and a smile. "Well, you guys be safe on the road, and don't be strangers."

Jex nods and smiles. "We won't. Promise."

* * *

Jex and Q are on the road, sun setting but still glaring down on them. The windows are open and the music is loud. Q is trying hard to keep it cool, but she is getting bored and she hates long silences anyways.

"Jexy, what's wrong? Why you so quiet?"

Jex shakes her head absently and says nothing. She messes with her septum ring nervously, but says nothing. The music is good, an old album by the Jam that Jex has on CD for some reason she could not explain if asked. She just knows she likes the music. The silence above the music continues.

"Where did you meet Eugene anyways," Q asks, "what with him

living all the way out here?"

"He didn't live here when we met. He was living in Echo Park. He was playing guitar in a band. That's where he knew my brother from. Their bands played on the same line-ups a lot. We met at a show somewhere. I think in Long Beach."

"Cool," Q responds.

"Yeah, his band was pretty rad. Really tight punk."

Q laughs. "No shit?"

"Oh, yeah. And Eugene is a huge Mountain Goats fan. Sometimes when I see him out there, all we listen to is tMG. Once, his band played *We Shall All Be Healed* from beginning to ending, but all electric punk."

"Hah, rad," Q exclaims. "That's hilarity. Awesome."

"Yeah," Jex agrees. "Those gigs were so much fun. Some of the first shows I ever went to. I was like eleven or twelve and my brother would sneak me in through the back door."

"That's cool," Q marvels. "I have to use a fake id to get my ass in a club." She shrugs with a smirk. "Not that that's any big deal."

"Yeah," Jex agrees lazily. "Anyways, he moved back home about, I don't know, eighteen months or so ago. The band split up 'cause Gary, the lead singer, OD'd and died."

"Oh shit," says Q with a slight gasp.

"Yeah," Jex agrees. "He went out like six months or so after my brother." Jex pauses, the pain of the recollection clear on her young face, which didn't seem so young in the brief moments when she spoke about her brother. "After that, I think Eugene had enough and just split the scene."

"Shit," Q says.

"It was good going out to visit him back then, though. Could really clear my head. Eugene spoke truth to me a lot. Like he speaks now."

Q nods her head in agreement.

"It was worse back then, taking the bus, though. Makes this old Ford Focus seem pretty rad, no?" She chuckles at the end of that.

Q agrees. "Shit's a fucking Rolls Royce compared to the bus."

The two laugh. "Anyways," Q continues. "Eugene's pretty hardcore. Sucks about his cousin. Another junky in his life."

"Yeah," Jex says, her eyes fluttering out again into quiet, into absence. Something had been brewing in her mind and her mind has for some reason returned to it. Q seems to sense this and sits back into her seat, her attention turning to the mountains passing by her window.

After a few minutes, Jex breaks the silence. "Shit," she yelps out. "Shit."

"What is it, Jex?" Q asks in surprise. "What is it?"

Jex shakes her head and repeats, "Shit."

"What, Jex, what?" Q urges.

Jex makes an unexpected swerve to the right and she is barreling down towards the next exit.

"What's wrong, Jex? Are you OK?"

Jex pauses a moment before answering. "Shit, Q," Jex says. "We gotta get back to the reservation. I think there's a problem with Eugene."

[What's the problem with Eugene? Will he be OK? Turn to page 183 to read Jex's diagnosis and the conclusion of the story.]

JENNY THE CHICKEN

BAWDY DYSMURFIA

JEX BLACKWELL LOVES PUNK MUSIC. That's all there is to say about that. She sits crawled in a ball on the floor of the L.A. Public Library's basement stacks listening to *Milo Goes to College* by the Descendants. The volume on her headphones is as loud as Jex can gamble without being heard. If her boss, the inimitable Ms. Thelma W. Tubman, catches her reading one more time, slacking off on shelving books, there will be hell to pay. Again. She can't put the volume up more than half the way without risk of exposing her hiding place. She is reading *Violence Girl* by Alice Bag for the fourth time.

The rubber on one of her Chucks distracts Jex from her reading momentarily. A small part of the rubber has been slowly peeling off like string cheese. Jex gently pulls on the rubber until it splits off completely from the sneaker. She holds it in both hands and studies it carefully, aimlessly. After a while, she returns to her book and slips away.

Soon enough, though, Jex is distracted again. It is that kind of day. This time, her attention is captured by the spine on a book near where she is sitting. The spine is gold and dusty. It is old and looks out of place. Jex straightens her septum ring and then, after running her hands through her hair, tugging at her ponytail, she reaches out to touch the book. It is scratchy on her fingers. She stares for a moment at it, and then turns back to *Violence Girl.*

The book is intriguing to Jex mostly because, maybe accidentally, it views Los Angeles in a romantic way, and its early punk scene as some kind of iconic moment in the city's history. And maybe it is all true. Maybe the city did have a pulse that powered its art scene; its punk scene. And maybe the art scene, the punk scene; maybe they powered the city back in some strange, surreal, hopelessly romantic way. Jex likes to dream it was so, and sometimes she wishes she had been there to be part of it.

And at the same time, she likes to dream that her time in the city is somehow also an iconic moment. Maybe her scene gets power from the city; maybe her scene powers the city back. And at some point in the distant future, some other girl in some other library will read books about this time in L.A., and wish that she had been here. Some days the city feels like it is straight out of a Raymond Chandler book. Some days it feels like Bret Easton Ellis. Mostly, though, it's just kind of a twisted Hannah Montana episode. Maybe someday, Jex thinks to herself, she could help to make it something real. Or at least something romantic.

"Ms. Blackwell. Exactly what do you think you are doing?"

Jex looks up. If she is surprised, she doesn't show it. It is Ms. Tubman talking, her face beet red and her hands on her hips. She is wearing a blue dress that accentuates her frame, which some would describe as frumpy; holding her large, rather sturdy body in a manner that is strikingly reminiscent of a 1950's era caricature; the angry librarian steadfastly chasing a truant library book. Her expression suggests that steam may soon literally spout out of her ears. Without waiting more than a moment for a response, Ms. Tubman repeats shrilly, "I said: what do you think you are doing?"

"Hi," responds Jex, nonchalance dripping as slow as molasses from each word. She stands deliberately and looks up at Ms. Tubman, who is several inches taller than her. "I was just inspecting this book," she states calmly, her words purposeful and precise. "It was shelved here in the history section, right here, near Napoleon. But, Ms. Tubman, it didn't look right to me as I was re-stacking books, and upon scrutiny it appears it may be a fine arts book. I was concerned it might be misplaced, and so I was inspecting it to try to make a determination." Jex holds the book out to Ms. Tubman. "See," she queries.

Ms. Tubman looks down her nose at the book and eyes the spine carefully. "Well," she sniffs. "This is the third time this month a ... 'fine arts' book has been ... 'misplaced,'" the skepticism thick in her voice. "I trust very much that we will not see these aberrations continue ... or I will have no choice but to investigate the matter much more deeply. Let's hope it does not come to that."

"Let's hope," Jex agrees firmly, the sarcasm of her words every bit as impenetrable as the skepticism in Ms. Tubman's had been.

"In any event, Ms. Blackwell," Ms. Tubman sniffs. "I was looking for you. We have a ... patron who insists that you are the only library employee who can competently tend to her needs. I find that difficult to believe. In any event, I thought I might find you here, 'inspecting' books of one sort or another."

Jex looks past Ms. Tubman's imposing figure and for the first time she sees a girl standing somewhat meekly behind her. It is Molly, the cousin of Jex's good friend, Eugene. Her skin is pale and she is thin. Her hair is long and pitch black with a flare of blue in the front. She is wearing black jeans and a black t-shirt with a cartoon of what seems to be Smurfette in somewhat cheeky vaudeville attire on the front. Her belly button is slightly visible, just a little. With a hint of surprise in her voice, Jex greets Molly. "Oh, hi Molly!"

"Hi, Jex." Molly offers quietly, her voice an embarrassed tin, every bit as meek as her appearance. "How are you doing?"

"I'm OK, how are you?"

Molly shrugs. "I'm OK, I guess."

"Well," Ms. Tubman interrupts stiffly, speaking to Molly. "I trust very much that you will be just fine in the … capable hands of Ms. Blackwell."

"Thank you," Molly mumbles, almost silently.

"And Ms. Blackwell. While I am quite delighted to see that you have your own personal following in our library, I would remind you that you are here as a library assistant. And your assistance continues to be required in the stacking of books."

"Yes, Ms. Tubman," Jex nods diligently.

"Lots of books."

"Yes, Ms. Tubman," Jex responds again, with no diminishment of determination in her voice.

"Very well," say Ms. Tubman, who seems to spin on one heel as she turns and walks purposefully away. Molly looks at Jex with more than a hint of fear in her eyes. Jex smiles. "Don't worry about Ms. Tubman. Her bark is worse than her bite."

"Oh," Molly says reluctantly. "Ok," her voice a little raspy.

"She's actually sweet. And she's right. I should be stacking books, not reading them. I'm getting paid to stack 'em." Jex smiles, and her smile is naturally, organically disarming.

"I didn't mean to get you in trouble," Molly apologizes.

"Nah," Jex says, waving her concerns off. "It's got nothing to do with you. She catches me all the time with my nose in a book. Either a punk book like this or some medical book." Jex lowers her voice in a mock tone of conspiracy. "Between you and me, I think she's secretly proud I read so much."

"Oh," Molly says hesitatingly. "That's cool."

Jex points at Molly's shirt, perhaps thinking it was time to just move on from the subject of Ms. Tubman – adult figures of authority appear to make Molly nervous. "I like your shirt. It's pretty rad."

"Oh, thanks," Molly replies, her face quickly brightening. "It's for my new band."

"Oh," Jex exclaims, recalling that when she saw Molly last, she was carrying a guitar. "You have a new band? That's headlines."

"Yeah," Molly agrees. "It's gonna be awesome. We are still working up songs. I'm playing bass. Power trio," she shrugs as if it's no big deal to her, though it clearly is. She is glowing. "Drums, guitar and bass. It's gonna be rad. We're called Bawdy DySmurfia. Get it?" She points at the cartoon on her chest, and then turns around to show her back, where the name of the band is written out. Jex pauses for a moment, putting the pieces of the pun together before smiling broadly.

"That's super rad," Jex agrees. "I love that name."

"Yeah," Molly agrees as she looks down at her shoes and fidgets with her fingers. There is an awkward pause before Jex continues the conversation.

"So, are you living in L.A. right now?"

"Yeah," Molly confirms, and then clarifies, "well, I've been staying in Echo Park with Leigh for the last week or two. She's the drummer of the band."

"Cool," Jex responds. "Echo Park is cool."

"Yeah," says Molly. "It's cool. I'm just living on the couch for now."

"Are you in school right now?"

Molly hesitates before responding. "Naw," she says. "It's not for me right now."

"That's cool. I went in and out of high school before I got my diploma."

Molly laughs nervously. "Yeah, but you're like Marie Curie or something."

Jex shrugs. "You don't have to be smart to finish high school. You just need all the bullshit in life to white out for a while so you can just focus on getting done all the crap they want you to do."

Molly agrees. "For realz," she says. "That crap is too much sometimes. And it's super hard to white stuff out sometimes."

"That's for sure," says Jex. "I'm really, like … lucky I made it."

Molly laughs again. "Yeah, right… Madame Curie."

Not one to accept compliments gracefully, nor to engage in casual chit-chat for any meaningful period, Jex laughs and changes the subject. "Yeah, so, anyways, what brings you to the library?"

"Well," Molly says, her words reluctant. "When we were out in the desert last month, with Eugene? You seemed to be really smart about medicine. And you know about my condition and all, right?"

Jex had been visiting Molly's brother earlier that year and recalls very well Molly revealing that she has Type I Diabetes. Eugene mistook her use of insulin needles as proof of illicit drug use and the misunderstanding soon brewed a nasty confrontation. It also turned out to be the night Molly learned that she had contracted TB, and had unknowingly passed it on to Eugene. It was a night of a special kind of awkwardness that Jex won't soon forget.

Type I Diabetes is a serious condition, Jex knows, and a hard one to manage; particularly for a kid like Molly, whose parents aren't around much and the temptations of Southern California are everywhere. If Jex had such a condition even just a couple of years ago, there's little doubt she would have managed it horribly, and maybe it would even have killed her. Jex is smart enough to know these things, and so a sense of concern with Molly is palpable in her words.

"Yeah, I remember," Jex confirms. "How is it going?"

Molly shrugs. "I dunno," she says. "Like, it's been hard I guess. I dunno."

Jex nods in the way she does, in a way that is calming and empathetic at once. "Yeah," she agrees. "It must be really hard."

"Yeah," Molly says. "Really hard," repeating Jex's words.

Perhaps sensing why Molly was here, Jex continues. "Do you want to sit somewhere and talk about it a little?"

"Yeah," Molly says instantly, enthusiastically. "That would be awesome."

"Cool," Jex says, looking around and grabbing Molly's hand. "I know someplace we can go where Ms. Tubman won't even think of looking for us." Molly smiles and follows Jex through the stacks, sharing a mischievous moment in the stilted silence of the library basement; the kind of moment that bonds people without words.

* * *

"So, anyways. There's this dude. He's in a band."

Not sure if a wise man said this once or not, but very few scenarios end well that start with "there's this dude. He's in a band." Though only sixteen, it is a lesson Jex already knows well. She and Molly are now secreted out behind a couch on the second basement level, by the patent section. It is a corner of the library that is seldom used, and Jex has exploited the floor's quiet nature to keep hidden from Ms. Tubman on only the most important occasions. She does not use it often for fear of being discovered and ruining her favorite secret place; but Molly seems sad and scared. She is worth the risk. They are behind the couch, Molly with her legs stretched out and Jex sitting cross-legged.

"So, this dude, he's been hanging out at this house I am flopping at. His name is Ian. You know, like Ian MacKaye from Minor Threat. We've been talking a bunch. He's older. Like eighteen or nineteen maybe. He does some shows, grindcore stuff."

"Ugh," Jex mutters under breath. Grindcore is not her scene. Molly shrugs. "I dunno, the music's kinda rank, but he's cute and he just makes me go all bonkers."

Jex smiles and plays with the rubber on the sole of her sneaker. "Yeah, I dig that," she says, though there is a hint in her voice like maybe she doesn't quite know; like she hasn't really met a dude that has made her go quite bonkers. Not yet, at least. There is a flicker in her eyes. Her focus on Molly and her story is clear, noticeable to Molly, and Molly seems invigorated in her storytelling by Jex's demeanor.

"So, anyways. Like, I don't know, the last few nights we have been hanging out at the house. Not just me and him. And, I don't know, he likes to drink these cognac drinks."

Jex furrows her eyebrows. "Cognac?"

"Yeah," Molly says. "Cognac."

"That's kind of a weird drink for a grindcore kid be drinking."

Molly looks down at her fidgeting fingers, nervous and uncertain. "It tastes good, I dunno."

Jex shrugs. "That's cool," in what is perhaps her least judgmental tone, kind of like she doesn't want Molly to freeze her out.

"But, that's the point. I've had a couple of drinks with him. And it's been totally cool. Just a couple each night … but …"

Jex throws Molly an understanding nod. "But you're worried how your diabetes might react to it?"

Molly heaves a sigh that is equal parts exasperation and relief. "Exactly," she exclaims and immediately realizes her volume is just a couple notches too high for the patent section of the library. She clutches her eyes tightly for a minute before opening them again and repeating, much more quietly, really in a whisper, "exactly."

"I get it," Jex said firmly. "It's a real concern. How well are you managing it right now?"

Molly shrugs and holds her head down, shaking it slightly from left to right. "I dunno. I've had this shit for like four years now and it's OK. But, the doctors are all douches and the whole thing is ridic and exhausting. Plus, with the meds for TB, which are super fucking overwhelming …"

"Yeah," Jex agrees. "I can only imagine." She knows that diabetes requires daily attention, and that Molly's TB diagnosis means that she will be spending many months on a carefully regimented diet of drugs, a literal cocktail of prescriptions to care for and monitor.

"I really can't remember everything all the time," Molly continues. "All the pills and log-keeping, I don't know, it's just not me. And now with maybe drinking every now and again, I don't know. I know I shouldn't be drinking but hell, I just want to, Jex. But, I feel, like, out of whack and I don't know what to do."

"Out of whack?" Jex repeats, studying Molly's face carefully.

"Yeah," Molly says. "Like something is not right in my head and my body. I mean, I try to monitor my glucose and take care. I know with TB it's more intense, and the chance of me … croaking are … higher."

Jex gestures softly in a shrug that is non-committal. She could tell Molly that the mortality rates for diabetics with TB is markedly higher than those without; that there is a growing epidemic of young people with TB and diabetes; that treating and managing these dual diseases is flustering doctors around the world. Jex thinks better of this and instead says nothing more. At least not at this point. She waits for Molly to continue.

"I dunno. It seems pretty bad to me."

Jex shrugs again. "It's not great," she agrees quietly.

"Anyways, yeah, my head's not been right the last couple of days, or my body. I've been sweating, shaking. I can't get my temperature right. I'm thirsty all the fucking time, no matter how much water I drink. I'm lightheaded or I'm dizzy. I'm either nauseous or I'm starving. I dunno, I feel like I'm pregnant."

Jex raises her eyebrows and looks carefully at Molly, speaking with her eyes but not saying anything. Molly hears what she is saying and shakes her head. "No, not pregnant. Not possible."

Jex nods and states the obvious conclusion. "Hypoglycemia," she states firmly.

"Yeah," Molly nods back, but then says, "Naw. I check my glucose levels really regularly and I'm OK right now. It teeters between being low and OK, but right now it's OK. A little low but OK. I'm worried about how much I can drink."

"Well," Jex says with humor in her voice, "I see why you don't want to talk to the doctors." She smirks. "I can't imagine they'd be too anxious to tell you how much booze is OK if you're diabetic with TB," she chuckles.

"Look, Jex," Molly says earnestly. "I don't want to get wasted. I don't want to get hammered and puke. I'm not into that. I see these dumb kids doing that, and I'm not into it at all. Like, at all. But Ian is drinking and all these cute little punk girls are drinking too, and eating whatever they want. And doing . . who knows what. I don't want to do who knows what, so I have to at least have a drink in my hand."

Jex chuckles again, and nods with understanding.

"Look, dude. I'm not going to be the one who tells you how much to drink, but there are plenty of places on the inner-webs that will tell you precisely what you need."

Molly grabs Jex's hand in exasperation, and points to her head with dire stabbing motions. "I know, Jex, I know. But there's something in my head that won't let me search. Every time I have tried in the last two days, I have gotten headaches and the screen looks black. I don't know." Tears well up in her eyes. "I think it's all just getting to my head. I can't use even my phone at all." She begins to cry, just a quiet one, though; almost like a weeping.

Jex taps on Molly's leg urgently. "Come on, Molly. Don't worry about it. I know this shit is overwhelming. Don't worry about it," she says reassuringly. "I can help you."

* * *

About forty-five minutes later, Jex and Molly are in the library's first floor café. Jex is drinking a Diet Coke and Molly is drinking black coffee. They are sharing a table and flipping through a big book that Jex pulled from the library, *Clinical Medicine* by Parveen Kumar and Michael Clark. Eighth Edition. Jex is pointing out little pieces of information about diabetes and Molly is taking it all in. "So, you see," Jex explains, "type 1 diabetes is increasing all over the place, see," she says, pointing at the page. "There's going to be 57.2 million people with it in ten years. That's crazy."

"Nuts," Molly agrees.

"And you see," Jex continues. "Diabetes is inherited. In other words, you can get it from your family. But, it's not genetically predetermined. See," she says, pointing. "Your chances rise if your parents have diabetes, but not that much."

"Mine never had it," says Molly.

"Yeah," Jex says. "It's just a few points, but it's super interesting."

"Yeah," Molly says, interested in the subject for what seems to be the first time. Jex moves on from the background.

"So, listen, Molly. I don't want to encourage you to drink, but the facts are you can. You can as a diabetic, and it won't kill you. It just won't. Just do it smart. You're not going to be one of the kids getting wasted and crashing out on the lawn."

Molly whistles through her teeth. "I don't have interest in that nohow."

"Yeah," Jex agrees. "No fun. But there are a bunch of tips to let you have a drink every now and then without knocking yourself into instant hypoglycemia. That's just the way it is. And how do you minimize the effects? It's pretty simple. Not much of anything you don't already know. Eat stuff, starchy stuff, throughout the night, if you drink."

Molly nods, taking in every word. Jex continues. "You shouldn't just start drinking at the beginning and keep drinking every night. Water is your friend. Alternate between booze and water. That's smart even if you're not a diabetic with TB. But if you are, it's super more important. For real."

Molly studies her fingers and considers what Jex says. "Totally makes sense," Molly says, turning her gaze out into the distance.

"And be smart about taking your glucose levels. Monitor both before you go to sleep and after – to make sure hypoglycemia isn't creeping in. I'm a little worried about some of the things you are saying you're feeling. Sweating, shaking." She reaches out and touches Molly's arm, which seems somewhat cold. "Those are pretty straightforward hypo symptoms. You sure you're cool?"

Molly nods. "Yeah, I'm taking insulin, and my pills . .. and monitoring my glucose levels. All that shit," she says with a chuckle, pulling her shirt sleeve up and showing the marks on her arms.

Jex takes her hand and quickly inspects her injection sites. She nods approvingly, though there is some hesitation in her grasp. Molly doesn't seem to notice. "Good," Jex says. You seem to be moving around in picking your sites. No fatty lumps or anything. No lesions or scarring, really."

"Yeah," Molly agrees. "I'm pretty careful not to leave marks," she says with a shrug.

"Ok," says Jex reluctantly. "Well, make sure you carry your monitoring system and some kind of hypoglycemic treatment in case you need it." Molly holds up her purse and pats it. "Got it covered," she says.

"And, Molly, for sure make sure that someone you are drinking with knows about it." Molly cringes but Jex continues. "For realz. It doesn't have to be Ian, but someone needs to know. If something goes wrong, somebody needs to be close by to know what to do."

Molly shrugs with resignation. "My girlfriend Sarah is cool. She knows. I can keep her kinda attached at the hip."

Jex smiles with a clear kindness. "Cool, boo. And remember, I'll give you my digits. You can always call me. Whenever, seriously."

Molly smiles. She reaches over and hugs Jex, the hug having that kind of texture that somehow demonstrates a particular kind of feeling. She is grateful.

"Now," Jex proclaims. "I need to get going, or Ms. Tubman is going to have a fit," she says. "What's your digits? I'll text you so you have my number." Molly smiles and they exchange numbers on their phones.

"Thanks, so much, Jex. I'm really mean it. I'm kinda freaked out about this whole thing. Ian and drinking and the TB and, shit, I don't know. It all seems so much." She is smiling and talking much more calmly, confidently, than she did when she walked in. The change is palpable. The two hug again and Jex watches as Molly walks down Figueroa Street. The sun is warm on Jex's face, and the pleasant feeling is not lost on her.

* * *

The night is dark in a way that some nights are wont to be. Stars pepper the sky but do little to illuminate the streets below. There is a street light here and there, but otherwise the street is dark. Jex tags in silence. Her eyes dart from point to point; she is somewhere else entirely.

Jex wouldn't know, if asked, how much time passes in the quiet darkness. All she would likely say if asked is that the silence was broken by a dumb question from Q. Jex never bought into that 'no stupid question' thing. Sometimes, a stupid question is just a stupid question.

"You see any cops around, Jexy?"

"No," Jex thinks to herself. "I don't. If I did, I would be a hundred yards down the street already." Instead, she just says, "no."

There is some more silence and Q breaks it, again, with this simple question. "You OK, boo?"

"Yeah," Jex nods absently, not distracting herself from her graffiti piece, which is kind of a mutation between her simple tag and a larger image that lies somewhere between a tiger and a muscular arm. "I'm just thinking about stuff."

"What stuff," asks Q.

Jex waves her off, clearly not wishing to talk about the stuff in her head. "Nothing. Just thinking." In an effort to change the subject, Jex raises her conversation with Molly from earlier in the day. "Hey, you know Eugene's sister, Molly? You know she's in a band now?"

Q nods with sudden exuberance. "Yeah, Bawdy DySmurfia," she exclaims. "They are totally awesome!"

"Oh," Jex says. "Have you heard them?"

Q shrugs. "Not really. I spent a night at a squat last week, one of the chicks in the band is staying there."

"Yeah," Jex says back. "I know that squat. Molly stays there sometimes. Eugene, too."

"Yeah," Q continues. "So. Molly was over and I heard them trying out a song. It sounded pretty cool." She pauses, thinking. "I think they were gonna call it: Physiology Not Fattyology," she says with a guffaw.

Jex nods and comments out of the side of her mouth. "Sounds like they're coming from a healthy place," sarcasm clear in her voice.

Q shrugs again. "Anyways, I like the name of the band: Bawdy DySmurfia. Makes me laugh all day."

"Yeah," Jex says quietly. "It's funny."

"You sure there isn't nothing wrong with you, girl," Q asks as she pauses her tagging for a moment to study her friend.

Jex shakes her head, almost bursting to make a rude comment about stupid questions. She refrains and leaves it at the head shake. She doesn't want to talk.

Q waits another moment but can't seem to stand the silence. "Molly's a cool girl. She made me laugh."

"Oh, yeah?"

"Yeah," Q nods, happy to be away from anything that might annoy Jex, who seems endlessly annoyable at the moment. "She is a total goofball, you know?"

"Yeah," Jex responds, seemingly back behind the cloak of absenteeism.

"Yeah," Q nods again, not prepared to give up. "She totally fell down the stairs, right in front of me. I thought she was like dead or something. Everybody in the squat was like ... whatttt?"

"Yeah," says Jex, her interest suddenly piqued. "She didn't mention a fall to me."

"Oh, she was OK. She jumped right up after like thirty seconds."

"Thirty seconds," Jex repeats in a voice that has become suddenly demanding.

"Yeah, maybe a little more, but not much. She was totally OK. She was laughing about it like the next minute. Man, she seemed like a bowling ball going down the alley, you know? Like her head hit the walls and the stairs and everything, you could totally hear it."

"No shit," Jex says, staring out to nothing, her tag trailing off, a thousand calculations suddenly spiraling around in her head.

"Yeah," Q confirms with a growly pitch to her voice. "She was totally OK, but there was a minute there where I was like, holy shit."

Jex's tagging stops completely and Jex is engulfed in silence. "No shit," she says in a whisper, not to Q or anyone else in particular.

"What's wrong Jex? Don't be worried. She is totally OK. I mean you saw her just today, right? She wasn't bleeding or nothing. She just got rattled around a little, like she tripped over her own feet or something."

Q barely gets out "her own feet or something" before she even notices that Jex is up and running. She jumps gracefully, urgently off the barrel she was standing on and she is running down the alleyway. Q is too shocked at the sudden action to move at all. She just stares quizzically as Jex tears down the road, disappearing almost immediately into the darkness.

"Jex," Q calls out quietly, more to herself than to Jex. She tilts her head in uncertain confusion and just stares out into the darkness where Jex was but was now nothing but darkness. It is not unusual for something to strike Jex as unusual; and it is not unusual for Jex to disappear into the night or even the day, following some tangent thought that rages without explanation into her head. But this was a fast exit, even for Jex.

Q shakes her head, and puts her hands on her hips in exasperation. The moon is bright above her but Jex's sudden departure renders the street particularly and unexpectedly empty. "Well," she says, chucking the spray paint can onto the ground. "Shit."

[Why is Jex concerned so suddenly about Molly? Is something really wrong? Turn to page 195 to read Jex's diagnosis and the conclusion of the story.]

LITTLE TOY SAXOPHONE

JEX BLACKWELL IS NOT IN THE HABIT OF CRITI-CALLY STUDYING HER BODY. Nevertheless, she stands in front of the long mirror in her bedroom, inspecting the image that reflects back at her. She is a mess. Tired. Gaunt. Almost skeletal. She peels off her gray sweatshirt and black v-neck t-shirt. They are drenched in sweat, and the a/c in her house has been shut off. She kicks off her Chucks and yanks off her socks; then her jeans and her underwear. She looks herself up and down. Her skin is almost translucent, scabs here and there, finger nails chewed down practically to the bone. She glares into her own eyes, which seem empty through her few years. Red and swollen, she can barely see the blue of her iris. She squeezes her eyes tightly shut for several seconds and then opens them, watching her reflection in the mirror emerge as the red and blue and green stars and lines fade in and then fade away.

There are very few things that Jex does without music, but she spends these several minutes with her mirror in complete silence, a weird soundtrack of its own. It's the eyes that get her, her own eyes, and she finds herself struggling not to cry again. It's an odd battle she has had to fight time and time again in the six weeks or so since she took Molly to the hospital. Before that night, she can't remember a time when it was even an issue. So be it, she thinks to herself. She turns away from the mirror and shakes her head as if to shake the thought away, her straggly blonde hair framing her thin face, locks flying this way and that. She throws on a clean t-shirt and a pair of basketball shorts, walks down the hall and lies on the floor of her living room.

Next to her is a Panasonic RX-FT500. Jex leans over and presses play, and the tape player begins to churn grumpily. The song by Johnny Hobo and the Freight Trains, *Whiskey is My Kind of Lullaby*, is a familiar one to Jex, having been played a hundred times maybe over the last few weeks, filling the emptiness of too many dark days, most of which did not find Jex leaving the house at all. She stares at the ceiling fan above her, watching it revolve as the tape grinds noisily. She tries to fade away.

She shuts off the tape before the song finishes and chucks it across the room; not hard enough to break it but far enough to make it kind of disappear. She has spent too many days – shit, too many weeks – being Johnny Hobo. It is time to spend some time being a little more Pat the Bunny. Damn, not even that. Something easier than that. It's time to be Ke$ha. It's time to be Taylor Swift. Well, hell, Jex thinks to herself, it's maybe not that bad. She settles on The Front Bottoms and has it on her iPhone in no time. The music, Jex finds, is somehow easier to fade away to than Johnny Hobo, which wasn't the case even two days ago.

Several songs on the playlist pass before Jex rubs her face and stands up. "Shit," she murmurs to herself and looks around. She walks over to the jeans she kicked off, picks them up and starts to rummage through the pockets. She finds her keys and walks them over to her kitchen, drops them into a dish near the sink, where she always keeps them. She goes back into the jeans pocket, pulls out about thirty dollars in crumpled bills and some change. She begins to deposit the coins into two jars next to the keys dish, as she always does, silver in one jar and bronze in the other.

As she sorts out the pennies from the nickels from the dimes and quarters, she comes across a bronze coin that is larger than a penny. She instantly recognizes it and sighs, dropping the rest of the change onto the kitchen counter. She fingers and rubs the coin, and through foggy eyes, she reads the stylized writing: "18" and "To Thine Own Self Be True." "Shit," she murmurs again, and shakes her head, strands of hair falling down onto her face. She looks back over to the kitchen counter, picking through the change. She picks up another coin, a white chip actually, and studies it as well. The bronze chip she's had for almost twenty months. The white chip she just picked up this morning. She shakes her head again and chuckles. Without a further thought, she tosses the bronze one into the garbage bin. She rubs and studies the white chip for a minute and then sticks it in her pocket. Grinning to herself, she sorts the remaining change and then walks back into the living room. She presses shuffle on the iPhone and lies down next to it on the hardwood floor. There is a pause of just a second and then music begins. *Sycamore* by Martha. Good deal.

As the music floats around her head, Jex smiles at the ceiling fan blades as they circle and circle around her. The music hits her and she can't help but jump up. Instantly she is dancing wildly, all alone, her small frame moving this way and that way in a delicate mixture of grace and earnestness. She bangs her head. She air guitars. She throws her hands into the air, a stupid grin all over her face. As the last notes of the tune play, she drips back down to the floor, lying next to her iPhone, now as quiet as the end of a playlist. She lets the silence syphon through. She is faded away.

The time Jex spends in silence lying on the floor is unclear, but after some time passes she sits up and looks around. The cigarette butts in the bottle. The dust in the corner. The stacks of clothes everywhere. Black-out curtains shut tight. Pizza boxes. The mess is cliché in its completeness. Jex just shakes her head. "Fuck," she mutters and picks up her pack of Camel Crushes. There is only one left and it is in the pack upside down; her lucky cig. Jex pauses for just a minute and then pulls it out and lights up. She never used to smoke in the house.

A couple of drags and Jex stands up. She walks to the front of the house and pulls the curtain to one side. The sun is bright and hurts her eyes. "Fuck," she repeats and closes them abruptly. She sighs. She takes another drag. She leans her back against the closed front door. She looks around from side to side and then to the iPhone in her hand.

"Fuck," she says for the third time and then opens her iPhone, dials some digits with her thumb. "Fuck," she whispers as the phone rings. "Fuck, fuck, fuck."

"Hey, Q," Jex says. She listens to Q on the other end of the line.

"Yeah, I'm sorry."

Jex pauses and listens.

"I know, I'm sorry. I'm OK." She grimaces.

Another pause.

"Uh, so … you wanna come over, just hang out?"

Jex nods her head.

"Uh hmm. Cool."

Jex looks around at the mess that surrounds and then at the clock on her iPhone. "Why don't you give me two hours," she says, surveying the cigarette butts and dust and stacks of clothes everywhere, the pizza boxes and more. She stubs out her cigarette in an old beer bottle. "Yeah, I'll see you in a couple hours. Cool."

Jex hangs up the phone and, as walks down the hallway and into the living room, she looks up and sees her reflection in the mirror. She is smiling. The smile broadens and with a quick flick of the thumb, the music of Thao and the Get Down Stay Down is emitting from her iPhone. She throws the beer bottle into the recycling bin and begins to dance again.

* * *

Q sits on Jex's living room floor with her legs crossed, engulfed mercilessly in a big old belly laugh. She lies back and holds Jex's white chip in her hand, her arms extended outwards so the chip is framed by the sun shining through the window. "It's beautiful, Jexy! I love it."

Jex shrugs and smiles shyly. She fingers Q's green chip, flips it in her hands. "Yeah, I don't know. I thought I'd never end up back there. Or that it would seem like such a long struggle back to this one," Jex says, waving the green chip in her hand, and then tossing it back to Q. Q just barely catches it and smiles as she holds it over her head in a celebration of the catch. Jex smiles a little wider and gives Q a quiet round of applause to recognize the catch.

"Yeah," Q says, nodding her head. "I never thought I'd get to this one. And to actually be hopeful that I might hold a blue one soon enough."

"You will for sure," Jex says confidently. "You're a super bad ass."

"Naw," Q says, suddenly shy and hesitant. "I'm not nothing compared to you. You're a superhero, you know?"

Jex chuckles. "I'm nothing but a dumb kid that's thirty hours into a white chip. Just a stupid kid," she says quietly, somewhere between a laugh and a whisper.

"No way," Q protests. "I knew you were gonna say that shit. It's just bullshit. You fell off, like a lot of people do. But you made it Jex."

Jex shakes her head and stands up. She smiles again and walks to the window, staring out into the back yard. "I don't know, Q. I feel, good, I mean." She laughs and says, "I'm hungry all the time. I guess that's a good thing."

Q laughs and says, "it's always good for me to eat, I think. You want to get something downtown."

Jex shrugs, suddenly pensive. "Yeah, maybe." She pauses. "Or maybe not, I don't know. I mean, I want to, for sure, but you know, I have a few things I have to do still." She pauses again. "Some things I have to fix up right away. If I can, I don't know. I'm stupid."

"Stop saying that, boo."

Jex waves her off. "You know what I mean. I am just a mess. I don't know what to do."

"You can do whatever you want. You are so smart, with all that medicine stuff and all that."

Jex shrugs again. "That's all just bullshit."

"No," Q protests loudly.

Jex waves her off and continues. "It is," Jex insists. "I'm just a fraud."

No," Q insists right back.

"Yeah," Jex shoots back. "It's kind of like, back when I was a kid, my family rented a house in Calabasas for a couple years, in this fancy neighborhood. I was probably seven or eight. There was this kid that lived next to me, probably about my age now, fifteen, sixteen. Something like that. Anyways, he was in a band, like a crappy band. Crappy cover band. So, they used to practice in his garage, like Blink 182 and Green Day covers, shit like that."

Q laughs. "That's awesome."

"Yeah," Jex nods in agreement. "Really awesome. My bedroom was on that side of the house, so I would hear them sometimes when I was in there hanging out. And I would always grab this little toy saxophone that I had. Just a little piece of shit, I don't even know where I got it from, I guess my dad or maybe my uncle. I don't know. Anyways, it was shitty but it worked, you know? Just enough to make a really horrid noise."

Q laughs aloud and nods. "I know exactly what you mean. That's hilarity."

"Yeah," Jex says with smile. "I really made a racket. But, hell, they weren't that much better without me, you know," she continues with a chuckle. "What could it really hurt? But this one day, I am in my bedroom, reading a comic book. It was Captain America, I totally remember it. And I hear them starting to play. They were making a go of *Buddy Holly*," she laughs. "You know, by Weezer?"

"Yeah," Q affirms. "Totally."

"And so I grab my little toy saxophone and run out there. I mean, How could they do that song justice without some horns, right?"

Q is laughing so hard she has to hold her belly, like maybe she will puke or something.

"But the thing is, I get halfway across the yard, and my neighbor's little brother Kevin, who is probably eleven or twelve I don't know, stops me like he's the gestapo. He tells me the band is practicing for a Battle of the Bands thing and it's really important and I'm a distraction and I should just turn around and go home. They were rehearsing, and the band didn't want me there."

"Oh, shit," Q exclaims in a low tone, her grin melting into a grimace. "Harsh."

"Yeah," Jex shrugs. "I guess so. I was crushed, of course."

"Yeah," Q concurs. "No shit. I would be, too."

"Totally crushed," Jex emphasizes. "And, I totally remember it, too. Kevin goes running back to watch the band play Weezer, and I am standing there with my little toy saxophone in my hand, completely broken. I ran back to my room and cried into my pillow for an hour. I never played that stupid thing again." She pauses. "I would put on my headphones every time I heard the band play after that. They sucked anyways."

"For sure," Q agrees supportively.

"They were right, though. I mean, that I was just a distraction. I didn't do anything but squawk and howl out of tune and melody. I was just a stupid kid for sure, and they were, too. They had every right to play their shitty cover songs in their garage without some silly eight year old nipping at their ankles and blowing a goofy little toy saxophone."

"Fuck those guys," Q states defensively. "I bet they're all in Imagine Dragons or some bullshit like that now."

Jex laughs heartily at that. "You're probably right, Q. But, still. They have every right to be all the Imagine Dragons they want to be without me bothering them. And a few days ago, as I'm coming out of it, you know, just being sick and getting through it, and I'm starting to feel better. Like my head is getting clear, you know?"

Q nods her head and doesn't have to say a word. Jex knows that she knows exactly what Jex means.

"Yeah, so I'm just getting into that clear feeling, and it's feeling good," Jex says earnestly. "And I start thinking about the hospital and Molly and everything I have done, and that feeling came back. The feeling I had when that little shit Kevin kicked me out of the band practice. Like I was just a kid with a little toy saxophone, making a horrible racket to entertain myself. But not actually doing anything but making other people's shit harder. You know?"

"Dude, whatever. You saved Molly's life, for sure."

"No way, Q," Jex retorts. "I just got in the way. I almost killed her. I really am just a dumb kid and I have to stop taking myself so seriously. I mean, it's OK. I'm sixteen years old. It's not a shock that I don't know so much, but I know just a little bit and it's enough to, I don't know, make me dangerous."

No way," Q insists. "All the doctors said it. If it weren't for you, Molly would be dead. Now she is out of the coma and out of the hospital and doing OK. And you know what, I know I'm not supposed to say it or put pressure on your or anything, but she really wants to see you. A lot of people do. I mean, it's just bullshit to think you're not smart, I wish you would just see . . ."

Q stops her words in their tracks. She knows she has gone too far. Jex smiles a hard grin. All she needs to say is in that look. Q is instantly flush with regret. "Jex, I'm sorry. I don't mean to interfere. I just ..."

"Don't worry about it," Jex interrupts. "It's cool. It's just stuff I'm thinking. I don't mean to sound down on myself. I'm really not. I am just . . . sorting things out. I probably should have waited a few days before calling you. I just, I don't know. I just missed you."

As Jex speaks, it dawns on her that she is about to cry, and she finds herself choking back her tears. Q jumps up and practically tackles her in a hug. The two embrace for a long time, with Jex not quite crying but also not quite in control of her emotions. Q is much shorter than Jex but she still manages to get her in a pretty strong bear grip.

After some time passes, Jex gives Q a stronger hug and then pulls away. Q's senses are good and she lets her go. That's the only hugging that Jex needs, at least for the moment. "Hey come on, Jex," Q says. It's dark now. Let's go downtown and do some tagging. It's gonna be a nice night and I know a couple good places that would be fun to hit."

Jex smiles and touches Q's arm. "Thanks, Q. I'm going to stay in tonight. I have a couple things I have to do, and I'm kind of tired. And hungry. I'm gonna scarf down a couple frozen pizzas and crash."

"You sure, boo?" Q asks with a sense of concern. "You OK?"

"Yes," Jex promises. "I'm cool. Stop by tomorrow and we can hang out. Maybe we can take a dip in the pool." She smiles and maybe it's somewhat of a forced smile. Sometimes a forced smile is better than no smile at all.

Ok," Q nods and picks up her bag. "Well you know I'm around if you need me." She kicks at her skateboard and picks it up by its front wheel axle. "I'm always around."

The two high five and Q finds the door. They exchange one more hug and then Q is gone. Jex turns around to face the emptiness of her house. She is glad she cleaned the place up; she is glad she showered. She walks over to the kitchen and picks her iPhone up off the counter. She punches the keys and sends out a text, before heading to the fridge and pulling a frozen pizza out of the freezer. She scratches her face as she walks to the oven. Maybe two minutes after her text, her phone rings. She walks over and reads the text, which brings a crooked smile to her face. On the other side of the text, Dr. Johnson seems happy to hear from her, and is available for a coffee the next day. Jex pecks at the iPhone some more to get some music into the room. She dances to Martha as the frozen pizza cooks. She will smoke outside tonight, not inside. It is going to be a long evening.

* * *

Jex didn't sleep much last night. Headaches and body pain, sick to the stomach, nightmares drenched in sweat. Tossing and turning, groaning and moaning. Crying. Tears. A hundred hours stuck in six hours. She waited and waited for real sleep to come. It never did. The rise of the sun comes early today, but Jex rose even earlier. She sits on the small terrace off the master bedroom, sips coffee she made herself in an ancient French press she's had forever. Coffee is good. It seeps through her blood, jolting her as it flows through her veins. The jolt is good. She picks the sleep out of her eyes.

It is not quite ten a.m. when Jex finally makes it to the County hospital downtown. She is slow getting out of her car, perhaps dreading her visit. She sits in the car, listening to music, maybe a thousand thoughts flying through her head; maybe none at all. Though lo-fi folk punk is her typical music, today she is listening to FM radio. At the moment, "Obsession" by Animotion is playing. The words don't mean anything to her necessarily, but she bops her head up and down to the beat. A little bit of fluff can go a long way.

The cruel hand of the clock gets the better of Jex and, after as much procrastination as she can reasonably muster, she drags her body out of the car. She shuffles haltingly through the sliding glass doors entering the hospital. She doesn't bother to stop at reception. She knows exactly where she is headed.

Down the sterile hallway, into the elevator – crowded with patients and doctors and visitors – and hesitantly gets out at the third floor. She looks left and right but not like she doesn't know where she's going. It is something different, almost like someone might be following her. She is uncertain, nervous. Her gait is reluctant. After an initial hesitation, she proceeds down the hallway. She stops in front of a door, and hesitates again. Again, it is not like she doesn't know where she is. Rather, she knows precisely where she is but she maybe doesn't want to be there. After that stutter of a stop, she knocks on the door. Her knuckles sound like a whisper on the wood, almost like she wishes she wouldn't be heard at all. No such luck.

"Come in," came the voice of a woman from behind the door, confident and strong.

Jex hesitates one more time, takes a deep breath and then opens the door. "Hi, Dr. Stephens," Jex says as she walks in the door. Her face is flush. Her skin is cold and clammy. They have not seen each other for weeks.

"Jex," Dr. Stephens says. "It's good to see you." Her voice seems genuine. Her eyes glimmer. Her face glows.

The conversation is warm, real. The two talk on and on like they are friends in grade school. Dr. Stephens tells stories about when she was in medical school, how she would cram the last few days and eat nothing but pizza and coffee and never sleep. Jex tells a story about how she would always wait until the last day to study for chemistry exams in high school, fourteen years old, and always ace it. Reminiscing. They talk about a George Clooney movie that the Doctor saw. Jex says that she will make sure to see it. They talk about everything. Everything but the last six weeks. There isn't anything to say about that.

"Hey," Dr. Stephens says after about twenty minutes of chit-chat. "I've got a patient at eleven. Want to get a quick coffee before that?"

"Sure," Jex says with a grin. "I'm always up for some hospital coffee."

"Not as good as Starbucks," Dr. Stephens chuckles. "But it gets the job done."

"Oh, I will take hospital coffee over Starbucks every day of the week," Jex gushes, her voice fuller and more confident than it was twenty minutes earlier. "I refuse to drink Starbucks corporate crap."

"Perfect then," Dr. Stephens responds with a smile. "Hospital coffee will be just what the doctor ordered then. Government subsidized crap." The two stand up and leave the room, walk down the hallway. As they walk, Dr. Stephens rubs Jex's back. "I don't want to talk about everything if you don't want to, but it would be not such a bad thing to gain some weight."

"Well," Jex shoots quickly back. "Maybe we could have coffee and chocolate cake, then," she says with a smile.

"Coffee and chocolate cake it is," says Dr. Stephens and they walk down the hallway. There is a skip to Jex's step as they walk. Dr. Stephens doesn't notice, or maybe she just pretends she doesn't notice. The two make it to the café, and as promised, Dr. Stephens orders coffee and chocolate cake (with strawberry frosting) for each of them.

The two share good conversation. Dr. Stephens talks about a patient she is seeing. Jex listens rapturously, kneading each word in her head like so many pieces of wet clay. The patient is a middle-aged woman, presenting with obesity and depression. She had fallen and broken her ankle about a year earlier, but she was not caring for it and the healing was slow going. Jex nods her head as Dr. Stephens gets into details.

"So, then," Jex asks, "is she showing any signs of aggravated knee pathology on the injured knee?" Dr. Stephens can't help but smile at Jex's intuitive question.

"Exactly," she confirms.

"Secondary to the ankle?"

"Exactly," Dr. Stephens repeats. "And now she is experiencing pain in the cruciate ligament … on the leg that wasn't injured."

"A tear on the non-injured knee?" Jex queries. "Because she is relying on it too much?"

Dr. Stephens smiles and repeats one more time. "Exactly."

Jex looks pensively up above, seeming to be crafting her next question in her head. "Well," she says. "What about …"

"Hello, Ms. Blackwell," a deep voice with an upper class accent interrupts her. Jex looks up and sees Dr. Cohen, somewhat looming largely over her, glaring at her down his nose. She looks up at him and her eyes can't help but bulge a little bit in nervous surprise, despite Jex's best efforts to show no reaction. After just a moment of a deer-in-the-headlights expression, Jex looks down at her plate and takes a bite of chocolate cake with her fork. "Hi, Dr. Cohen," she says quietly, almost in a whisper.

"Good morning, Dr. Stephens," Dr. Cohen sniffs, turning his attention to his colleague.

"Good morning back, Dr. Cohen. What brings you slumming all

the way from Cedars-Sinai?"

"I," Dr. Cohen retorts, extending his "I" in a manner that can only be described as pretentious, "am tending to a patient that is not able to travel to my hospital at the moment. So I, quite cordially, am spending the afternoon in this fine establishment."

"Well, bully for you," says Dr. Stephens. Jex can't help but giggle a little bit at her tone.

"Indeed," Dr. Cohen sneers. "Well, I won't interrupt your chatting any longer. Good day, Dr. Stephens."

"Good day, Dr. Cohen," Dr. Stephens sneers right back.

Dr. Cohen quickly turns his attention from Dr. Stephens to Jex. "And you, Ms. Blackwell." Jex gulps and looks up at Dr. Cohen. Despite her best efforts, she can't help but be filled with something resembling dread as she waits in stilted anticipation for the sharpness of Dr. Cohen's impending barb at her.

"I trust you won't be away from us for so long any time soon?"

Jex gulps again and doesn't even seem to notice this time how her eyes bulge at Dr. Cohen's unexpected words. "I won't."

"Well," Dr. Cohen says in a snooty way that masks the sudden kindness in his eyes. "I certainly hope not." He pauses and then lowers his tall frame just slightly, his voice lowering to a whisper. "It is good to have you around again."

Jex smiles awkwardly, and swallows before saying, "Thanks. It's good to be here."

"Very good," Dr. Cohen snaps and pulls his body quickly up and rigidly stands at attention. "Good day to you both." He turns on one heel and disappears out of the café without waiting for any kind of response.

Jex looks over at Dr. Stephens, her eyes wide and her face slightly flushed. "Yikes," Jex says hoarsely. "That's not what I expected."

"Meh," Dr. Stephens harumphs and waves. "He's a crusty old S.O.B., but he's one of the good ones." She scrunches down a bit, her elbows on the table. "He was worried about you. We both were."

"I know," Jex says meekly. "I'm sorry."

"Don't be sorry," Dr. Stephens states firmly. "It's in the past."

"Yes," Jex says, just as firmly. "It's in the past." Her words are a little wobbly, but the sincerity of them is unmistakable.

Dr. Stephens pulls out her phone and checks the time. "Jex, I need to be getting back."

"Ok," Jex responds instantly, not wanting to be a burden.

"But, here's the thing, Jex. I mentioned that particular patient for a reason. I'm the head of surgery in this hospital. I don't typically see patients with broken ankles."

"Yeah," Jex says. "That was actually what I was thinking."

"And," Dr. Stephens continues, "it doesn't really matter why I took the interest, other than to say that I think she needs a little more personalized treatment, and I've taken a liking to her and her husband."

"Ok," Jex says, not knowing what else to say.

"And, well, I think it's important that, after your break, that you get right back into it, Jex. Two months ago, you were seeing patients with me, shadowing me. And, Dr. Cohen. I've spoken to the patient. And her husband. She has agreed to provide consent for you to participate in my examination of her today. I would like to invite you to come with me. I think it would be good for the both of you."

Jex pulls her head back in surprise. "Me?" she says with a start.

"Why me? What could I do that is unique or personalized?"

Dr. Stephens smiles slyly. "Well, sometimes patients can benefit from a different perspective."

Jex's eyebrows rise at the thought, and she almost feels a shudder down her spine. "I don't know," she says, rubbing her hands through her hair and grabbing at the ponytail that dangles down her neck. She looks down at her plain gray sweatshirt, jeans and Chucks. "I don't think I'm dressed right."

Dr. Stephens smiles again. "You're fine, Jex. Don't worry."

Jex shrugs and says, "Well, at least there aren't any holes in these jeans," inspecting herself.

Yes," Dr. Stephens says with a grin, "at least we have that," winking at Jex.

Jex shrugs and tips her head. She rubs her face and then, with a practice hand, puts two fingers on her septum ring and shoves it up and into her nostrils. It disappears easily.

"Wow," Dr. Stephens says with a nod. "Impressive."

Jex smiles. "It's not my first time."

"I'm sure it's not. Come on," Dr. Stephens says as she rises to go. "We don't want to keep the patient waiting."

Jex hesitates for just a moment and then stands to follow Dr. Stephens. "Ok," she says slowly through her teeth, a nervous twinkle in her eyes. "Let's do it." Jex's walk turns briefly into a jog as she catches up with Dr. Stephens, whose gait is fast and purposeful. The two walk out of the café, chins up and eyes determined.

* * *

The examination room is cold and sterile. Ms. Basira Awad sits on the examination table in a niqab, her eyes visible but she is otherwise completely covered. Her husband, Ammar, sits in a chair next to her. The two are silent. The discomfort in the air is tangible.

Dr. Stephens walks purposefully into the room and Jex follows behind, wearing her nervousness on her sleeve. She is surprised by the sight of Ms. Awad in her niqab. Jex momentarily panics but quickly regains her composure, kicking herself in her mind for letting something so irrelevant and natural throw her off kilter, even momentarily. She looks on steely as Dr. Stephens goes through a brief introductory statement.

"Ms. Awad, it is good to see you again."

"Thank you, Dr. Stephens," the woman says. "It is good to see you, too." Jex senses that maybe she is smiling behind the cloth, but she can't say for sure. Dr. Stephens turns to the man next to Ms. Awad and greets him, as well.

"And Mr. Awad. It is also good to see you."

"Dr. Cohen," says Mr. Awad, nodding his head in a respectful way. "Thank you very much for seeing us. We very much appreciate it."

Dr. Stephens smiles. "It is not a problem at all." Dr. Stephens turns to Jex with a slight wave. "Ms. Awad," Dr. Stephens continues. As I mentioned to you before, this is Jex Blackwell. She is a volunteer at the hospital who is preparing to enter college and will likely focus her curriculum on pre-med. I have asked for your consent to allow Ms. Blackwell to participate in the examination today, and you have agreed to that. This is done with the understanding that I will be in the examination and will lead the examination, even though Ms. Blackwell may be conducting portions of it. Of course, there may be elements of the exam that I may do a second time, so this may extend the time of the exam slightly, but not much. You are free to withdraw your consent to Ms. Blackwell's participation at any time, just by letting us know and I will take over from there, or begin the exam again, depending on what you would like. I would be grateful if you could confirm that consent."

"Yes," Mr. Awad states firmly, looking at Dr. Stephens and Jex in a manner that seems curious but also sad in some understated way. "We have spoken and we consent to the procedure you describe."

Dr. Stephens eyes Mr. Awad politely, but responds just as firmly. "Thank you, Mr. Awad. But, your wife is the patient and I really do need to confirm consent with her directly."

Mr. Awad awkwardly nods again, and says, just respectfully as before, "Of course. My apologies."

"Not a problem, Mr. Awad," Dr. Stephens smiles. "Just following procedure." She turns to Ms. Awad and asks her, "So, Ms. Awad. I would be grateful if you confirm your consent as previously described."

"Yes," Ms. Awad says. "I most certainly do." Again, Jex senses that Ms. Award is smiling.

"Very good," Dr. Stephens says with a nod. "Ms. Awad, we are going to ask you to disrobe. Your husband is welcome to stay if you like and you consent that, but if you would like to be examined alone, that is completely your choice and right to do so."

Mr. Awad seems to turn red, and speaks his words quietly. "With all respect, Dr. Stephens, I have every confidence that you and your young colleague are quite competent to conduct this examination without myself being present. My wife and I have discussed this and, if it is all the same, I will wait outside and return once the examination is completed."

"Of course, Mr. Awad. Thank you very much."

Mr. Awad moves towards the door but pauses a moment next to his wife. He reaches out her hand and she reaches back, touching hands slightly. "I will be right outside, my dear. You will be fine."

"Thank you, Ammar. I will ask them to bring you back in once the physical examination is complete."

"Thank you, my dear." He turns and walks towards the door and says, "Thank you again, Dr. Stephens."

"Thank you, Mr. Awad," Dr. Stephens repeats.

"And thank you, Ms. Blackwell." He speaks to Jex while looking straight in her. He speaks to her like an adult. "I am quite confident that you will see that my dear wife receives excellent treatment."

"Thank you, Mr. Awad," Jex says, mimicking Dr. Stephens.

Mr. Awad leaves the examination room. Dr. Stephens turns to Ms. Awad. "OK, Ms. Awad. You've come today because your left ankle continues to ache, even though the injury occurred over a year ago. Is that correct?"

"Yes, ma'am."

"And, also, you have noticed pain in your right knee, is that fair to say?"

"Yes, ma'am."

"OK, well. Ms. Awad. We are going to conduct an examination of your knees and ankles today and see what's going on, is that OK?"

"Yes, ma'am."

"And we've done these kind of examinations in the past, right?"

"That is correct, ma'am."

"And so you know that in order to conduct this examination

properly, you will have to disrobe down to your undergarments. Is that OK?"

"Yes, ma'am."

"OK, well, Ms. Blackwell and I will step out of the room so that you can disrobe privately. We'll come in about five minutes or so. Is that OK?"

"Yes, ma'am. Thank you." Jex and Dr. Stephens walk out of the room and close the door behind them.

"You OK, Jex?"

"Yes," Jex beams. "I'm doing great." She does seem to be beaming.

Dr. Stephens touches Jex's shoulder lightly. "You ready to conduct the exam?"

Jex does not hesitate. "Yes, for sure. I'm totally ready. Totally."

Dr. Stephens smiles. "Good, Jex. You're going to do great. Just keep focused and stay calm."

Jex smiles back. "I promise. I will."

The two stand in silence as the minutes click away. After about five minutes, Dr. Stephens says, "You ready?"

"Ready," Jex confirms. "Let's go."

The two walk into the exam room. Ms. Awad is standing in the middle room, wearing only her bra and underwear, unashamed and unapologetic. She is middle-age and overweight. Her face is beautiful and her eyes sparkle like a young girl. "Well, hello there you two. I thought you would never come back."

"Hello again," Dr. Stephens says cheerily. Jex chimes in as well, "Hello."

"Well," Dr. Stephens continues, "as we discussed, Ms. Blackwell is going to be performing some exams today, and I will be supervising. If you have any questions, please let us know. With that, I will hand you over to Ms. Blackwell."

Ms. Awad nods to Dr. Stephens and turns to Jex with a look that blends expectation and perhaps some level of amused, vicarious pride. "Ms. Blackwell, I look forward to your exam."

"Thank you, Ms. Awad," Jex says, her chin up and her eyes locked with her patient. "As Dr. Stephens said, my name is Jex Blackwell and I am not a doctor but a volunteer at this hospital. I have been trained for the examinations that are going to be conducted, that will focus on your knees and your ankles, and I would like to confirm that you consent to those exams."

With a smile, Ms. Awad confirms, "Yes, you do, ma'am."

"Great. Dr. Stephens will be supervising and if you have any questions or want me stop at any time, I will. Just let us know. Is that OK?"

"Yes, ma'am."

"Great. So, the first thing we are going to do is just ask you to walk from the edge of the exam table to that wall and back again. Just walk normally, not fast or slow – just the way you would typically walk."

Ms. Awad complies with the request as Jex watches with unrelenting focus. She observes the height of her steps, her ankle movement, the position of the foot and placement of the arches as she steps. She cocks her head a bit as she watches Ms. Awad walk, which can be described somewhat as a stilted gait. As she turns around and walks back towards Jex, Jex nods her head approvingly, saying, "Great. Very good. Now, can you just stand here for a minute. I'm going to examine your knees and legs and ankles for any swelling or scars or things like that, ok?"

"Yes, ma'am."

Jex bends down into a squatting position and looks carefully at each of Ms. Awad's legs and ankles, feeling here and there, each time prefaced with something like, "I'm going to squeeze below your knee for a moment, ok?" or, "I'm going to touch you right at the ankle for a moment, is that all right?" Each time, Ms. Awad affirms her consent with a "yes, ma'am." Jex studies each portion of Ms. Awad's legs fastidiously. Dr. Stephens observes each step with a sharp eye. Jex stands and, in a manner that belies her mere sixteen years of age, says, "Great. You're doing great," and speaks to Ms. Awad while looking her directly in the eye. Ms. Awad smiles back.

For just a moment, Ms. Awad's large, middle-aged frame juxtaposes in Jex's mind with her own slight frame that she was observing carefully just this morning. She remembers feeling gaunt, almost as if she were disintegrating away. Ms. Awad, although overweight, seems vibrant and alive, spry and sprightly, even. It resonates in Jex's eyes as she feels a sense of comfort in speaking with and examining Ms. Awad. In her eyes is a sense as though she is exactly where she is supposed to be. She smiles back at Ms. Awad and says, "why don't you just lie down on the examination table, on your back. We're going to run through just a few simple exercises to see how you're doing. Is that OK?"

"Yes, ma'am," Ms. Awad says in her knowing way and complies with Jex's request. So far, Dr. Stephens has not said a word, but watches carefully.

"Great, can you please extend your knee, fully? Great." Jex holds Ms. Awad's left ankle between her elbow and right side. She applies force to the knee with her right hand, towards the left. "Ms. Awad, I'm just applying what's called valgus force and varus force to your knee, to test your ligaments. To see if there's any issues there, OK? Does that cause you any pain?"

"No, ma'am. Not really."

"OK, how about if I go this way," Jex asks and applies slight force in the opposite direction.

"No," Ms. Awad says, watching Jex with the same sense of curiosity and amused pride she displayed earlier. "It doesn't hurt."

"OK, great. Now, I'm just going to try one other thing." She flexes the patient's knee to about ninety degrees, examining it while Ms. Awad's foot is held in place by the side of Jex's thigh. "Does that hurt?"

"No, ma'am."

"No discomfort?"

"No, ma'am."

"Great. You're doing fantastic."

Ms. Awad, smiles. "Thank you, you remind me of my son."

"Oh, thanks," Jex responds cheerfully. She does not see Dr. Stephens wince slightly behind her. "How old is he?"

"Well, he would be eighteen, but he died three years ago unfortunately."

Jex's body tenses but she otherwise does not show any reaction to this news. Dr. Stephens takes a step forward as though to intervene in some way, but she stops herself before she does. Jex doesn't seem to miss a beat.

"Oh, Ms. Awad. I am very sorry to hear that. That was three years ago?"

"Yes, ma'am. He unfortunately was involved in a car crash. He did not survive." She smiles in a way that covers her sadness but does not seem to betray her grief. It is a smile that somehow manages to respect the grief without being overcome by it.

"That's really sad, Ms. Awad," Jex says, looking again directly in her eyes. "My father died a few years ago, and it really hurt me badly. He was only forty eight when died. Cancer."

"That is very young, Ms. Blackwell. I am sorry."

Jex shrugs. "I still deal with it, I guess, but I had to put it behind me," she says bluntly. "The first year or so was terrible. I didn't even really want to get out of bed."

Ms. Awad smiles. "I know how you feel."

"That must be very hard on you, still."

"Yes, my dear," Ms. Awad says. "It is still very difficult."

"I am sure," Jex says. Dr. Stephens watches the interaction closely. Jex has returned to her examination while she is talking, almost without anyone even noticing. As she speaks with Ms. Asad, she peppers the discussion with instructions for the exam.

"Ms. Awad, can you please flex your left knee." Ms. Awad complies. Jex rotates the foot externally and abducts the upper leg at the hip. She keeps the foot towards the midline, creating a stress at the knee. As Jex guides Ms. Awad's leg to extend, she listens closely and hears a click. "Is that uncomfortable, Ms. Awad?"

"Yes, ma'am. A little bit."

Jex rotates the foot the other way, internally, and abducts the leg a little lower on the hip. She listens and hears a click. "Is that uncomfortable, too?"

"Yes, ma'am. A little."

"I see. OK, well we won't do that again," Jex says, with a smile.

"Thank you," Ms. Awad says with a slight smile, watching Jex closely.

"Yeah," Jex says, as she continues to prod and examine the knee. "So, I was totally bummed when my dad died, and everyone was like, you gotta get out of bed, you gotta get out of bed. But I didn't want to. I ended up failing the seventh grade," Jex chuckles. "I ended up passing though."

"I am quite sure you did," Ms. Awad says with a smile.

"Yeah, but they were right, even though I didn't want to admit it. It wasn't doing me any good just lying in bed."

"No," Ms. Awad says quietly. "I am sure it wouldn't be."

"OK, now I'm just going to extend your knee and push what's called the patella laterally, OK?"

"Yes, ma'am."

"Please flex that knee for me again, OK?"

"Yes, ma'am." Jex observes carefully as she does so. "Great, no resistance," Jex says. "You're doing great."

Jex continues her examination, having Ms. Awad turn her knee and ankle this way and that, first the left and then the right, instructing her to flex in various ways as Jex observes every motion. They continue to talk here and there, some about the exam and some about Ms. Awad's son. There is both sadness and acceptance in her voice as she discusses this.

After some time, Jex stands up and says, "Well, Ms. Awad, you did great. Just great. Thanks very much for being so patient. As I bet you could tell, I'm kind of new to this."

"Well, Ms. Blackwell, I'm no expert but I think you did pretty great."

Jex smiles, as Dr. Stephens looks on, with a smirk of satisfaction on her face. "Thanks, Ms. Awad. I really appreciate it. You can go ahead and get dressed. We'll give you a few minutes and come back and talk about what we found."

"So," Ms. Awad says with her grin. "Am I going to make it?"

"Yes, I think you are," Jex confirms with a grin. "From what I can tell …"

"Oh, can you just wait a minute," Ms. Awad interrupts her with a cute little shake of her hand. "I would very much like Mr. Awad to be in her with me, if that is OK? He will get very nervous if he's not listening in. He dotes on me very much that way."

"That's fine," Jex says and then catches herself. "I mean it's OK if it's OK with Dr. Stephens." The two look over at Dr. Stephens, who has been silent but observant the whole time. She smiles.

"We will of course honor your request to have your husband with you. Jex, are you comfortable giving your diagnosis in front of a crowd?"

It is Jex's turn to say "Yes, ma'am," now. "I am confident I have it right," she says in a manner that comfortably walks the line between confidence and arrogance.

"Great," Dr. Stephens says. "Ms. Awad, go ahead and get dressed. We will get your husband and bring him in when we come back in about five minutes."

Dr. Stephens and Jex leave the room as Ms. Awad begins to get dressed.

[Will Jex properly analyze the symptoms of what is ailing Ms. Awad? Turn to page 214 to read Jex's diagnosis and the conclusion of the story]

ANA GNORISIS

THE LIBRARY IS A SANCTUARY FOR JEX **BLACKWELL.** The stacks are a womb. The carpet is warm, safe; a reliable comrade in the endless war against everything. The low buzz of the ceiling fans emits the perfect white noise that dulls away all distractions. Every hallway and fire exit. The door on the fifth floor that has a lock that works in a funny way, which if Jex jimmies just so, she can sneak onto the roof and watch the city shuffle by beneath her. The old ladies reading Lilian Jackson Braun while the old men with funny hats pretend to read biographies of Churchill and spend all their time flirting; beautiful clichés. They are all friends to Jex, family in a weird way, whether they've ever shared a word with her or not.

And the books. The books. They are everything of course. Joan Didion and Thomas Pynchon; James Joyce and Toni Morrison. Sir Arthur Conan Doyle (her secret favorite) – Jex has read those a hundred times, maybe more. All of them her best friends. Poe and cummings and Virginia Woolf. They represent the one consistency in Jex's life. And Henry Gray, of course. The hours that Jex has spent in the downtown L.A. Public Library with the words of Mr. Gray and his intellectual colleagues and progeny are too many to contemplate. In this way, the library is not just a safe haven for Jex. For Jex, it is home.

It is, therefore, with an uncomfortable weight that Jex sits on the first floor, in an uncomfortable wooden chair, outside the office of the library manager, Ms. Tubman, preparing to fight uncomfortably for her job as a library assistant. Jex has been absent without leave from the job for weeks now, fighting demons. The demons seem to be at bay, for now, at least. She disappeared without notice from her duties, though, and provided the library more than enough reason to fire her. Jex wouldn't blame them at all if they didn't consider her back at all. Jex wouldn't be surprised if they had already hired someone else. But, if Jex doesn't have her job at the library, one of the very foundations of her existence will be gone, and there aren't many left. Jex pulls at the short pony tail that holds her dirty blonde hair back. She straightens and re-straightens her wrinkled gray sweatshirt and ruffled jeans. The uncomfortable weight on Jex's spirit, as she waits for her chance to advocate for her job back, is a heavy one indeed.

The office door opens suddenly and Ms. Tubman thrusts her head out into the waiting area. "Jex," she beckons. "Come in. Please." Her words are abrupt and serious. Jex stands and hesitates for just a moment in sort of a 'fuck all this' kind of way, but it doesn't last long. She shuffles into Ms. Tubman's office. Ms Tubman closes the door behind her and the two sit down. Ms. Tubman offers some water to Jex. Jex declines.

"So," Ms. Tubman says, looking across her messy desk at Jex, a stern look on her face. "It's nice to see your ugly mug again."

Jex smiles awkwardly, just a tiny smile, no more than a reluctant grin, really. She plays with her fingernail and says, "Ms. Tubman,

I'm really sorry I went AWOL. I don't really have an excuse, I just
…"

"Jex, please," Ms. Tubman interrupts, her voice as hard as nails. "I
didn't ask for an excuse and I'm not looking for one. Your excuses
don't matter to me."

Jex recoils just a little bit, stuck somewhere between remorse and
rebellion.

"I'm sorry," she stutters. "I don't know …"

"Stop it," Ms. Tubman interrupts again. She looks Jex straight in
the eyes, hard and firm. "I don't want to hear it."

"OK," Jex says, extending the word in a clumsy fashion that is
either obstinate or scared, maybe a combination or both. "I don't,"
she tries to continue but Ms. Tubman stops her again.

"Don't, Jex, just don't."

"OK," Jex say. She is, apparently, just here to listen. She thinks for
a moment that she might just get up and leave, extend a middle
finger and just leave the library behind. Leave everything behind.
Despite these instincts, the kind of instincts that grow in you as a
kid and never leave, she doesn't follow them. She just sits there and
waits.

"My emotions are very strong, Jex, they always have been. I'd like
to think that they don't rule my world, but that would be a lie.
Maybe if they didn't, I could be somewhere other than this old
library. Not that it's so bad, but emotions can be a tough thing.
That's my point."

She pauses a moment, as if to measure how well Jex is following
along. "OK?" is all Jex could say in response, and that's just enough,
maybe, and so she continues.

"Emotion can be a tough thing," Ms. Tubman repeats. "And emotion can be limiting. But I've found over time, though, that if you follow emotion, there will be more good than bad. It's OK to trust in your emotions. There is good and there is bad. And it's your emotions, your instincts, if you follow them, more often than not, you will find right, not wrong. I believe these things."

Ms. Tubman doesn't ask Jex this time whether she understands her point, but she does study in a way that suggests she is trying to see if Jex gets it. Jex doesn't respond and Ms. Tubman never asks. She just continues.

"Jex," Ms. Tubman continues. "I am not one to judge or criticize. I believe in good and bad. And I think you do, too. And I believe in you."

There is a long pause and Jex says all she can think to say, which is: "thank you."

Ms. Tubman doesn't respond this time. She just says this: "Can you come in Tuesday, ten to four?"

It takes Jex a second to break that sentence down. She pauses in a way that seems more like making sense of it rather than hesitating at the offer. Jex shakes herself out of it and says the only thing she can say: "Yes, I am. I mean, yes, I can."

"Good," Ms. Tubman says, without any hesitation on her side. "Tuesday, ten to four it is." Ms. Tubman stands up and walks over to Jex, who also stands up.

Ms. Tubman embraces Jex, and it feels warming and comforting in a way that Jex did not expect, nor does she feel understand. She hugs her back, which is all she can really do. "Oh, you've gotten so skinny, Jex."

"Just a few pounds," is all Jex can say. She knows it's a few more than that, and that she couldn't really afford to lose even a few pounds before she disappeared. She doesn't think about it much, or much other than the comforting feeling that Ms. Tubman's hug provides. She doesn't articulate it though, and neither does Ms. Tubman. The hug finishes and Ms. Tubman walks Jex to the door. "OK, Jex, see you on Tuesday."

"Thanks, Ms. Tubman," Jex says, a mature earnestness obvious in her young voice. "I really appreciate it."

"You're welcome, Jex. The library is delighted to have you back."

Walking out of the office through the library halls – her most comfortable stomping grounds – Jex can't help but smile. Behind her, out of her eyesight, Ms. Tubman can't help but smile, too.

* * *

The café in which Jex sits is no Starbucks. It is blunt and simple, more dirty than clean. Like the café in which it is served, the black coffee Jex drinks is purely utilitarian, no flower made of foam lingering coyly on the surface. She drinks it from a white mug, unadorned and unembellished; no plastic cup with a pithy phrase running down its spine. It is the best coffee in L.A. that seventy-five cents can buy. There's no commissioned soundtrack flowing smoothly from overhead speakers, hidden from view; just the tinny sound of Otis Redding straining from a tiny radio behind the counter. The sound is lo-fi. Jex likes it that way and she chooses to listen to it while she drinks her coffee instead of disappearing into her ear pods. She likes, too, the clattering of dishes and mumbling of the dozen or so people that populate the fairly sparse greasy spoon.

As she sips and thinks, Jex sketches absently in the pad that is resident in her oversized messenger bag. The pad itself is something to see, with a cardboard cover completely covered in green-ink drawings and black sharpie tags. The edges of the pages are tattered and torn, and the pad seems nearly full of drawings, doodles and sketches.

Inside the tattered pad, Jex draws what she likes to draw best: anatomical figures. At the moment, she is sketching a side view of the human heart. She takes great care with the curves of the coronary artery; spends minutes on the complex map of fine capillaries, studying each capillary carefully, recognizing its individuality and character before moving on to the next. The broad arc of the left auricle, still beautiful in its simplicity. No more than a fuel pump, straightforward as that. The little circles that stand proud as crowns on the aorta. The elegant lines of the inferior vena cava. As she completes each section of the heart, she carefully labels them in compact, neat lettering.

Jex focuses so intently that at first she doesn't hear the drumming and chanting growing louder outside the café. She goes over each pencil line carefully in pen, picturing the red and blue slopes and twists and coils as though they were real, replaying in her head as she draws the photographs she'd seen in books and videos she watched endlessly on YouTube. She is in her own world.

"Now, what in the world is that," says a waitress behind Jex, and Jex is momentarily distracted from her sketching to look at the waitress, who had walked past Jex and was now looking out the front window. Jex follows her gaze and sees a growing crowd in the distance. The chants and drums suddenly come into focus in Jex's head and instantly command her attention. Jex sees colorful signs and banners in the crowd, which is starting to morph into something that seems organized. The drums grow more distinct and begin to sound more robust than just stark percussion. It is starting to sound like music.

"Oh," Jex says with a note of abrupt recollection. "Shit."

The waitress looks back at Jex. "What's up, sweetheart?"

"Oh geez, Jo," Jex says absently, as much to herself as to the waitress. "I think I'm late." Jex fumbles through her bag and pulls out the flyer she received the prior week. It is dated today and the time is 3:00. Jex looks at her phone and sees it is 3:15. "Oh, shit," Jex repeats, and stands up. She stuffs her hand into her hip pocket and pulls out a fist of crumpled dollars. She drops two bucks on the counter and says, "Sorry, Jo. I'm super late. I gotta go."

Jo shrugs. "You gotta go, girl, you gotta go. Don't be no stranger, now."

Jex smiles as she opens the door. "Never, Jo. I promise." She rushes out and heads north toward the crowd. The waitress Jo watches Jex as she goes, a reluctant grin on her face.

* * *

By the time Jex gets to the protest, the passion is already hot and Pershing Square swells with people. There are protesters everywhere, of every size, seeming to be protesting about every issue imaginable. Anti-government; anti-racism; pro black power; pro Native American power. On the flyer that Jex found, the protest advertises itself as an anarchist battle against poverty, and it seem that anarchy is the road map of the day. Everyone seems interesting in having their say.

Drum beats, the whole square seems to pulsate to the drum beats, which are morbid and loud; frenetically paced. And over that, "Testify" by Rage Against the Machine blares from a sound system somewhere in the park, Jex can't quite see where. The dueling rhythms of the song and the drums don't quite match, instead melding together into a tinny cacophony of angry sound. Jex's heart seems to race with it, and she looks around the mad crowd, the din of outrage loud in the air.

Jex promised Eugene and Molly that she would meet them at the southwest corner of the Square, but that was twenty minutes ago and the crowd is practically a mosh pit at this point. "Shit," Jex says out loud but not loud enough for anyone to hear over the shouts and chants. She's never going to find either of them like this. She pulls out her iPhone and clicks Molly's number. It rings and rings and goes to voicemail, though Jex wouldn't have been able to hear her voice if she had picked up. The sound is outrageous.

"Oh, well," Jex thinks to herself. "I guess I'm on my own on this one." She looks around at the crowd; some people screaming at each other and some chanting together in unison. There are protesters and anti-protesters. The sun is hot above. Jex looks around in a three hundred sixty degree circle. She sees that police encircle the entire perimeter of the square. Jex is not sure if it is ominous or comforting; maybe neither, maybe both. Perhaps it just depends on who's looking, she guesses. She looks around, surveying her surroundings. She sees a group of about a dozen women, mid-fifties or so, some black and some white. They are holding hands in a straight line and marching with determination through the crowd, almost like a left-wing conga line. They dress sensibly, sneakers and comfortable slacks. The woman in the front holds a sign that says: "Stop Anti-Woman Violence." The group is chanting loudly in time, "Say it once, say it again! No excuse for violent men!" Jex shrugs. "Makes sense to me," she thinks and heads to the back of the conga. Someone hands her a sign. It says, "My body, my choice." Jex grabs it and thrusts it into the air. "Say it once, say it again," she chants

ANA GNORISIS

along in her gruffest voice. "No excuse for violent men!"

Fifteen minutes or so pass, and Jex savors each one of them as she snakes her way through the crowd. She looks ahead and the woman in front of her looks back at her and smiles. She seems slightly older than the rest of the women in the line, maybe sixty or so. Her smile is sweet. "Thanks for joining us, kiddo!" the woman shouts. "I was protesting when I was your age, too. My body, my choice!"

"My body, my choice!" Jex repeats loudly, with a big grin. She is having the time of her life. She scans the crowd again, studying every face carefully. White faces. Black faces. Brown faces. Red faces. Yellow faces. Everyone having their say. Everyone having their moment to shout; their moment to scream at the top of their lungs. The people and the voices melt together into one. The result is a dreamy mess of surrealism. Jex is not sure if she is awake or asleep. She feels alive, though. That is good enough for her.

"Jex!" The voice is loud and clear over the roar of the growing, excited crowd. Jex jolts around at the sound of her name. Her friend Eugene stands behind her, his face nothing but a grin. "How are you, girl?"

"Eugene!" Jex shouts back at him and gives him a big hug. Eugene is a big boy, with large shoulders. His hair is pulled back and his eyes are wide. He has a large red sign that says "Free Leonard Peltier" on it in black lettering, surrounding a black stencil of Peltier's face. "I'm sorry I'm late," Jex shouts. "I got distracted."

Eugene chortles. "Of course, you got distracted, Jex. Of course! You always get distracted! It's OK with me! As long as you made it, I'm happy!"

"I wouldn't miss it," Jex confirms. She looks around, her eyes wide. "It's amazing, isn't it?"

Eugene nods his head, enthusiasm and sweat dripping from his body. "It is totally radical. There are so many groups represented here," Eugene shouts. "There really is an uprising on the way, and this is where it starts, Jex. This is the breeding ground for a new society!"

"That's awesome," Jex yelps. "You are such a bad ass!"

Eugene shouts with a laugh. "Nah, I'm just doing my part. You know Native Americans are gonna start getting some proper representation in this town now, right? Everybody has to do something, right Jex?"

"That's right," Jex agrees, her eyes glimmering.

"You're going to do something great, Jex," Eugene says, putting his hand on her shoulder. "You are going to help a lot of people with your head,

" he says and then pauses, before tapping his own chest lightly. "And with your heart. You need both of those things, right, Jex?"

"Yes," Jex says, nodding her head in agreement, in a way that fairly gushes with pride and determination. "I understand."

Eugene holds up his hand, and Jex pauses. He looks over his shoulder, listening to something in the distance. After a moment, a look of satisfaction takes over his face. "Yes!" he says emotively. "This is the Sex Pistols playing."

"Yeah," Jex agrees. "'Anarchy in the UK.'"

"Exactly," Eugene explains "Boy do I have a surprise for you!"

'What's that?"

Eugene is nearly imploding with excitement. "I know the DJ here, DJ Somethin' Kool. He's part of the revolutionary vinyl movement, playing loud, mean songs at protests."

"That's cool!" Jex says.

"Yeah, well that's not the coolest part. He owes me a favor and he agreed to play one of Bawdy's songs after he played the 'Anarchy in the UK'!"

Jex is delighted. Eugene's sister, Molly, plays bass for Bawdy DySmurfia. "What," Jex exclaims. "No way! How?"

"I snuck him a copy of their new seven inch. It's their first release."

"What!?? No way. I knew they recorded it but I didn't know it was out yet."

"Well," Eugene say slyly. "It's not released formally yet, the record label is doing a little release party in Echo Park next month." Eugene winks," but I know someone in a position to get me an early copy. DJ's gonna rock that shit right after this song. The crowd is going to love it."

"For sure," Jex agrees. She is about to ask what songs they ended up putting on the seven inch – they had several to pick from and she is personally hoping for "Anarchy isn't Just a Fanny Pack with a Circle A on it" – when her conversation with Eugene is interrupted.

"Hey, brother," says a large young man in a flannel shirt, touching Eugene's arm slightly. "We're late and we gotta go."

Eugene pulls his phone from his pocket and checks the time. "Shit," he says. "I didn't know it was getting so late. We gotta go." He turns to Jex. "Jex, we gotta go. We're going to have ten minutes at the microphone and we have to finish coordinating what we're going to say." He pulls a folded up piece of paper from his breast pocket. "Trust me, though. We have plenty to say."

Jex smiles, "I know you do," she says and pats him on the shoulder.

"Stay safe," Eugene says as he turns to go. "This place is cool, but vibes can change quickly. Take care of yourself."

"I will," she says with a wink. "I'm pretty good at taking care of myself."

Eugene nods and turns to leave."Oh, wait," Jex says. "Where's Molly? I want to find her if I can."

"Yeah, dude. For sure. I just saw her. I am pretty sure she is headed to the DJ table. She wants to be in prime listening position for when the song comes on. It's that way," Eugene says, pointing to the northwest corner of the park, where Jex can just make out some turntables set up on a raised platform.

"Which song are they going to play?" Jex asks.

Eugene grins. "Fanny Pack!"

"Cool!" she shouts, with a grin equal in size. She gives Eugene a final hug and watches as he walks away. The conga line is long gone, so Jex is on her own to make it through the thick crowd over to the DJ stand. She makes it about a hundred feet before she hears the unmistakable bass riff. Bawdy's song is starting. "Whoop," Jex yells, and quickens her pace to the DJ stand as the first lyrics start to drop.

Anarchy! Anarchy!

Direct action! it's the time!

Anarchy! Anarchy!

Always gaining traction! Crossing every line!

Five guys with black bandanas covering their faces run past Jex, waving tall red flags recklessly through the crowd. They are yelping out some words that don't seem to make any sense, almost like speaking in tongues. Jex shakes her head in momentary annoyance and continues her trek to the DJ stand. The song continues to jam, as the drum circle picks up its pace, closing in on the rhythm of the track.

Anarchy! Anarchy!

Moving forward! Never backwards!

Anarchy! Anarchy!

Grooving towards you! Bearing swords!

A man dressed all in black, with a black and white keffiyeh around his neck, shouts out that Israel must pay, and that genocide must end. His eyes swarm about in a way that, from the corner of Jex's eyes, seems off. She keeps walking, not taking the time to think more about it. She really wants to get to Molly before the song ends and, like any good punk song, it's not very long. Time is of the essence.

Because anarchy isn't just a fanny pack

With a Circle-A On it.

Not your Walmart Guy Fawkes mask.

We don't need your poseur scene.

Jex spots the conga line of women again, about half way across the park, almost in the center. She pauses for a moment and considers heading back to meet up with them, convinced she will not make it to the DJ stand before the song ends. It seems like a much easier walk and the crowd seems to be largest and most rowdy around the DJ stand. Still, she thinks, she'd like to say hi to Molly and she knows Molly will be stoked to talk about the song. So, she continues onward as the song and the drums get louder and louder.

We will tear down those goddamn barricades

And show you what we mean!

When the first explosion hits, no one mistakes it for anything other than an explosion. The bang is like a cannon blast, and the ground vibrates. People are on the ground. People are in the air. Dirt and bricks fly around in a tornado of dust. Dirty paper floats up and down like big pieces of confetti. Trees are uprooted. Limbs are torn off. The Square sits in shocked silence, only the faint, robotic whirl of car alarms in the distance.

It is a child that begins to scream first. A woman's cry follows. Within seconds, there is moaning and weeping and yelling. "Help!" squeals a nameless face. Someone else, some other anonymous voice, screeches out in pain. Smoke rises from close to the DJ stand. A chorus of other voices begin to crackle in a thousand individual tones. Pain. Fear. Anguish.

When the second explosion hits, thirty seconds later, all of these emotions strip away and melt together into one single emotion: panic. Sheer, mad panic. It is not intuitive, perhaps, to fear a second blast immediately after a first blast occurs. It is, however, much more predictable to consider a third blast after a second one. And so in these moments, there is nothing in the air but panic.

But not Jex. Jex is cool as a cucumber.

The Square is a mess and it is easy enough as a matter of practical triage to divide the mass of people into two groups: those who flee and those who shelter in place, including the immobilized injured. There are the dead, too, of course. But, at the moment, they don't really matter. Only the living matter. And with her instincts now suddenly commanding her, it is the living to whom Jex tends. Even before the smoke clears. Even before the last piece of dirt falls to the ground. Even before anyone knows whether there will be a third, or even fourth explosion. Even before she knows whether any of her friends are OK, whether they are alive or dead. Even before all of that, Jex begins to tend to the living. She ducks those that are fleeing, and focuses on those she can identify as immobilized injured. She picks her first patient the old-fashioned way: she responds to the closest person screaming for help.

"Help," the woman wails. "Help me, please."

Jex blinks twice, rustles her hair with her hand, and in a small crouch, she jumps to the woman, who is sitting on the ground with her legs to the left side. "Hi, I'm Jex. What's your name?" she asks in a firm, confident tone. There is no hesitation in her voice.

"Ann," the woman says.

"Hi, Ann," Jex continues, calmly. "What hurts?"

"Everything hurts," the woman chokes out.

"I know," Jex says patiently. "What hurts most?"

"My arm, sweetheart. My arm and my wrist."

"Which side," Jex asks.

"My left side."

"Why don't you stay seated, Ann, but put your legs in front of you. Can you sit up without supporting yourself with your hands or legs?"

"Yes," Ann says, as she moves her legs around. "I think so."

"Thanks, Ann. That's great." Jex continues to look at Ann's arms and body, but does not yet touch anything. Jex reaches back in her head to the rescue medicine books she has read, and the course she took on mountain rescue the prior summer. Some things in life make fundamental sense to Jex, and in that way, they instantly become part of her internal memory chip. One of those things is ABC in a trauma situation: airway (is it open), breathing (are they breathing) and circulation. The point is simple: make sure the person you are examining gets enough blood into their body, or else hypoxia will set in, followed by cardiac arrest and that's it. So, everything else is secondary to that.

A: Airways. Jex knows that the airway is clear simply by the way that Ann is talking. Check. B: Breathing. It's not just a blocked airway that can affect someone's breathing; many things can. So, Jex takes a moment to observe Ann as she speaks. She does not appear to be struggling abnormally for breath, particularly in light of the stressful situation, nor does she exhibit any clear signs of respiratory distress. Jex moves on with a silent check. C: Circulation. Jex takes Ann's right hand. "That's not the hand that hurts," Ann says, protesting slightly. "I know," Jex says in a reassuring but still firm tone. "I'm just checking your circulation." "Oh," Ann says. "I'm sorry." Jex doesn't respond, but focuses instead on her work. She applies pressure to the fingertips, and then releases, watching the blood flow out and quickly in, demonstrating proper circulation. She checks her pulse with her hand on Ann's uninjured wrist, with the stethoscope head placed slightly above. About 80 beats per minutes; on the high side but not unusual in a stressed situation. She looks carefully at Ann's face, hands and fingers; not unusually cold or discolored. Circulation: check.

"And can you tell me what happened to you? I mean, I know what just happened. But, what happened to you."

"I was just standing there, I don't even care about politics. I just saw all these people milling about, and I didn't have nothing to do, so I just walked over, doing some people watching. Next thing I know there is some dang explosion over there." She nods slightly with her head. "And it's the loudest thing. I just bent over and put my hands over my ears. Next thing I know, there's another bang and something hits me on the back of my head. Right here," she gestures the a spot right above her neck. "That didn't hurt none, but it made me lose my balance. I fell on my left arm. And now I'm here."

"OK," Jex says. She pulls her messenger bag over and pulls out an otoscope and a stethoscope. She wraps the stethoscope around her neck like a necklace.

"OK, Ann. First things first. I know you said that whatever hit you on the head didn't hurt, but before we get to your arm, I just want to check you out and make sure your head is OK, OK?"

"OK," confirms Ann, not particularly being in any place or mood to argue with the point.

"No pain?" Jex asks. "Headaches?"

"No."

Jex takes the otoscope from the pocket of her hoodie and turns it on. "I'm just going to take a quick look in your eye, OK?"

"OK," Ann agrees.

Jex points the light of the otoscope in both of Ann's eyes. The pupil of each side constrict quickly when focused on the light. Good sign. Jex smiles, winks at Ann and moves on.

"OK," Jex says. "I think your noggin is just fine."

"Thanks."

"Now, that arm," Jex continues, looking at the left arm. It is beginning to swell from the wrist to at least above the elbow, under the hem of Ann's dark t-shirt. "You're going to have to go to a hospital, of course, but let's just immobilize that thing a bit for now, try and minimize that pain."

'Oh, thank you," Ann gushes. "It hurts so badly, all the way up the arm."

"I understand," says Jex. "Can you just bend your elbow a little bit for me?"

"Yes, I think so." Ann moves the elbow so it is at almost a forty five degree angle. "Great. Let me just unhitch that watch from your wrist there, or else it's going to swell up and hurt real bad. I can just stick it in your bag there, if that's ok?" Ann agrees with a head nod. Jex removes the watch without resistance, and drops it into Ann's handbag, which she is clutching with her healthy hand.

Next, Jex pulls a roll of cloth bandage out of her messenger bag. Sitting directly in front of Ann, Jex pulls out a long piece of bandage and rips it off with her teeth. She folds the cloth in half diagonally and forms a triangle. She folds the lower part of the bandage over Ann's forearm. She brings the upper part of the bandage down over the upper edge of Ann's shoulder, and then ties the two pieces together in a reef knot. Jex tugs at the improvised sling slightly, and nods in approval at her handy work. "How's that," she asks Ann.

"It's OK," says Ann. "Thank you very much. What did you say your name was?"

"My name is Jex."

"Jex, thank you, but I will survive here. You should be using your skills with others who are more injured than me."

Jex blinks. She looks around. It is a battlefield around her. She didn't even notice; didn't see it, didn't hear it, didn't smell it. Not when she was focused on Ann and what she could do to ease her pain. But now, the pungent odor around is overwhelming. As is the sounds of crying and screaming, sirens and roaring. Wailing and moaning. Gore everywhere. Jex blinks again and then stands up, shoving her otoscope into her bag.

"I gotta go, Ann. Please, just sit. There will be nurses or doctors or rescue people coming with more supplies. They will be able to get you to a hospital and get that arm checked out. And make sure you tell them about the hit on the head, even if it doesn't hurt." She squats down in front of Ann, looking her straight in the eyes. "Are you sure you're OK?"

"Yes, thank you so much. I'll be OK. I'm just shaken up."

Jex touches Ann's good arm, smiles and then goes. She looks around. Another woman approaches her, similar in age and body size as Ann. She has also injured her wrist by falling, just like Ann. Jex takes a third of the time with her. She runs a quick ABC test and satisfies herself that there is not a concussion or other serious head injury that needed assistance that minute. She focuses on the wrist and, with just a moment of examination, fashions another arm sling and fits it onto the woman. She barely waits for a thank you before turning to head closer to the DJ stand, where the turmoil seems to be focused. She looks for those in pain.

It doesn't take long. It is a young girl, maybe thirteen or fourteen. She is covered in dirt and is absolutely petrified. Her words are barely making sense and she is shouting them out to nowhere. There are a bunch of "helps" and "pleases" in between the indecipherable stuff. She must see the stethoscope around Jex's neck because she beelines right towards her. There are more "helps" and pulls at Jex's arm. Jex tries to to start some kind of dialog, but it quickly becomes clear that she is not looking for herself. There is someone nearby hurt much worse than her. "Show me where," Jex says once she figures out what the girl is saying. The girl spins on her heel and is off, with Jex firmly attached to one hand. Jex follows with no hesitation.

The two travel through a hundred feet of humanity. There are people lying on the ground, covered in blood. Jex sees a woman wrapping a cloth around the upper arm of a man who appears to be missing the lower part of that arm entirely. The smell is the most remarkable thing, something Jex will never forget. It smells like sulfur and burning skin.

They arrive at the edge of the sidewalk to find a man, late thirties, in a blue polo shirt and khakis sprawled out on his back, staring up at the sky. His eyes are wide open. His arms lie flat on either side of him with their palms down, and his toes are pointed straight up. He glistens with sweat underneath the afternoon sun. The girl that sought out Jex kneels down behind her silently, terror in her eyes. There is so much darkness and death around, it is hard to remember that the sun still shines.

Jex squats on her knees next to the man. "Hey there, what's your name?" she says, taking his hand and holding it in his. "Is this OK if I hold your hand like this?" It is clammy and cold to the touch.

The man doesn't answer. He does not move his head, but his eyes slowly turn from where they were looking, into nothing, and shift towards the rough general area where Jex kneels. He does not speak or seem to clearly acknowledge Jex's existence. The girl, frozen silent before, now begins to speak frantically.

"We were just standing there, reading everyone's signs, and a bomb goes off. It knocked us both over, but I didn't see any blood or anything. When the second explosion or whatever went off, we were on the ground. I don't know, he's not bleeding or anything. I don't know what to do. Can you help us? Can you help him?" She turns away from Jex and turns to the man. "Daddy, this woman is going to help you."

Jex puts her hand on the girl's shoulder. "What's your name?"

"Alyssa."

"Ok, hi Alyssa. I'm Jex. I'm going to do whatever I can to help get your father stable until a doctor or nurse shows up. I'm not a doctor or nurse but I have some medical training. I can help. But you have to calm down and back up a bit, let me examine your father and I will see what I can do."

Jex's voice is so smooth and her words are so considered, Alyssa has almost no choice but to calm down. She immediately backs up a few steps and mouths silently, "I'm sorry." Her eyes are wide open, the fear and terror clear in them. Her father is injured. She doesn't know what to do. Jex looks her in the eyes and says, "It's OK. I know you're scared. I'll do the best I can to help your dad right now. Trust me."

"Thank you."

Jex nods and returns to the man. "What's your name, sir?"

He doesn't respond. "What's your dad's name, Alyssa."

She stutters for a second and then says, "Bill Carter."

"Mr. Carter, can you hear me?" She tries to look him straight in the eyes. He doesn't look away but doesn't seem to really focus on her either. He doesn't respond verbally or with any facial movement. His face is pale, almost like a ghost. She puts her hand on the back of his head, tilts his head and lifts his chin. His airway seems unobstructed. She looks at his cheeks and put her ear to his mouth. His breathing is fast but shallow. She takes his wrist and attempts to take a pulse. It is faint, almost non-existent. With the noise behind her, Jex can't really feel it at all. She pulls her stethoscope from around her neck but it doesn't help much.

"Mr. Carter. I'm having trouble getting a radial pulse. The pulse in your wrist."

"Oh, my God," says Alyssa. "He doesn't have a pulse?"

Jex looks up and stares Alyssa hard in the eyes. "Alyssa. He has a pulse. I just can't get it because it's too loud here. And your screaming when I have a stethoscope in my ears doesn't help at all."

Alyssa says, "I'm sorry," with a start, perhaps not even realizing she had spoken.

"Mr. Carter," Jex says, "I can't get the pulse in your wrist. I'm going to put my hand on your neck so I can try and take your carotid pulse, the pulse in your neck. Is that OK?" For the first time, he appears to try to provide a response, nodding his head just slightly up and down in agreement. Jex smiles.

"That's great, sir. That's just great."

Jex puts her hand on the side of Mr. Carter's neck and pauses there. "OK, it's weak and it's fast, but it's steady." She holds his hands and squeezes his fingertips, examining his hands closely. She pulls her otoscope from her pocket and looks into his eyes. She watches as his pupils dilate. "Good," she says. "Good."

"OK, Mr. Carter," she pauses, and turns to Alyssa. "And Alyssa. Both of you listen to me. Mr. Carter, I think you are suffering from shock. That means we have to get some blood to your head and calm you down, but you're going to be OK." She focuses specifically on Alyssa. "He is going to be OK. I don't know if there's something internal that's damaged or not, I can't say that, only a doctor can, but for now I think the scary symptoms you are seeing are from the shock. We need to get blood to his head, and let him lay flat for now, OK?"

"OK?" Alyssa says, not knowing quite what this might entail for her.

"OK, great." Jex says. "Here, is that your bag," she says, pointing to a backpack lying on the ground next to her.

"Yes," Alyssa says with a nod, and she grabs it, passing it to Jex. Jex quickly takes it and puts it under Mr. Carter's feet, raising his legs by about 10 inches.

"OK, Alyssa." Jex says. "That should help a little." Jex opens her messenger bag and pulls out a bandana and a bottle of water. She douses the bandana with water, squeezes out some of it, and places it on Mr. Carter's head. She looks up at Alyssa, her eyes big and wide, and holds out the bottle for her. "Here. Take this. Drink some. Try and get your dad to drink some. Grab a doctor or nurse when you can. The good news is he doesn't have any external injuries. He is bleeding a little bit about the eye, but that's no big deal. Here, grab that blanket," Jex says, pointing at a blue blanket about ten feet away. Alyssa jumps at it and hurls it at Jex who catches it effortlessly, and wraps it around Mr. Carter's body. "Keep him warm." She turns back to Mr. Carter. "You have to stay warm for now, OK? You'll be OK, but you need to get to the hospital." She looks him in the eye. He nods softly and manages a little smile. In the tiniest of voices, he says, "thank you." Jex smiles.

"OK, Alyssa, you're in charge."

Alyssa's eyes grow wider. "You're leaving?" she says in horror. "You can't go."

Jex grabs her by the hand and stares her hard in the eyes. "Alyssa, there is nothing more I can do for your father that you can't do. Keep him warm, stay by his side until the EMTs or someone can get him to a hospital for a check up. But they will look at him just I did and they won't find him to be a priority, because his vitals are stable. You might be here for a while but this is nothing you can't do. Keep him warm, keep his legs elevated, make sure he drinks water and you drink some, too. You'll be OK. OK?"

Alyssa nods slowly, her eyes in a way revealing that she understands and is willing to take the responsibility. "OK," she says.

Jex stands and does not hesitate. "Good luck. You'll do great." With that she turns and leaves Alyssa and her father. She leaves them safer and more comfortable than when she found them and heads back into the inferno like a fire fighter returning to the blaze.

There are helicopters hovering above, and by above, only a few hundred feet above. The wind from their blades rustle Jex's hair as she walks through the crowd, which seems to have begun full force of recovery, no third explosion having materialized. She continues her walk to the DJ stand. Police and firefighters and doctors and nurses seem to have materialized from nowhere, which is in reality not a real surprise, considering that both a police station and a hospital are within a mile of this blast scene. Jex walks towards the DJ stand, which is only a couple of hundred feet away now, maybe less. She eyes her surroundings. She is confident but careful, not wanting to get in the way of anyone but ready to help if needed.

Jex freezes about fifty feet from the DJ stand. There, to the right, maybe twenty-five ahead, are a pair of boots. Connected to two legs. Connected to a body. A body that's not moving. In her mind, Jex hesitates for an eternity. In reality, there is no meaningful hesitation at all. She makes a beeline straight to the person.

The man is completely non-responsive. His body is cold to the touch, clammy. He does not respond to Jex's verbal cues. He does not respond to her grabbing his hand. Or squeezing his arm. She examines him quickly and just as quickly sees the injury to the back of his head. There is blood on the ground but he doesn't seem to be bleeding much. Anymore. Not good. His airway is clear but he does not appear to be breathing.

Jex grabs the man's hand and gently pulls his arms towards him. She puts her forefinger and middle finger on his wrist, looking for a radial pulse. She finds none.

She does not panic. From the moment of the first explosion, Jex has not panicked. Not a single time. Finding no radial pulse, she does not hesitate. She remembers the training. She remembers the books. She remembers the thousand times she has done it in her head. All at once. She acts instinctively. She moves her two fingers from the wrist up to below the elbow. She is looking for a brachial pulse. Again, she finds none. She pauses there, perhaps a moment longer than she should. Hoping a pulse, even a slight one, would appear. Nothing.

Still, she does not panic. It doesn't seem real to her. She leans over the man and brings her two fingers softly to his neck and presses down. She is looking for a carotid pulse. Anything. She finds none. She kneels down and her hand goes back to the man's hand, looking again for a radial pulse. Again, she finds none. She finds nothing. She pulls at one of his eyelids and looks at his eyes. She pulls out her otoscope, desperate perhaps, and turns it on. She shines light in his eyes. Nothing. No dilation. No sign of life. Not even close.

This man is dead.

If Jex were to narrate the next few moments of her life, she would probably compare it to that scene in every war movie since *Saving Private Ryan*, where the whole scene switches instantaneously to slow motion and the sounds are all garbled and slurred. It is meant to symbolize shock; that moment after something terrible happens and the protagonist momentarily loses control of their senses. That is Jex.

As she stands up and steps back, she is somewhat out of control but on her own two feet. She lives in that instant of stunted reality. Where movements are slow and detached. Where speech is incoherent. Where thoughts are nonexistent. Where action is frozen. Where skin is pasty and stinging all over. Where ears are buzzing. Where eyes see swirls of rainbow colors, but no shapes or forms.

"Jex," the deep, dark, raspy voice shouts, in half-speed, though at first it is barely an echo in Jex's head. Slow and indistinct, like a dream. Jex's brow furrows deeply as though she is trying to connect that voice to something real. She looks at the dead man that is laying on the ground, not ten feet from Jex's feet.

"Jex," the voice screams again, lighter though, higher in pitch. It is clearer this time, more real perhaps. Jex's head cocks sideways, as if she is reaching out to the voice, to somehow put some context around it; some perspective.

"Jex," the shouts again, louder and clearer still, not dark or deep at all. This time, the sole word is punctuated with another word: "help." "Help," the voice says. "Help, Jex! Help!"

And in one of those moments that lasts forever but is over so quickly it barely constitutes a moment, clarity returns to Jex. Her flirtation with desolate panic ends before it even begins. "Molly!" she shouts back, recognizing her old friend, who is kneeling over someone that Jex can't quite make out. She does not look back at the body behind her but instead runs to Molly's call for help as fast as her shaky legs will take her.

"Oh my God," Jex lets out with a start as she reaches Molly and grabs her in a hug. "I was so worried about you. Tell me what's up?" To the point, as Jex always is. No panic. No hesitation.

Molly is in shambles, though, and Jex can see she is nothing but a bunch of puzzle pieces that need sorting. She is covered in blood from her waist down but it doesn't seem to be hers. Jex looks for entry wounds or injuries but finds none. She tries to look into Molly's eyes but they are just slits in her face from the crying.

"Molly, slow down. Please slow down. It's OK. Take a minute."

Molly shakes her head violently from side-to-side. There are no extra minutes to be had, she seems to be saying. Snot is running down her face and her jaw is shaking badly, her lips aquiver. She tries hard to find words through her agitation. "It's Marcus," she manages to eke out through the phlegmy coughs and tears.

Jex looks down and sees him for the first time, lying on the ground beneath Molly. He is covered in blood, skinny and shirtless. He appears barely conscious. His left leg below the knee is missing. There is a bloody cloth, maybe a torn t-shirt loosely wrapped around his leg above the knee, tied limply like a shoelace.

Jex does not vacillate. She is immediately on her knees and rummaging through her messenger bag. "No," she says in a resolute tone. "That's not right." She lightly puts one hand on Marcus' leg and the other on Molly's wrist, pulls Molly's arm off of Marcus. "Don't elevate the leg right now. Keep it level with his body."

Jex removes the cloth, soaked with blood, from around his leg. She pulls out a roll of thick cloth gauze and rips off a long piece with her teeth. She folds it in half lengthwise so it is about 15 centimeters wide. She looks around quickly and then spies what she is looking for hanging lazily from Molly's neck. She points. "Your bandana, Molly. Give me that bandana."

Molly blinks twice through her tears, seeming to run through Jex's words in her head and then looks down to see the blue bandana tied around her neck. She shakes her head and pulls the bandana off, handing it to Jex. Jex grabs it, folds it and wraps it just below

Marcus's knee joint. She then wraps the gauze around the leg twice and then pulls it tight. With one hand holding the gauze tightly, Jex uses her other hand to dig some more in her messenger bag. Quickly, she finds a sharpie pen. Deftly, she ties a half-knot with just the gauze and then, once that is loosely secured, she places the sharpie into the cloth and finishes wrapping the gauze around the leg. Once wrapped, she turns the sharpie pen, causing the knot to tighten securely. As she does so, Marcus moans a little bit from the pain.

"I'm sorry, Marcus," Jex says to the young man. "My name is Jex and I'm just trying to stabilize you a little bit. The tourniquet you had wasn't tight enough so I just made you a new one real quick. I know that hurt but that part's over now, OK?"

Marcus doesn't respond verbally but manages to offer a shallow nod of recognition. Molly is crying hard now. "I'm sorry," she screams. "I didn't know what to do."

"You did great, Molly. You did great. It served its purpose. It's better now but you did fine. Marcus, can you hear me? Can you hear me, Marcus?" She pulls open his half-closed eyelids and checks his eyes, which dilate fine. He opens them a little wider at her touch, and makes eye contact with Jex. She smiles thinly and says, "hi, there."

"Hi," Marcus says weakly.

"It's good to hear you speak."

"It hurts," he whispers.

"What hurts?"

"My leg," he says through a choke. "The lower part of my left leg really hurts."

Jex pauses for a split of a second and then continues through her teeth. "Anything else."

"Yeah," he says. "My ribs really hurt, or my stomach. Somewhere in between my ribs or stomach or something. Really bad."

"Ok," Jex says with a nod. "Does your head hurt? Or your back or neck?"

"No. Just my leg and my stomach. Am I going to be OK?"

"Marcus, I promise I'm going to do everything I can to get you the treatment you need, OK?"

"OK," he murmurs, his eyes closing slightly.

"Stay with me, Marcus, OK. Please stay awake and stay with me. There's going to be an ambulance soon." Jex looks around her as she says, noticing in her head that she is actually quite in the dark as to when an ambulance may come that has room for Marcus. There are people running everywhere, still screaming and yelling. To the quick glance at least, there seem to be more injured people than treating people. The park is a disaster, a crime zone, and a war zone at once.

Jex looks back down at Marcus. "Are you there, Marcus?"

"I'm here," he confirms quietly. "I'm OK."

"That's great. Marcus. Stay with me. I just want to test a couple things, OK?"

"OK," Marcus agrees.

Jex takes his left hand and lightly strokes her finger from the top of the palm to the bottom. His fingers jump a little in response. "Do you feel that," Jex asks Marcus.

"Yes," he confirms.

"Great. Can you wiggle your fingers?" He wiggles them weakly. "Great," she repeats. She does the same thing with the left hand. His fingers similarly respond. "Feel that?" she asks.

"Yes," he confirms again, and though his voice is strained with pain, he wiggles his fingers at the same time.

"Perfect. Hold on one second."

Jex scurries down to his remaining leg and unties the laces of his Doc. She pulls the boot off and the sock underneath it. She strokes the bottom of his foot from top to bottom. "Feel that?" she asks.

"Yeah," he grunts.

"Can you wiggle your toes?"

There is a stilted pause. Slowly, the toes begin to wiggle, not much but a little. It is enough. Jex smiles. "Good, Marcus, that's good."

She looks Marcus again in the eyes. "You're doing great, Marcus. You're doing great. One more quick thing. I know you're in a lot of pain but I just want to see if there's anything wrong that we need to worry about. Can you move your neck side to side? Slowly? Even a little."

Marcus pauses as though he is gaining strength. His eyes look straight up to the sky, open wide. Slowly, he turns his head partially to the left. "Good," Jex says, "good." Just a slowly, he straightens it out and turns again, this time to the left. "Good," Jex says as he straightens out. Marcus coughs and wheezes. "Where am I? Why does my stomach hurt?" he asks.

Jex puts her hand on his check, which is cold and clammy. "It's OK, Marcus. You've been in an accident, OK? Do you remember?"

Marcus looks at her, with maybe half the focus he looked at her three minute earlier. "An accident?" he asks and pauses. "An explosion," he says. "I remember that I think."

Jex nods her head. "Right, an accident. I'm Jex, remember? I'm just checking you out, see if I can see any other injuries."

"You're Jex?"

"Yes," she says. "I'm Jex."

Marcus doesn't say anything but nods a little.

"Is it OK if I look you over a little bit, Marcus?"

He pauses and then nods. "It's OK," he whispers.

"Thanks, Marcus. I'm just going to lift your shirt and see if I see anything amiss, OK?"

Marcus nods again but does not say anything.

"Staying with me, Marcus?"

"Yes," he confirms in a whisper.

"Great."

She pulls his shirt up and he doesn't resist. She visually inspects his chest and stomach. There is bruising dotting the entire flanks of his body, from the top of the hips to the bottom of the last rib. The bruising is dark blue, almost purple, splattered in nature but deep in its color, almost thick in texture. "Shit," Jex whispers to herself, too quietly for Marcus to notice, who is looking up at the sky, gritting his teeth in pain. He is beginning to sweat.

Jex looks over to Molly, who has turned away from Marcus and is huddled up in a low crouch. "Molly, I need your help." She doesn't respond.

"Molly," Jex says again, louder. "Come here." Again, she doesn't respond.

"Molly, you OK?" After a moment, Molly responds, choking her words out between tears and moans. "Where's Eugene? I want Eugene."

Jex doesn't hesitate. "Shit, Molly. I'm sorry, I don't know. I'm sure he's OK but I need to take care of Marcus right now, and I need your help. I need you to hold Marcus' hand while I find a doctor."

Molly doesn't move. "I want Eugene," is all she says.

"Shit," Jex mutters to herself. She pauses and then quickly makes a decision. "Marcus, I have your back, I promise. I need to find a doctor to look at you and I need to do it now, OK? I'm going to make sure you get the best treatment to make you OK, but I have to go find a doctor. I will just be a minute. Is that OK?"

"A doctor?" Marcus asks.

"Yes," Jex says firmly, her eyes locked in place with Marcus'. "A doctor to look at you. To make you feel better."

Marcus pauses before responding. "OK, you have to find a doctor. I'll be here," he says weakly with a faint glimmer of a smile.

Jex smiles. "I promise you I will be back quickly."

"OK," Marcus says.

Jex is up and moving in a flash. She jumps over Molly and heads out into the carnage, targeting any doctor with legs and arms. Most are bent over bodies that are screaming and yelping. She sees an EMT here and there, carrying a stretcher, but not nearly enough. She doesn't see a single ambulance. The resources here are overwhelmed.

Jex spies a man in a doctor's coat twenty feet away, his hands on his hips and looking down despondently at the ground. Probably not her best audience but any port in a storm, she thinks. Jex beelines it to him.

"Excuse me, Doctor, I need your help."

"What is it," the doctor snaps. "I'm taking thirty seconds before I have to return to see the wounded."

"I know it's terrible, I know you're busy but my friend is hurt and I think it's a lot worse than they think."

"Where is your friend," the doctor half-sneers, looking down his nose.

"Over there," Jex says, pointing to where Marcus is lying, maybe thirty feet from the smoldering DJ stand.

The doctor shakes his head. "We have already triaged everyone in that section and everyone there has already been prioritized for evacuation to the hospital. We have a shortage of emergency vehicles. They will deal with him in order."

"No," Jex protests. "You don't understand. I know his leg ..."

"Listen, young lady, I don't really care what you know or don't know. Medical professionals have examined your friend, like all the other injured, and they have prioritized him appropriately. If you want to comfort him, please do. I have other patients to tend to."

Jex is instantly in rage. "Yeah, I see that they examined him. Nice job on the tourniquet by the way. Built to last, eh. What they failed to see in their examination is..."

"I don't have time for some punk girl's sarcasm or grade school criticism of our work," the doctor sniffs. "Go be with your friend but leave me alone or I will have you arrested." The doctor turns on his heel and disappears.

"Shit," Jex says, not anywhere near a whisper this time. She looks in every direction but sees no other doctor that is not elbows deep into an injured person. "Shit," she repeats. She turns and heads back to Marcus, not knowing her next move.

As she approaches the spot where Marcus is lying, her heart skips a beat. Eugene is holding Molly tightly in his arms as she sobs uncontrollably. One of his friends stands by, looking curiously at Marcus.

"Eugene," Jex screams as she gets to him. He holds out his arm and pulls Jex into his hug with Molly. All three of them break into tears, bawling and crying.

"Shit, you two. Shit, shit. I didn't think I'd see you again. Thank god for you. Thank god for us."

After a moment that lasts for an eternity, Jex breaks away.

"Eugene, it's too early for prayers. Molly's friend Marcus is hurt, hurt bad, and the only doctor I could even find to speak to basically just told me to go fuck myself."

Eugene's expression turns quickly from relief to darkness. "Where is this doctor?" he asks, menace deep in his voice. "I'll get him to help us, guaranteed."

"No, Eugene. Don't bother. They're taking care of patients, too. We need to get Marcus to the hospital now. For real," she lowers her voice, "or he may not make it. Is your truck nearby?"

Eugene blinks and then responds. "Yeah, we're parked right at the foot of the park. All the roads are closed, but if you need me to get Marcus to the hospital, trust me, we can get Marcus to the hospital in my truck."

"Good," Jex says, looking around the crowd. "We just need to find a way to get him to the truck. He is not exhibiting signs of spinal injury, but we still need something flat and firm to transport him."

"We have our surfboards in the back of the truck. How does one of those work?"

"Perfect. Go get one and let's do this."

As Eugene and his friend run to get the truck, Jex surveys the scene, hopeful to find the lost limb, though she thought to herself that the likelihood of successful reattachment was low, but never give up hope. The morbid search is in vain though, and by the time Eugene has returned with the surfboard, she has given up. Eugene and his friend move Marcus clumsily to a surfboard. and they begin to move, Eugene walking backwards and Jex guiding them through the busy crowd. Within two minutes, they have Marcus to the truck and they gently lay him in the truck bed. Jex and Molly jump in the back. Molly just curls up. Jex holds the surfboard steady.

The trip to the hospital is bumpier than Jex would like but it is quick. They pull into emergency as an ambulance pulls away. Two nurses are standing there and quickly run to the truck. Jex jumps out to greet them. One of them looks over the side and into the truck bed and looks at Jex. "Severed limb. Did you preserve it?"

"No," Jex says softly. "We couldn't find it."

The nurse shakes his head. "OK, we'll get him checked out and into the ER as soon as we can. There's a long line."

"Wait," Jex says. "There's more than just the leg to worry about. He needs an ER immediately. Right now. If it's not already too late."

The nurse turns to Jex in irritated resignation. "What more is there?"

[What is the emergency issue that Jex identified in Marcus? Will the young injured drummer be OK, or is it too late to help him? Turn to page 221 to read Jex's diagnosis and the conclusion of the story.]

Diagnoses

FREE-STYLING

"Betsy," Jex says firmly. "I don't think there's really much doubt about it. Ben has bacterial meningitis."

Betsy turns pale, seems weaker than before, maybe about to fall over. "Oh, holy shit. What does that mean?"

Jex puts her hand up. "It's OK – it's only been about twelve hours, I think you said, since he began to show symptoms. There's time. He's going to be fine. But, right now, for sure, we have to get Ben to a hospital to diagnose it and start treatment if I'm right. They need …"

"Oh, man, I just can't do hospitals. Q, I thought you said your friend could fix Ben?"

Jex interjects. "I definitely do not have the ability to fix Ben. He needs a doctor; a real doctor. And a hospital and all its resources. I …"

"See, Q, why do I even want to listen to some punk kid about this? Look at that ratty sweatshirt, and you know what, she stinks. I can't be going to a hospital right now. With all respect, I am not taking this kid's advice," Betsy continues nervously. "I am sure it's just a cold or flu or what have you."

Q protests. "No, Betsy, you're wrong. Come on, don't be like that. Jex is the real deal, I'm telling you, if she says you should be going to a hospital, I think …"

"Betsy, listen to me," Jex says firmly. "There is only one thing to do here. And that one thing is to bring Ben to a hospital immediately." Her tone leaves no doubt to consider. "There is no other choice."

Loudly, but with an assurance that seems slightly diminished, Betsy rebuts. "There is a choice. There is always a choice. I am his mama and I am the one who gets to choose what's good for him and what's not."

Jex does not back down, knowing there is no time for a delicate bedside manner. "You may be the one who chooses who makes the decisions for him, but you don't get to choose what's good for him. What's good for him is treating his meningitis. There is no doubt about that. It will save his life. The layers of his brain have become inflamed by a bacteria and if he doesn't get antibiotic treatment, things are guaranteed to get much worse – and fast."

Q butts in, having watched the exchange with growing despair. "We could call child protection. I bet they would demand Ben be taken . . "

Jex interrupts her before Betsy can. "I am not calling child protection on anyone. Period, Betsy. Period."

Q looks startled but shuts her mouth. Jex continues, looking directly into Betsy's eyes, whose emotions Jex reads as a roller coaster of anger, fear, confusion and helplessness.

"Betsy, no one is calling child protection. The decision is yours. You're his mama. But as his mama, please, please just listen to me for three minutes. Literally three minutes."

Betsy squints her eyes in doubt and cynicism, but there is fear behind those eyes, too, and she mutters quietly. "What you got to say?"

Jex doesn't hesitate. "There are pretty straightforward symptoms of bacterial meningitis. Fever, sluggishness, lots of crying – those are some of them, but those could be a thousand things."

"That's right," Betsy agrees, a bit more stridently. "A thousand things."

Jex nods her head in agreement. "But Ben has more symptoms from that. He's crying mostly when you hold him, or anyone even touches him. I tried. And he stops crying when you stop holding or stop touching him."

Betsy winces at the thought, but it is obvious in her eyes that she knows this is true. Jex continues.

"That is what the doctors call paradoxical pain. That's not so common, not like the other symptoms. But it is common in babies with bacterial meningitis."

"That's it?" Betsy whispers. "That's why you think he has this. Because he won't let me pick him up? What do you know? Babies go through their fits sometimes. You're just a kid. That's all you have?"

Without hesitating, Jex pulls from her backpack a tattered paperback book, littered with dog ears and folded over post-it notes, marking page after page in the book.

Jex flips immediately to a page in the book she seems to know from memory. "This is the Oxford Handbook of Clinical Medicine. It is in every doctor's bag out there and it sets out the symptoms very clearly. You can look if you want," Jex declares, waving the book around like a piece of evidence in a trial. "He has an aversion to light. The light hurts his eyes. That's called photophobia and it is a key symptom of meningitis," Jex declares, pointing at the dirty and tattered pages of the paperback. "And remember the fontanel I described. The soft spot on his head?"

"Yeah."

"It's bulging out. It's swelling. That's because the layers of his brain are inflamed. Like I said."

Betsy's eyes pop out. "His brain is inflamed? Bullshit."

"No, it's not bullshit. It happens in adults, too, with meningitis, but you can see it easier in babies because the four plates of their skull haven't fully connected yet. See? There? It is clear as day. I am tracing it with my finger. See? You can see it with your own eyes. Just look. You can't tell me he was like that two days ago."

Betsy doesn't look at Ben and she doesn't look at Jex. She looks down at her own two feet and shakes her head slowly, barely, from side to side.

Jex is relentless. "And that seizure, the one you say you barely noticed. I hate to be the bearer of bad news, but those are just going to get worse. And fast. Like, anytime. Minutes, a couple of hours. Not more. Fever, sluggishness, crying, paradoxical pain, photo-phobia, a bulging of the brain, seizures. That is textbook bacterial meningitis and it needs to be treated right now. If we take Ben to a hospital, they can give him general antibiotics and it will begin to destroy the bacteria right away. Right away. They will take a quick culture and in two days they will know the precise antibiotic to switch to that is designed to destroy the specific bacteria that is causing this. He will be fine but he needs antibiotics right now. Right now."

Jex pauses and both she and Q study Betsy carefully. She is just shaking her head from side to side. Tears drip from her eyes and her fists are clenched. "I can't go to a hospital," she says, barely audible. "I can't."

Q walks up to Betsy. Betsy grabs onto her and nearly collapses in her arms. "I can't go the hospital, Boo. I just can't."

"Yes, you can, girl. You are strong and Ben needs you to do this."

"Q…"

"You can do this, Betsy. You can…"

"Q …"

"Betsy, you can…"

"Q, I'm on probation and I'm not clean, OK? If I go … If I go to a hospital, they are gonna make me pee and I am not clean. My PO is a son-of-a-bitch and he will lock me up and take Ben away. I can't go to a hospital. I can't let that happen. I am sorry. I am so, so sorry."

Betsy collapses onto the couch and digs her head into the pillows, the force of her own revelation knocking her off her feet. "I am sorry," she repeats, crying softly. Q sits next to her, holds her leg tightly. "No, Boo, no," is all she can say.

Q looks over at Jex, desperate for answers. She is surprised to see Jex texting away furiously on her iPhone. "Jex, what you doing? We gotta help Betsy. This is some urgent shit. Get your nose out of your phone."

Jex does not avert her eyes from the glowing screen, her brow furrowed in concentration. "Hold, please," is all she says. Jex seems to be doing all kinds of finger acrobats on her phone, her face flush with light in the otherwise dark apartment. She does not seem to notice Q or Betsy at all, who are still collapsed on the couch, Q stroking Betsy's leg as Betsy gazes out into nothingness, biting her fingernail and, here and there, shaking her head side to side in disbelief; but otherwise still.

A ping from Jex's phone fills the silence and Jex's eyes scan it quickly. She does not smile but her eyes fill with triumphant satisfaction. She does not hesitate, walking with purpose to the couch where both Betsy and Q have turned their unflinching attention to Jex. Jex squats down next to the two and looks Betsy straight in the eye.

"Betsy, I know you don't trust me but this is what I have to say. I just texted Dr. Stevens at County – you know, the hospital Chief Medical Officer I talked about earlier. She is a friend of mine. Dr. Stevens confirmed to me what I already knew: they are not going to pee test you or blood test you or anything test you – and they are not going to call your probation officer. You are safe at the hospital. It is a safe zone for you. I don't know what to say to you to make you trust me, but it's true."

Betsy doesn't respond but she stops shaking her head side-to-side. Her eyebrows curl up and it looks like she might cry again.

"Listen, Betsy. I know you're scared. I know you're confused. But Ben is not going to get better without treatment. He is going to get much, much worse. And treatment is just a couple of miles away. My car is outside and it fits a baby seat really easily. Dr. Stevens is expecting you, and no, I haven't told her your name yet, I wouldn't do that without you OKing it. But she is expecting you and I can drop you off at the hospital."

Q chimes in. "Boo, come on now. If you don't trust Jex, trust me. I know Jex and she has never done me wrong. If she says Ben has to go to the hospital, Ben's gotta go. You know it's right. You know it's right."

There is a long silence. Q opens her mouth, but Jex touches her on the shoulder and nods to her to give Betsy some time. The tension in the air is palpable. Another moment passes, and Jex is the one to break the silence this time.

"Betsy …"

Before she could continue, Betsy stops her. "Let's go, OK, let's go."

Q puts her hand around Betsy's arm. "Betsy, that's the right cho. . ."

Betsy cuts her off, standing up quickly. "OK, I said OK. Let's go. Let's go." Q turns to Jex for direction and Jex is already heading towards the front door.

"Grab his baby seat. My car is out front. I will have the engine running and ready to go. Let's go." And just like that, she is out the door, as Q and Betsy scramble to collect Ben and his things. In a moment, they are off.

* * *

It is two hours later. Jex sits in her beat-up Ford Focus outside downtown County hospital and thumbs through her well-worn copy of the clinical medicine handbook. She has read it cover to cover a hundred times over; replicated every drawing in her sketchbook, memorizing every word. Its pages are barely legible under the dim glow of the streetlight. Dawn and its light is still some time away. She thumbs the cover and reads and re-reads the section on meningitis.

Ben is not the first case she had ever seen, but it was as close in physical proximity as she had ever been. She rubs her fingers together and recalls the shape and size of Ben's fontanel, the softspot, closing her eyes and going through the texture and the curves, ensuring it is burnt into her memory. She remembers Betsy's words; and her eyes; and her tears. The heat on Ben's forehead; the piercing of his crying. With every thought, Jex yearns to learn more; to do more; to be more. Graffiti is awesome, and punk rock, too, she thinks to herself. But science and medicine. Man, Jex loves science and medicine. Since she could talk, she was learning about science and medicine. She loses herself in the words of the book, her dreams slipping in and out of each letter.

The sudden knock on the passenger window startles Jex. She looks up quickly and sees Dr. Stevens looking down expectantly. The two exchange smiles, and then there is a short, rather uncomfortable silence as the two look at one another. After a moment, Dr. Stevens points at the lock of the car door. Jex smacks her head with her hand and immediately unlocks the door. Dr. Stevens opens the door and gets in. "Sorry, Doc, I was distracted and didn't think about the door being locked."

"No worries, Jex. How's it going?"

"Yeah, it's going OK, you know. Not up to much."

"Seems like you were up to quite a bit with Ben, no?"

Jex just shrugs. "I didn't do anything. I happened to know some symptoms and told his mother about it. Q really was the one who talked her into going to the hospital."

"Not surprised you knew the symptoms, with all you read in that book," Dr. Stevens says with a sly smile. "You know that book better than I do."

Jex smiles. "Well, that is sure not true, but those symptoms are pretty simple, so I felt pretty confident. I'm right, aren't I? It's bacterial meningitis, right?"

"We did the initial culture and its gram positive diplococci. Blue as can be. So, yes, it's bacterial meningitis. Probably streptococcus pneumoniae, though we have to get the culture back from the cerebral spinal fluid to know for sure. We've already started an intravenous broad spectrum general regimen of antibiotics." She pauses and then continues. "And, again, as you surely know," Dr. Stevens continued with a wink, "we'll decide on a specific set of antibiotics once we have identified the specific bacteria after the culture comes back from the lumbar puncture."

Jex thinks for a moment. "Yeah, heh-heh, I didn't mention the lumbar puncture to Betsy when we were talking about coming to the hospital."

Dr. Stevens laughs. "So I learned. Probably a smart idea, but Betsy was none too happy to hear about it."

"Yeah, not looking forward to the drive home. I am sure I will catch hell from Betsy for leaving out telling her about the excruciatingly painful needle that was needed to get a culture."

"Oh, well, you might get a little bit of a respite from that, Jex. I came out to tell you. We are going to have to keep the baby here for a bit, and one of Betsy's roommates has agreed to pick her and Q up when we're done. So, you're free. And for the record, I think Betsy is pretty grateful to you for what you've done. And Ben surely is, too."

Jex just shrugs. "It was nothing. I wish I could do more."

"Someday, Jex, someday soon."

She shrugs again. "I don't know. We'll see, I guess."

Dr. Stephens pauses before continuing. "How about you come in and get some food? The café is open. A full, proper meal on me."

Jex scrunches up her face and declines as politely as she can. "That food is grisly. I'd rather eat socks... .oh, but thank you for the invitation. I really do appreciate it."

Dr. Stephens smiles that smile she saves mostly for Jex. "No worries, Jex. I hope you get some rest. It must have been a long night."

Jex shakes her head. "Naw, I'm not tired. There's a sunrise yoga class near Venice Pier. I think I'll check that out. Oh, and there's a food truck there that has vegan burritos. I'll eat then."

"Are you sure, Jex?" Dr. Stephens protests. "Come on in, and relax for a bit before going out again."

"Thanks, Doc, but a yoga class on the beach seems about as relaxing a thing I could hope for. The hippies are annoying but I'm pretty good at ignoring them." She winks. "I'll sleep when I'm dead. Besides," Jex continues, gesturing out into the Los Angeles horizon. "The sun is already starting to rise. Early morning is my favorite time here. It's so quiet . . . calm."

"Fair enough, Jex. Fair enough. Well, I won't keep you," she finishes up, rubbing Jex's arm before reaching for the door handle. "Thanks again for stepping up for Ben. I don't like to think what would have happened if you didn't get him here."

Jex shrugs a final time. "Anyways, it was nice seeing you. I'm sure you will see me soon – I can't stay away from the hospital."

"You're always welcome, Jex, and whenever you want to talk about your next steps, just let me know how I can help. I don't mean to be a cliché or a broken record, but you have gifts, Jex. There's a next step for you out there, Jex. Do what you want to do, but don't forget to take the next step."

Jex smiles and says only, "Right now, I'm just free-styling." A pause. "Anyways, it was good seeing you." Dr. Stephens nods and smiles. After a moment, she gets out of the car and steps to the curb. "It was good seeing you, too, Jex."

Jex turns on the car and pulls away. Dr. Stephens waves and smiles again as she sees the bumper sticker-ridden 2001 red Ford Focus pull away, battered and broken but plugging away strong as a heart. She shakes her head affectionately and watches as Jex drives down the road, away from her.

Jex doesn't look back in the rear-view mirror as the sun begins to rise around her. She plugs her iPhone into the cassette adapter and switches to her favorite playlist. "In the Aeroplane Over the Sea" by

Neutral Milk Hotel has been rattling around her head all night. As the sun rises and she vanishes westward into the empty L.A. streets, the song rings through her joyfully, echoing through the car window and into the crispy air, like freedom. She smiles to herself, and sings along, out of tune and for no one else to hear.

After Leviathan

"Look," Jex says earnestly to Joe, looking him right in the eye. "Dr. Cohen is one of the best cancer doctors in the world and Cedars-Sinai has the best cancer resources in the world. Like I said. If Dr. Cohen says his treatment is the only realistic treatment, I have no doubt he is right."

"Yeah," Joe says with resignation. "I know that."

Jex continues. "There is definitely nothing I've seen in your file to suggest some other remedy that can help you. There are all kinds of alternative treatments and things, maybe they work, I don't really know. I can't really give you any direction on that. But I believe in science and Dr. Cohen is a true scientist. What he says makes sense." There is empathy in Jex's tone, but also an air of certainty.

Sam sighs and grunts and for a moment it seems that maybe he is about to engage in another outburst. But he keeps his cool and just looks down at his feet. Joe shrugs. "It didn't make sense until you spelled it out." He pauses. "But you're not telling us anything we haven't already heard, Dr. Jex, so don't worry about it," he says with a smile that seems somewhere between forced and natural. "You just say it in a way that we understand. And we appreciate it."

"True dat," says one of the two other guys.

"So, that's that. We get it. Thanks a lot for coming," Joe says, his voice firm, a touch of despair inside the resignation.

"Well," Jex says, "hold on maybe just a minute. Just because treatment is unlikely to be successful, doesn't mean you have to fritter your last days away in a hospital bed, moping and doping."

Joe's eyebrows raise for the first time. Sam's head is up and he is suddenly focused on Jex like a laser beam. "What do you mean," Sam asks. "I thought you said that treatment was the only option, and it wasn't going to work anyways."

"No," Jex counters. "I said the treatment Dr. Cohen put together is the only treatment, not the only option. Did Dr. Cohen talk to you at all about palliative care?"

Joe curls up his brow. "What kind of care?"

"Look," Jex explains. "You said earlier that the cancer is making you sick in all these kinds of ways. That's not literally true. When you go through chemotherapy treatment, it kills off white blood cells in your body – including these cells called neutrophils. They protect your body normally but when the chemo kicks in, they are seriously reduced so you're not protected as much . It's called neutropenia. And so you get sick the way normal people do – the flu, things like that – but you get it a lot easier and you get it a lot worse."

"So," Sam says with disgust. "It's the treatment that is getting him sick, not the cancer."

"It's a trade-off," Jex clarifies. "If the chemo works, the cancer goes away, goes into remission. If it doesn't, at least you tried."

"So wait a second," Joe stops her. "So what if I don't get anymore treatment? Do these cells grow back?"

"Yeah," Jex confirms. "They should. Neutropenia reverses itself pretty quickly. In other words, the number of white blood cells goes up again. See, there's a difference between symptoms and side effects. You know, symptoms are things that show you things about the disease – like pain in your stomach can indicate a tumor in your abdomen. That's a symptom. But things like losing your hair, reduced white blood cells... those are side effects. A lot of that goes away after you stop treatment for a couple weeks. So, like the nausea or diarrhea I saw on your chart. That stuff would go away if you stopped doing treatment."

"Heh-heh, diarrhea," murmurs one of the two other guys. Jex ignores him. "And I saw you're anemic now. You had to get two blood transfusions, right?"

Joe groans just a little under his breath. "Yeah," he says. There is a pause for a moment, and then Joe continues. "Hey, this tingling in my fingers, is that a symptom or a side effect?"

"Yeah," Jex nods. "That's called peripheral neuropathy. It can be mild or it can be pretty bad.

Joes seems pained as he responds. "It's bad. It makes it hard to play guitar. That's the worst part. By far."

Jex nods again. "Yeah, that's a side effect of the treatment. It's not a symptom of the cancer itself. It should theoretically go away within a few weeks if treatment were to stop."

"No shit," Joe asks incredulously.

"Well, no guarantees, but I've read a lot of articles on that. Peripheral neuropathy... that tingling, it should recede in just a bit if treatment stopped."

There is a sudden hint of glow in Joe's eyes glow for the first time since Jex walked into the room. "That's rad. I thought that was permanent."

"No," Jex says, shaking her head. "It shouldn't be at all."

Joe takes a moment and takes that information in. The room is quiet. Sam looks out the window. He sees a flock of blackbirds fly by. "So, wait a second," Joe says after a moment, breaking the silence. "If I stop treatment altogether, I'll feel better. But if I do this treatment that Dr. Cohen wants me to do, I'll keep feeling sick, catching a bunch of diseases. Puking and shitting everywhere?"

Jex nods slowly. "At least until after the treatment is complete. If you got those side-effects the last time, it's likely you'll get them this time, too. They can treat some of them, like with anti-nausea pills, but yeah, you'll probably get sick."

Sam chimes in. "and if we stop doing anything, he'll be fine?"

"No," Jex quickly responds. "He won't be fine at all. He has a very advanced form of sarcoma. Like Dr. Cohen said, if he doesn't begin a treatment, it will spread more and it will quickly be fatal." She lets that sink in for a moment, her words hanging in the air like a jury verdict. "But he will feel better, for awhile at least. He would probably have to take some meds to fight off some symptoms, but for a little while, at least, he'll feel better."

"What's a little while?" Joe asks, putting the obvious question out there. Jex just shakes her head.

"I really can't say. It typically ranges to a few months before the cancer itself starts to make you really sick in a way that the symptoms can't be treated any more. But sometimes, a lot less or a little more."

There is another pause before Sam asks, "could he play gigs?"

Jex shrugs. "I don't see why not, but that's something Dr. Cohen would have to talk to you about."

"Well," Joe says firmly. "I want to talk about it. Talk about it at least. Shit man, I don't want to stew away my last days in this fucking bed."

Sam quickly agrees. "Let's at least talk about it. Maybe we could do a final tour." He pauses and then raises both hands in devil forks. "The Sarcoma Diarrhea tour," he announces proudly, sticking his tongue out. The two other guys snicker their Beavis and Butthead snicker. Jex holds her hands out.

"Well, hold on a second. How about if I see if I can go find Dr. Cohen and chat with him first. He can come in and talk to you about it. And, who knows, maybe I'm a complete idiot and got your hopes up over nothing." She scrunches her nose up. "So, you know, don't get your hopes up."

"We won't," Sam and Joe both say in unison, hope in their voices. They laugh at each other. "But we trust you, Dr. Jex!" Joe proclaims.

"It's just Jex," she corrects again. "And I'm not so sure I'm worth your trust. I've just read a bunch of books. Let me go see if I can talk to Dr. Cohen."

"Go girl," Sam urged, a smile on his face. As Jex leaves the room to find Dr. Cohen, she hears an excited Sam whisper to the rest of his band. "Sarcoma diarrhea!" There is laughter as the door shuts behind Jex. She can't help but smile a little bit.

* * *

It is twenty minutes later. Jex has finally tracked down Dr. Cohen. "Well, Ms. Blackwell," Dr. Cohen greets her in his Harley Street British accent, a slight bemusement in his tone. "It is delightful to see you in our hallways, as always. What sort of mischief are you finding yourself in these days?"

"Hi Dr. Cohen," Jex responds brightly. "I trust you are doing well," somehow painting her words with the precise degree of bemusement with which Dr. Cohen greeted her. He smiles in recognition of this fact. "Quite well, Ms. Blackwell. I trust you are the same."

"Quite," she responds with her own smile.

"Have you decided which university you will be attending?"

She shrugs, suddenly uncomfortable. "Well, I haven't even decided whether I will be attending college."

Dr. Cohen's smile turns coy. "Tough life, indeed, with the range of choices you have. A perfect SAT score is quite a nice thing to have in your back pocket, no?"

Jex sighs and shrugs again. "It's never bought me a meal."

"Someday soon it will, trust me on that."

She has no response to that and looks away, out into nowhere. Sensing, perhaps, that he is pushing too far, Dr. Cohen pivots away from the clear tenderness of the subject. "So, Ms. Blackwell. Are you in our hospital saying hello to old friends, or is there something we can do for you?"

Jex immediately brightens, grateful for the reprieve from having to actually talk about herself. "Actually, Doctor, yes. I do have a couple of questions for you."

Dr. Cohen chuckles. "Why does this not surprise me?"

"Yeah," Jex says, kind of looking to the side and smiling. "Just a couple quick questions. So, I have some friends whose friend is Joseph Foster, and I was just speaking to them about what he's going through and what, maybe, some of what his options are."

Dr. Cohen's face quickly turns dark. "Some of what his options are? And what exactly might his options be?"

"Well, I looked through his charts, and I see he has been diagnosed a PNET, and I know that is super rare but has a decent survival rate in some circumstances, but Joe's ..."

"Ms. Blackwell," Dr. Cohen abruptly interrupts. "You are fully aware, I am certain, that I cannot discuss a patient's ongoing treatment..."

"Not without his express consent," Jex just as abruptly interrupts. "I understand that. I am sure he would give that to you, but I am not asking you to discuss it with me right now. I just want you to listen to me. That should be OK under any reasonable interpretation of the AMA's ethics guidelines."

Dr. Cohen studies Jex's face up and down. "You," he says with a note of snarkiness in his voice, "have been spending entirely too much time with Dr. Stephens, haven't you. You are both two clicks too clever for your own good."

"No, it's just that I read of lot of books. And I'm right, aren't I?"

Dr. Cohen sighs just a little bit. "Please proceed, Ms. Blackwell. If you must."

"I must," she responds cheerfully but stubbornly. "So, he has PNET and a category of T3 N1 M1b. That's pretty bad in and of itself. PNET is super rare, which is probably how a guy like Joe managed to get himself treated at Cedars-Sinai. Too unique a research opportunity for a hospital to pass up, right?"

Dr. Cohen glares at her but says nothing.

"Anyways," she continues, not waiting to see if an awkward silence might melt into a response. "It originated in the abdomen but like all determined soft tissue sarcoma, it spread quickly. His latest lab results show it spread well past the sentinel lymph node, got itself into other regional lymph nodes and is now attacking the liver and lungs. At that stage, both you and I know there is nothing really left to be done. Joe doesn't say it straight out, but he knows it, too."

"What, Ms. Blackwell, is your point, exactly?"

"Well, Joe is lead guitarist in a band, they're called Water of Chaos. They're like totally metal and say they're punk but really they're just metal. I checked them out on bandcamp. Anyways, their music is not really my cup of tea, but they all seem like decent guys. Joe's parents are both dead and he doesn't have any other family. The band is kind of it for him."

Dr. Cohen lets out something between a sigh and a grimace, but doesn't otherwise respond.

"Anyways, so I'm not sure how much time he has, I'm sure you have a decent prediction. But I bet it's not too long, even with that treatment. None of them want to see him go through that procedure, get sick again. He can't even really play guitar right now because of the peripheral neuropathy. All they are dreaming about is a last tour. One more time to get together on a stage and play to an audience. It seems to me that with the way Joe's cancer has spread, and where it has spread to, and how quickly it spread, maybe it makes sense to help him do that, and, maybe, I don't know, worry less about treatments that almost certainly won't work."

"You are suggesting," Dr. Cohen says softly, somewhere between a sneer and a sigh, "palliation as a treatment path for a man as young as Mr. Foster? You don't think he should have a little bit of hope that the current treatment we have proposed might actually work?"

"Look, Dr. Cohen, I know it would be awesome if he was treated with the state-of-the-art processes Cedars-Sinai, but medicine is about reality, not Vegas-odd of success, right? I've read Huxtable. I've read Jeffrey. Shouldn't he at least have the choice to do that, if he wants? He's an adult. He's competent, and so he's autonomous, right? In any event, he's pretty smart and level-headed." She pauses for a moment. "Even for a waxhead-metalhead."

Dr. Cohen strokes his chin and his sneer evolves slowly into a slight sort of smile that wobbles between amusement and bemusement. "You really have been spending too much time with Dr. Stephens."

Jex shrugs. "You're the doctor, but I spoke for a while to all those guys. They get it. I mean, you were talking about medical ethics just a minute ago. Didn't Huijer and Van Leeuwen say that a patient's treatment has to be considered in the context of the patient himself, and not just clinical evidence. He wants to spend his last time with his band, playing music. Maybe it's time to discuss palliative care. "

"Is it, indeed?" he queries rhetorically, his crooked smirk struggling not to show itself.

"Well, maybe. I mean, Cicely Saunders said it's just as important to focus on the quality of the remaining life and a good death, not just solely on clinical stuff. There's nothing in his chart to suggest he isn't competent or autonomous. But, I mean, he's your patient."

"Indeed he is. Thank you for recognizing that."

"Well, there you go." Jex concludes. "I've spoken my mind. If you don't think it makes sense, you're the doctor."

"Yes," Dr. Cohen agrees, looking pensively away from her. "Indeed I am."

A long pause passes. Dr. Cohen says nothing else and Jex doesn't try to interfere with his thoughts. He pulls a pen out of his pocket and plays with the tip for a moment. He looks back out into nowhere. Finally, he breaks the silence.

"Very well, Ms. Blackwell." He turns without further comment.

He walks towards Joe's room without having to look at his notes to identify where it is. Jex hesitates for just a moment and then turns and follows Dr. Cohen. She gets to the door just before it closes and she slinkers in without touching the door, allowing it to shut naturally. Joe and Sam and the two other guys were talking loudly in a semi-circle around Joe's bed but stop instantly when Dr. Cohen walks in.

"So," Dr. Cohen states, instantly in control of the room. "I understand you have all been speaking to my friend, Ms. Blackwell, correct?"

We know Dr. Jex, for sure," Joe affirms.

"Like I said before," Jex interrupts, almost defensively. "It's just Jex."

"Just Jex," Joe agrees. "Anyways, she's helped us make a lot of sense of whatever it is you told me," realizing as soon as he says it that it sounds a lot more snarky than intended. "I mean she just speaks our language. No offense intended."

Dr. Cohen smiles his gruff smile. "No offense taken. Ms. Blackwell has quite a special way of making herself understood."

"That's for sure," Joe agrees.

"In any event, Mr. Foster, I would be quite grateful if you and I could have just a couple of minutes alone, without your ... carers and Ms. Blackwell, so we can have a quick discussion about your options. And then, perhaps," his thin smile grows slightly wider, but just slightly. "And then perhaps we can have a discussion about . . ." his last words dripping with an odd kind of disdain that probably tracks back to childhood, "heavy metal."

* * *

It is three weeks later on a Tuesday. It is the Whiskey on Sunset and Waters of Chaos is on stage, playing louder than hell and having a hell of a time doing it. There are maybe forty metalheads on the floor and maybe ten or fifteen in the balcony. In the defense of the band, most of the heads are banging. Jex is at stage right, taking in the scene with mild bemusement. As she said to Dr. Cohen, the music is not exactly her style Still, the passion is real on stage and the crowd seems into it, so who was Jex to judge anyways?

The set is lively. Jex is genuinely enjoying Sam playing to the crowd, and Joe shredding his Flying V like there is no tomorrow, inside knowing there might not be too many more tomorrows. The other two guys are the rhythm section and, again, though not Jex's favorite genre, she can't help but enjoy the musicianship and the passion.

"OK," Sam screams into the microphone. "This is our last song of the night. Thank you all for coming tonight, to see us on our Sarcoma Diarrhea tour, whoop!!"

Jex shakes her head but smiles bemusedly at that line.

"I'd like to dedicate this song, this is a new one, to Joe here," pointing to Joe and his Flying V. "He is the baddest mother fucker out there and his guitar has saved my life. Playing in a band with him is the best experience in my life, and I am grateful everyday for him. Love all your brothers like they are brothers, motherfuckers. And live for today. This one's called 'Lucifer is My Fuck Buddy.' Thank you L.A. Thank you Whiskey. Metal, always," he concludes, his right hand raised in a fist. The final song begins. It is fast and hard and is played by four men in love with music. It's not Macedonian punk, thinks Jex, but tonight, on the Whiskey's tiny stage, it is the best band in the world. For the band, at least. And her.

After the set, Jex hangs out, watching the scene and wondering whether she has the energy to stick around for the next band, Slunt. She doesn't know anything about them, but the name gives her a laugh. Maybe tonight is just a metal night, she thinks. Every once in awhile you need a good metal night, she thinks.

Her thoughts are interrupted by Sam. "Hey, Dr. Jex. You're here!"

"Yep," she says. "It's me. I'm here. Just Jex."

Sam looks at her from the side of his eye. "I know it's 18 plus tonight but my recollection is that you're not quite that."

Jex shrugs. "I have my ways," she demurs.

"Oh, yeah, what are those ways," Sam asks with a smile.

"Ask me no questions, I'll tell you no lies."

"Fair enough," Sam says with a laugh. "Fair enough. But at least you could have told us you were coming. We could have gotten you on our guest list. Saved you twelve bucks."

"Nah," Jex says. "Happy to support the bands."

"Yeah, you should stick around for Slunt. They're pretty rad."

"Yeah, maybe. I'm just deciding now what to do next."

Joe walks over and says, "hello, Jex." He is wearing a backwards Dodgers cap, with a black t-shirt and jeans.

"Hey, Joe. Nice set. I enjoyed it."

"Thanks a lot. It feels great to be up there."

"How many more dates do you have?"

"Three more in SoCal in the next two weeks," say Sam. "Two in SD and another one up here in LA again. And then, depending on how our man is feeling, we're headed up north to maybe hit SF And maybe even Sacramento. We'll see. The Sarcoma Diarrhea tour is never-ending."

"That's the truth," Joe affirms and they all laugh an awkward laugh, somehow comfortable in their collective weirdness.

"And then," Sam continues, "we have like four or five new songs ready to go. We are going to record some and get ourselves a new EP. It's going to be hot and won't take but a couple of days to record in my basement. Want to know what it's called?"

"Sure," says Jex, willing to take the bait.

"After Leviathan."

Jex smiles, remembering her critique of Mastodon and amused that Sam remembers it as well. "That's pretty rad."

"Thanks," Sam and Joe respond in unison, their voices filled with optimism over the thought of recording their songs.

"Yo, Jex," says one of the two other guys, who is up on the stage breaking down the drum set.

"Hey, man," Jex responds, waving over her shoulder. Both of the two other guys wave back.

"Yeah," Sam says. "We should finish up tearing down the set so the next band can set up. Maybe we'll see you a little later."

"Maybe," Jex shrugs. "If not, it was good seeing you all and I hope you have a good rest of the tour. And that it lasts a long time. I'll keep an eye on your Facebook page and try and make some other dates." She moves towards Joe and gives him a hug. She offers the same to Sam. It is the first time she has hugged either of them, but she somehow feels like she has known them a long time.

"Yeah, Jex," Joe says. "If I don't see you before you split, listen, thanks a lot for helping us out with Dr. Cohen. It was some hard shit and you made it a lot easier."

"Yeah," Sam agrees. "It is literally true that if we hadn't met you, we wouldn't be here right now."

"That's for sure," Joe follows up before Jex could even protest. She shrugs again.

"Anyways, it was good meeting you guys and I hope you stay in touch. I'm always around if you have any questions or anything."

"Oh," Sam says, clapping his head with his hand. "Hold on. Before you go." He reaches over into his bag and rummages around. He pulls out a t-shirt and checks out the size on the tag. "Here," he says. "This is a small. It should fit fine."

"Cool," Jex says, holding it up to see a large sea creature of some type, with a red beast of some sort in its clutches. "How much do I owe you?"

"On the house," Joe responds, Sam nodding his head in agreement. "You get free t-shirts and guest list spots and anything you want for life," says Sam. "Oh, and take this sticker, too. Waters of Chaos owes you forever."

Knowing resistance is futile, Jex just says, "thanks guys. Have a great night," already knowing she won't stay for the next band. Live music is awesome for Jex, but the room is getting crowded and she is over it. She walks away from the two and doesn't look back. She walks out onto Sunset towards La Cienega. Her little Ford Focus is parked not too far away. She unlocks the door, but pauses and goes to the back of the car. She pulls the Waters of Chaos sticker out of her back pocket and studies it for a moment. Then she pulls it from its backing and slaps it onto the back of the car, next to a Ramshackle Glory sticker and below a Misfits sticker. It is the eighteenth sticker on the car, she notes always careful to remember the number for some reason she couldn't explain if asked.

She gets in the car and plugs her iPhone into the tape adaptor. She plays with it for a minute and finds AJJ. "Rejoice." She turns it up loud. She pulls a one-hitter from the glove compartment and fills it with a pinch of weed. She lights it and inhales deeply. She takes another hit and then one more. She stares out into space and then looks around bleakly, suddenly alone. She shakes the thoughts out of her head. She pulls into traffic and soon she is gone. She sighs, headed downtown. There are walls to be tagged. The music is loud. She signs along.

JENNY THE CHICKEN

"Hey guys, what's up?"

Eugene is surprised to see Jex and Q back at his front door, but he gestures without a second thought to welcome them back into the house. Jex walks right in without hesitation, her backpack now hanging over her left shoulder. Q follows along but her gait is substantially more restrained, cautious perhaps, as though tip-toeing through a haunted cemetery.

"Eugene," Jex says firmly, standing with her neck straight and her body tense. "I want you to answer some questions for me," looking him directly in the eye.

"Sure, Jex," he responds in a mixture of confusion and slight hurt. "You know I'm always straight with you."

"When you coughed earlier, into your handkerchief, you coughed out blood didn't you?"

Eugene looks surprised and backs up a bit. "Why do you ask that?"

"It's true, isn't it?" Jex demands quietly. "I noticed you tried to hide it from us but I didn't think much about it at the time. But it's true, right? You coughed up some blood?"

He shrugged defensively. "Just a little. It's been happening for a couple days. Just a little bit. I figure I got to lay off the generic cigs for a bit. I'm smoking Marlboro lights for a couple weeks."

Jex shakes her head. "Whatever. And you said you've been waking up in the night sweating, recently, right?"

"Yeah, Jex, but ..."

"Let me feel your forehead," she demands and, without waiting for consent, slaps her hand on his forehead. "You're hot," she declares.

"Yeah, Jex., but..."

"How long have you had that cough?" Her tone still quiet but no less demanding, it is not an optional question.

"I don't know, Jexy," Eugene responds, now sounding somewhat nervous and even perhaps a little guilty, as though he did something wrong but did not know what. "Maybe two or three weeks, you know?"

"Is it two weeks or three weeks? It's not my cough to know."

Eugene pauses, trying to think. He coughs. "I don't know, maybe closer to three weeks?"

"And your cousin. Molly. When did she come back from San Diego?"

Eugene pauses again. He coughs again. "About three weeks ago. Why?"

"Has she been coughing like that, too?"

"Why?" He coughs again, nervous this time.

"She has, hasn't she? Since she's been here? The whole time? And you know she's been using intravenous needles?"

Eugene is getting either scared or angry; probably both. "Why Jexy? You're starting to freak me out."

"Look, man," Jex says calmly but firmly, looking Eugene right in the eye and holding her hand on his arm. "I'm not trying to freak you out. But a cough like that, for that long. And coughing out blood. Night sweats. Fever. Fatigue. Chills. Losing weight without meaning to. I think it's worthwhile for you to at least get tested for tuberculosis."

Eugene stops for a full ten seconds. "Tuberculosis," he mutters quietly, his eyes turning slightly black.

Jex stands firm. "I guarantee you I am going to get tested now. And so should you. And I'm going to make goddamn sure that Q gets tested immediately, too."

Q shrinks back in horror. "Jex, WTF?"

Eugene's eyes turn darker. "You mean because you spent an hour with me? You think an hour with me is enough to infect you, like I'm some kind of leper, now?" he murmurs accusingly.

Jex does not falter. "Yes," she confirms. "For exactly that reason. Not like a leper but you may be very infectious right now."

Eugene raises his hands in exasperation. "Jex, for real? What the fuckin' fuck?"

"Look," she says, "Let me just listen to a couple things in your chest."

Eugene scrunches up his face. "What?" he says, confused. "In my chest? How?"

Jex shakes her head. "No, it's no big deal. I just want to listen with my stethoscope." She unzips her backpack, reaches in and pulls out her stethoscope. "Just a stethoscope, see," she reassures him. "You've seen it a thousand times, no big deal."

Eugene hesitates but doesn't outright say no. Jex continues to prod, with her steely determination clearly on display.

"It's no big deal, Eugene. I've done it a hundred times volunteering. Trust me. Just take off your shirt and I will done in no time ..."

"Take off my shirt, Jex, are you for fucking real?" Eugene's face turns instantly red. He coughs hard and spits into the corner of the room, too embarrassed to care that he is spitting in his own house.

"Dude, I have done this exam a thousand times." This does not convince Eugene, who has turned and is walking out of the living room and into the kitchen. "Fuck this shit," he says. "I just have a cough."

Jex doesn't give up and follows Eugene into the kitchen. "Come on, Eugene. Don't be like that. Coughing is one thing – coughing up blood, that shit could be something else. Trust me."

"No, fuck this." He says, continuing to walk through the kitchen and out the other side, back into the living room. Jex turns to meet him as he completes his circle.

"Hey," she says in a raised voice, almost yelling. "You know Native Americans have a rate of tuberculosis that is over ten times higher than Caucasians."

It stops Eugene in his tracks, and he looks earnestly at Jex. "For real?"

"For real," Jex says with the tone of certainty that is hard to debate. "And I'm not talking historically. Historically, that shit is a much bigger differential, like totally ridic. I'm talking right now. Today.

The Native American has a rate of tuberculosis that is ten times higher than a white person."

Eugene looks at Jex in his thoughtful manner, instantly calmer. "No, Jex," he says. "I did not know that."

* * *

It is ten minutes later and Eugene is sitting on a chair, his undershirt still on, with Jex kneeling next to him on one knee, her right hand pressed firmly on his clavicle. She is tapping the middle finger of her right hand with the index and middle finger of the left hand, which she holds tightly next to one another.

"So, this is called percussing. The point is to see whether there's fluid in your lungs. It doesn't seem that way, but the apex of your lungs is above your clavicle. So, by tapping on it like this, I can get a sense of whether your lungs have fluid in them or not."

"My lungs go up that far?" Eugene, asks with a disbelieving tone in his voice.

"Yeah, it's just the apex of them, but that's enough, just by two millimeters or so, not much. But enough."

She does the same thing to his chest, under his right nipple and on a lower part of his lungs. "Your lung is separated into different lobes – different sections. I'm checking on each of them."

She places her hands on either side of his neck, straight out as if in a karate chop. "Can you please say ninety nine for me?"

"Ninety nine," he says. She puts her hands on his back, under his shoulder bone and asks him to do the same thing; followed by the same exercise but with her hands on his lowest rib, the twelfth rib. He says "ninety nine" each time as requested.

"How is it?" he asks but she doesn't answer.

She pulls out her stethoscope and places it below his right nipple. "Can you say it again, please?"

"Ninety nine," he repeats compliantly. She repeats the same exercise on other spots on his chest and he complies each time as requested. "Eugene, I'm listening for bronchial breath sounds and other areas that might be abnormal."

As Jex listens to the last part of Eugene's chest, his cousin Molly walks in the door. She is dressed all in black, save for a shock of blue on the left portion of her dark, shoulder-length hair. She seems pale and thin. She wears long sleeves and is holding a guitar case. She looks at the scene quizzically.

Chuckling slightly, she asks, "what are you guys doing?"

Eugene slaps the stethoscope away from his chest and stands fully upright, his full body towering over Jex, Q, and Molly. Molly instinctively backs up one step but otherwise holds her ground. "What are we doing?" Eugene bellows at Molly, pointing his finger accusingly at her. "I'll tell you what we're doing. We're checking to see if I have motherfucking tuberculosis. Which, by the way, it looks like I do."

Molly pulls her head back in confusion. "Tuberculosis? What the fuck?" She chokes on her words just a bit and begins to cough.

"There," Eugene roars. "That cough. That stinking, infected, disgusting junky leper cough. That's where I got it from."

"Eugene," Jex says calmly, holding her hand on his arm. He pulls away and Jex does not try immediately to disengage.

""What are you talking about?" Molly demands, her eyebrows now furrowed in anger, fear.

"You, you goddamn junky. You gave me tuberculosis. Now I'm nothing but a goddamn old lunger like some homeless person or junky like you." The vitriol is clear in his words.

"A junky?" Molly blurts out defensively. "Who you think you are, calling me a junky?"

"Don't lie to me, Molly. I know. I know. I seen your needles around. I tried to be cool and supporting and brought you into this house, but you don't just hurt yourself. You hurt me. Being a junky hurts everyone around you. For real."

Tears well up in Molly's eyes. Her face turns red, but in that way it turns red when you are angry, not when you are upset or embarrassed.

"Stop calling me a junky," she screams. "I'm not a junky." She is almost shaking in her anger. She turns to her left side and kicks a small lamp. It flies off the cabinet and cracks into a thousand shards of blue and white. The light flickers for a moment and then disappears.

"Stop lying to me, cuz, I saw your gear. I seen it with my own eyes." Eugene's face is contorted with anger and sadness and fear. "I saw your needles, cuz. I saw your needles."

"I am not a junky, asshole!" Molly scream back. "I'm diabetic, OK? Are you happy now? Now you know." She coughs hard. "I'm not a junky for Christ's sake." She cries harder and coughs on her words. "I'm diabetic and have to take those stupid shots every day. I'm not even allowed to drink. And I hate it. I fucking hate it, all right? But I'm not a fucking junky."

As she speaks, Eugene's hands slowly rise to grasp his head, and the anger and fear drips out of his face, leaving behind only the clear luster of sadness. His eyes redden and turn wet. Tears begin to drip down his face.

After Molly finishes speaking, Eugene turns his head just slightly, slowly. "Cousin Molly," he says, coughing out his words, nearly blubbering them, the words salty wet. "Cousin Molly, I'm sorry."

That is all it takes for Molly to burst out in tears. She breaks down and her shoulders lean inwards. Eugene walks across the room in less than three steps and grabs her in a bear hug and they cry together, weeping in sadness; weeping in joy. "Cousin Molly, I am so sorry. I never should have doubted family. I was just scared. I never should have doubted you."

"It's OK, Geney," Molly whispers through her tears in a raspy cough. "I know you love me. I would never do anything to hurt you. Or dishonor this family. I promise."

He pulls her away from him and looks her square in the eye. "You, Cousin Molly. You could never dishonor our family. You are the future of this family. We are the future of this family."

The two embrace for a long minute. Jex hesitates, and then delicately interrupts. "Uh, guys, this is awesome and all, but one or both of you might be, like, highly contagious and it would be awesome if we could all go to the hospital and, you know … get checked out."

Eugene pauses for just a moment and then steps back. He surveys the room quickly and then claps his hands loudly. "Right," he exclaims. "Let's get this show on the road. "I'll drive me and Molly. The hospital is a fifteen minute ride. Jex and Q, you follow in Jex's car. We don't know how long we'll be and you guys don't have to stay if you don't want to." He waits a second, contemplating, and then adds, "and, plus... Well, we're maybe contagious and all, so maybe separate cars are a good idea"

Jex shakes her head. "Yeah, anyways. Let's go. We'll follow you."

* * *

An hour later, Jex is sitting in an exam room with Eugene, both wearing surgical masks. Molly is being examined separately in another room down the hall. Q has been forced to sit out in the waiting room, to her endless consternation.

Eugene shakes his head at Jex. "Yeah, 'cause we wouldn't have already given it to you if we have it."

Jex chuckles. "Just a precaution."

Eugene shrugs. "It can't hurt I guess." He looks down at the mark on his forearm. "So, what, this thing is supposed to turn red or something if I have TB?"

Jex nods her head, looking down at the mark on her own forearm. "Yes and no. This is the Mantoux tuberculin skin test. They inject this thing, a purified protein derivative under the top layer of your skin. If it turns not just red, but also forms a big, firm bump, you probably have it. It's a pretty common way of detecting whether you have TB. But it won't tell you whether you have active or latent TB."

"What's the difference?" Eugene asks coughing strongly and looking less well than perhaps he did just a couple of hours ago.

Jex smirks. "I'm pretty sure you have the active kind. Latent TB infection is actually totally common. Like, a third of the population has it."

"For real?" Eugene asks incredulously.

"Yeah, but most of the time it never becomes active. And if it's not active, it has no symptoms and it isn't contagious."

"So, if this dot turns redder, it means I'm active?"

"Well," Jex clarifies, "no. If it is red and a firm bump, that just means that you have the underlying infection. It shows that there is mycobacterium tuberculosis in your system. That's what the infection is called itself. For short it's called M. tuberculosis."

Eugene shakes his head and coughs roughly. "Man, Jex. M. tuberculosis. It feels almost as bad as M. Ward sounds."

Jex chuckles and nods her head in agreement, studying the mark on her forearm. "So, just because you have M. tuberculosis in your system, that doesn't mean you have active tuberculosis. It might just be latent. Those chest x-rays they took, they should be a bitter indicator, you know?"

"Yeah?"

"Yeah. I read about this, like, a year ago or something. The x-ray is a posterior-anterior chest radiograph. It's looking for abnormalities like lesions in your chest. They can be all kinds of sizes, but if they are there, it's a good sign that you have active TB. And they pretty much cause all the coughing and stuff you have. Then they'll take your loogie and check it for what's called acid-fast bacilli, I think. It's pretty easy to do with a kit but they'll send it out for a culture, too, to confirm."

"But you think I got it?"

Jex shrugs, not showing any cards. "We'll see."

"Shit, Jexy, if I got this, I'm super sorry I exposed you to it. I feel just terrible."

She just shrugs again. "Don't worry about it. I love sickness." She laughs. "I mean, it fascinates me. If I get it, it will just be something I can use to learn."

Eugene shakes his head. "I love your positivity, Jexy. For real.

That's the kind of positive vibes I try to emanate, you know what I mean?"

Jex laughs. "You are a thousand times more positive than me. I'm a born misanthrope. Hopelessly cynical."

Eugene laughs back. "No way, Jex. You're an inspiration. I hope you'll spend more time with Molly. She can use a positive role model. Hell, we all can."

"Whatever, you're my role model for sure."

"Yeah," Eugene says with a shrug. "I'm not no one's role model for sure, but this is a learning experience for me, Jex, that's for sure. I am going to educate people about the disparity of this disease between Native Americans and whites. People need to know that. It's a disparity that is pervasive, man. Pervasive. Suicide. Alcoholism. HIV. TB. Shit, even I didn't know about TB."

"Yeah," Jex says. "It's not very common, even in Native Americans. So, it's not too surprising that it's not any anyone's radar. But the ratio is fucked, that's for sure."

Eugene shakes his head. "It's unjust. Just unjust."

Jex nods her head in agreement.

"So," Eugene continues. "This treatment. You say it's long term, yo?"

Jex shakes her head. "It's long, but it's not long term, really. Like around six months or so. Maybe up to a year for the infection to die."

"Shit, man," Eugen marvels. "That's a hella strong bug."

"Yeah," Jex agrees. "And you have to take a bunch of drugs, not just one."

"Oh yeah," Eugene responds, his eyebrows lifted.

"Yeah. The doctor can tell you. I'm not one hundred percent sure. But, it's on regiments, you know, like a series of different drugs in a batch. They figured out which ones work best." Jex clenches her eyes tightly and thinks. "Let's see," she says, counting on her fingers. "There's Isoniazid. Rifampin. Ethambutol. And … Pyrazinamide. I think those are some of the big ones – they're called first-line anti-TB agents."

"No shit. Like they're the guys out in the trenches."

Jex smiles. "Exactly. But it's a pretty precise concoction. So if you don't take it exactly like they say, I'm going to drive out to the desert and kick your stoner ass. You better comply, for realz."

Eugene laughs his big laugh. "I promise, I will. I will." And then he gets deadly serious. "And if Molly has it, you can make goddamn sure she will be compliant. No joking around. We are blessed to have you, Jex."

"Ha, ha," Jex laughs. Let me tell you something about … "

Jex doesn't have a chance to finish her sentence. The door opens up and a doctor walks in. He is about fifty years old, and is clearly of Native American descent.

"Well, hello there," the doctor says with a smile, looking at Eugene and Jex and then back at Eugene. "I'm Doctor Williams. Let me guess," pointing at Eugene. "You're Eugene."

* * *

It is three days later and Jex is on the floor of her living room. Alone. Flat on her back on the oriental rug, as chill as the Dude listening to past bowling matches. Her iPhone rings and she lets it go to voicemail. When the tone goes off, indicating a message, Jex sighs and grabs the phone. She dials voicemail and listens.

"Ms. Blackwell, this is Doctor Williams, from West Desert Hospital. I am calling to check up on your TB test. You were supposed to come in this morning and we didn't see you. I'd be really grateful if you could call me back so we could chat. Oh, and Ms. Blackwell. I understand that it was you that identified the initial symptoms of TB in Eugene and Molly. And that Eugene was scheduled to attend a rally with over a hundred people the night you brought him in. You could have prevented quite an epidemic there. Job very well done." There is a pause. "Please call me back, Ms. Blackwell. I'd just like to talk and make sure your test came out OK."

Jex smiles and stares up at her forearm, which she has raised lazily above her head. The area where the TB test was taken is completely clean and free from redness and swelling. No red; no bumps; No TB – and Jex knows it. She smiles her easy smile. She raises her torsos and sits cross-legged. She grabs her lighter and the purple bong with the Pat the Bunny sticker. She takes a hit, then another. She releases the second hit and then pulls the headphones on. She presses play. Jex looks up at her ceiling and into nothing, visions of infections and bacterium floating around her head. Pat the Bunny's "A Song for Jenny" begins to play, and wraps itself around her visions. The music drifts on, into the chaos, and helps Jex pretend that tomorrow will never exist.

Bawdy DySmurfia

Jex runs south down Seventh Street, Broadway behind her. Her gait is a desperate but intentional one. The moon is bright and the street lights, too. Jex's mood is as dark as they come. The inches seem like yards and the yards seem like miles. Molly's squat is about two miles away from the alley off Grand Street where Jex had been tagging. Jex runs at full speed the entire way. Even if Q had the quickness of wit to have immediately run after Jex, she never would have had the stamina to keep up.

Jex is on the front stoop of the squat, a dilapidated old place down the street from an abandoned warehouse, and in through a front window, silent as a mouse. She is smart enough to not have tried to knock first, because who knows who would answer, or what mood they are in. Or what they might be hiding. Or who they might think you are.

Unfortunately for Jex, she does not know where in the squat Molly is flopping or, frankly, whether she is even flopping there tonight. Her schedule is not traditional, to say the least. And even if Jex finds her, she doesn't know whether she will find her alone, or with someone else. Or what condition she might be in. That last one, that's the one that worries Jex the most.

Jex is in the living room and, half-crouched, she looks around through the darkness. She seems intentional but calm, giving her eyes a moment to adjust to the house, which takes time even though it is dark outside. Once she is able to see more than a few inches in front of her eyes, enough to know she is not immediately about to trip over something – or someone – she moves purposefully through the room, from one side to the next. She finds no one and nothing to really suggest anyone is even there. She pulls out her iPhone and turns on its flashlight. She points it down towards the ground and only a little bit in front of her. This minimizes but does not eliminate the risk that someone will see her before she sees them.

Jex is down another hallway and in the kitchen. There is nothing of interest to see here and she doesn't meander long; just long enough to confirm there is nothing of interest to see here. She flashes her light quickly into an adjacent room, which has a table in it with a bunch of dishes but nothing else, other than an old Smiths poster on the wall.

Deliberately, Jex moves on to the next room. She opens a door carefully but it's just a closet with a bunch of bowling pins stacked on shelves. They nearly fall when she opens the door but Jex gets lucky and they don't. She lets out a short, steep breath and closes the door quietly. She backtracks through the front hallway until she comes to a flight of wooden stairs. She does not hesitate and begins to climb them. The first one squeaks pretty badly, though, and stops her in her tracks. Damn old wooden stairs.

Jex takes a moment on that first stair, contemplating perhaps how to best distribute her weight and minimize the pressure on the steps. It is not, to say the least, a very scientific way of moving forward, but Jex doesn't have time for precise calculations. In any event, she isn't feeling particularly scientific at the moment. She just feels scared. Scared for Molly.

With Molly in her mind, Jex does not hesitate long. She tip toes as delicately as possible, taking each step carefully, deliberately. Though the trip is not without its squeaks and creaks, Jex manages to make it to the top of the stairs with just a little bit of noise. She keeps her light pointed down low, desperate to find Molly and still cognizant that she doesn't quite know exactly where she is, but she knows for sure she isn't supposed to be there. She has no idea how welcome or unwelcome she will be if she runs into a dweller she doesn't know.

Slowly, Jex finds her way down the hallway. She sees two closed doors on one side of the hallway, and a third closed door on the other side of the hallway, which turns left and into pitch black just a little bit past the farthest door. Shit. This is not good. Each step is an exercise in faith, with no way to know whether the next step would be met with someone or something that would radically change the temperament of the hallway. Jex creeps down the hallway and comes to the first door. She stands as quietly as possible and just listens for a moment. Is anyone there? Is anyone awake? Shit.

And in that tense dark hallway, a voice that is just inches from Jex pierces the silence, whispering shrilly but clearly, "hey!" Jex can't help but yelp out in response; something indecipherable but strong, all reflex and no intent at all. As if she is suddenly fighting a knife fight with nothing but her voice.

* * *

"Jex," she hears the other voice continue. "Is that you?" Out of sorts and in a sudden defensive posture, Jex struggles to gather her thoughts. Who is saying her name? Where are they? Who are they?

Instead of asking one of these quite fair questions, a sound something like "argh," is all Jex musters through her uncertainty and confused defensiveness.

"Jex? Jex? It's me, Sarah."

Jex collects her senses enough to focus on the dim figure in the room and after a moment she recognizes her, Molly's friend Sarah. They had met a couple times before, probably at this squat, now that Jex thinks on it.

"Sarah, holy shit, you scared me."

"Jex, oh my god," Sarah continues, and Jex notices her tone is a manic one. Her eyes seem to bulge behind her blond bangs. "I am so glad you're here. You're like a guardian angel. I'm so glad you're here," she repeats.

"What do you mean? What's wrong?"

"It's Molly, Jex. I can't wake her up. Follow me. Please. Please."

Without another second passing and without waiting for a response, Sarah turns and bolts past Jex and the three visible doors, down the hallway and takes a left turn into darkness. Jex does not hesitate in following her. The two move so quickly that neither of them see or hear the door on the left open as they pass it.

Jex walks firmly into the darkness and spends a moment in a darkness that is complete. Her heart skips a beat, as though she might be in a trap or something, but she does not falter. The moment lasts for minutes but is really just a moment before a door opens and allows just enough moonlight in so that Jex can focus on where she is headed. She sees Sarah walk through the doorway. Instinctively, she follows. The smell of mold hangs in the air. Old laundry. Unwashed dishes.

Inside the dark room, Molly lies in bed, motionless, her skin pale under the dim moonlight. Jex runs to her. Sarah stays slightly behind and starts to cry, holding her left hand to her face, covering her mouth. Jex moves quickly. The seconds tick like hours as she struggles to find a pulse; first in Molly's wrist ("Radial, arrhythmic"); and then under her elbow ("brachial, faint"); and then to her neck ("carotid, thready … at best"). "Thready," Jex murmurs to herself. "At best," she continues, again to herself, barely speaking at all.

"Is she OK, Jex? Jex, tell me she's going to be OK." Sarah's tone is a desperate one.

"She's alive, but just barely. She has a traumatic head injury. She's going in and out. Molly, can you hear me? Molly? Squeeze my hand if you can hear me." Jex has Molly on her back, inspecting her ears and mouth, pulling up her eyelid, checking her eyes. She pinches her arm. "Molly, can you feel that?"

Sarah emits a low, gurgle, and her crying gets louder.

"Sarah, you really do have to shut up. I need to focus here."

Sarah cries louder. "I don't know what to do."

Jex's tone is firm and clear. "Sarah, I will tell you exactly what to do. Pull out your cellphone and call 911. Nine-one-one, not nine-eleven. Nine-one-one. Tell them there is a fourteen year old girl here with a traumatic brain injury, thready pulse, and unconscious. We need an ambulance and paramedics immediately. Do that now."

"No," booms a loud and gruff voice from behind Sarah, which causes both Sarah and Jex to jump back with a start. "No one's calling the cops."

Stunned, Sarah pulls her hand out of her pocket, where it had previously been reaching for her cellphone. There is a long pause of silence as Jex takes in what is being said. She collects herself and responds.

"Not the cops, I didn't tell her to call the cops. We need to call the paramedics. Molly is hurt really badly."

The dark figure, who the moonlight is just beginning to identify – a skinny guy maybe in his late twenties, dark shirt, torn shorts, scruffy hair – responds. "Paramedics, cops, they'll all be here. No one's calling 911. Can't have pigs here. And besides," he says, looking over at Molly. "She's fine. She's just sleeping something off."

"Traumatic brain injury," Sarah blurts out. "Do you really think so? She was fine two hours ago? This isn't because of her falling down the stairs is it? She said she was fine."

Jex lashes back. "Does she look fine? Does she? Yes, I am very sure it's because of the fall down the stairs. There's often a delayed reaction and she has all the symptoms of it, and has all day. I missed it because she's diabetic and so I screwed up identifying what's wrong with her, but there's no doubt this is what she has. A traumatic brain injury."

The dark figure scoffs. "Ha, you confused diabetes for a head injury. Can I call you Doctor Stupid?"

Jex stands up and goes toe-to-toe with the dark figure, who is at least a foot taller than the diminutive Jex. Three other people – two girls and a guy – fall in line behind the dark figure, each of them clearly just awoken by the noise.

"Call me doctor whatever you want," Jex shoots. "I'm not a doctor at all, and yeah I confused them. But I know I'm right at this stage, and for sure it's because of that goddamn fall on the stairs. If I knew about it yesterday, she'd already be in the hospital. Here, try and wake her up," Jex continues, pointing at Molly. "You won't be able to do it, and she's not sleeping something off. She's dying right now."

"Says you," the dark figure says.

"Yeah," Jex says. "Says me and says science."

"You're just a kid," the dark figure retorts.

"Yeah, so is Molly. She's fourteen. And she's going to die here if we don't get her to a hospital. That's for sure. How's your shit going to go if you got a fourteen year old dead girl in your squat?"

"Oh, god," moans Sarah. "Somebody do something."

One of the other dark figures pulls on the first dark figure's sleeve. "Blake, we can't let her just die in here."

Blake waves him off. "She's not dying, this kid is just emo. And we can't have cops in here."

"They're not cops," Jex screams. "They're paramedics and Molly will die without help, goddammit. I don't have a car here and I can't bring her myself."

"Blake," another one of the dark figures urges. "We can't have no little girl dying in here."

"And it's not right, either. That's not what we're about," says another dark figure.

"Whatever," Blake says in frustration. "We can't let no cops in here."

"Paramedics," Jex states again, more firmly. "Paramedics, not cops."

"Yeah," Blake says, "but with this shit, the cops will come anyways. You're a dumb kid, but you're not that dumb, right?"

Jex does not back down. Her voice is loud and hoarse; not desperate but determined. "She needs a doctor now or she is going to die. End of thought."

"Blake," says one of the dark figures in a quiet voice. Blake holds up his hand and the quiet voice quickly trails off.

"OK," he says. "OK. We can take her to the hospital in my truck. We'll drop her off."

"No," Jex protests. "I just got her airways stabilized. We have to keep her neck immobilized and…"

"Listen, girl," Blake interrupts. "We can take her to the hospital and get her a doctor right now, or we can keep arguing about bringing cops to this house. You are not going to win that argument, though, so how do you want to play this?"

There is a long pause as Blake and Jex trade fearsome glares. Sarah's sobs don't relent. A dog begins to bark somewhere.

"Shit," Jex says, looking at Molly, weighing the limited options. "Shit," she says again, and then hesitates no more. "Let's go."

* * *

"What the bloody hell is wrong with you?"

Jex sits in the small examination room in L.A.'s downtown hospital, her legs curled up close to her body and her head laying delicately on her knees. She wants to be anywhere but here. The sun is beginning to shine outside, but all Jex wants to do is climb into some dark hole, disappear into nothingness.

The person doing the yelling is Dr. Cohen. His English accent is not so charming during a rant. He is ruthless in his criticism.

"Of all people to know this, Ms. Blackwell, you all of all people should know that. You hover around these hallways endlessly enough. A person who presents with these sort of symptoms" — he angrily shakes the folio of paper in his hand — "must get referred to an emergency room immediately. Immediately. Without delay. Without exceptions. And you … you give her drinking instructions? Are you a loon?"

Jex doesn't respond to this, which is probably for the best as it does not seem to be the type of question that is intended to elicit a response. The silence is awkward. Jex picks at her fingernail, her face contorted into a protective scowl; it seems almost second nature to her.

"Not to mention," Dr. Cohen continues, "that you moved a person with an obvious head injury. That wouldn't seem bright even to a plumber, for goodness sake. Have you heard of 911, Ms. Blackwell?"

"She was in a squat," Jex explains in a meek whisper, as though this might cause Dr. Cohen to relent. It does not.

"In a squat," Dr. Cohen repeats with exasperation, his hands making quotation marks around the word "squat." "In a squat," he seethes through his teeth again, shaking his head. "Well, that is just lovely, isn't it? What exactly are you doing in a squat in any event? You are fifteen years old."

Jex shrugs. "I went in to help Molly. She's only fourteen."

Dr. Cohen shakes his head. "Well, I never …"

"Perhaps, that is the problem, Dr. Cohen. That you never."

Dr. Cohen turns around abruptly to find Dr. Stephens standing behind him, her brow furrowed; her hands on her hips.

Dr. Cohen sighs at the site of Dr. Stephens and shakes his head. As he speaks, the tone of resignation in his voice is as clear as the condescension in the shake of his head. "Well, if it isn't Dr. Stephens, the ward's most popular enabler-in-chief."

"Well," Dr. Stephens retorts with lightning speed. "If it isn't the ward's most reviled Monday Morning Quarterbacker."

"You are too easy on the girl," Dr. Cohen cracked back, just as quickly.

Dr. Stephens shakes her head in anger. "And you, our favorite armchair general."

"It doesn't take a general to recognize what went wrong here, a pint-sized detective who fancies herself a doctor."

Dr. Stephens sneers defensively. "All the hindsight in the world won't change what happened here."

"Au contraire," says Dr. Cohen, every bit as defensive, his voice gaining in pitch and volume. "Perhaps some hindsight in one of the hundred other circumstances in which Ms. Blackwell comes storming into our institution with some ragamuffin or another that she has decided to save." He again uses hand quotations marks, this time to emphasize the word "save." "Perhaps," he continues, "if we — or more precisely you — would have nipped this little phenomenon in the bud earlier, young Ms. Blackwell would have done the right thing," he raises his voice and pivots his glare to directly address Jex, "and simply called an ambulance when she heard of this young girl's symptoms." Jex looks away, out into nothing.

Dr. Stephens does not relent. "Yes, Dr. Cohen," Dr. Stephens chides in a tone that forces Dr. Cohen to return his gaze to her, "I am quite sure you would have rushed a diabetic to the hospital after initial complaints of a headache and thirst. That is quite by the book, isn't it?"

For the first time in the conversation, Dr. Cohen stammers. "Well . . I . ." and a word that sounds awfully similar to "harrumph," and then, "I will tell you, Dr. Stephens ..." His words are still somehow caught in his throat as Dr. Stephens jumps in, her words slicing with the sharpness of a switchblade.

"That's quite enough," Dr. Stephens declares. "If there's some basis to admit a thirst patient into the emergency room, I would be pleased to hear it."

"Well," Dr. Cohen yells back, finding his words. "I can tell you that whatever I would have done, it would not be counseling a four-teen year old diabetic on the strategies of drink!"

"And that fourteen-year-old diabetic had a zero point zero blood alcohol content upon admission, Dr. Cohen. I am quite sure you would have seen that in her chart."

"Well, yes," Dr. Cohen ekes out, stammering again. "But . . ."

"But what are the chances," Dr. Stephens interrupts, overtaking Dr. Cohen's response and changing its direction. "what are the chances that this child would have survived the night if Ms. Black-well had not quickly put the pieces together – based on additional data the patient had not disclosed upon initial assessment – and broke into that squat" – she messily puts air quotation marks around the word "squat," mocking Dr. Cohen's prior gesture – "where exactly do you think the patient would be at the moment?"

"Well, uh, Dr. Stephens, you know that's not the point at . . ."

"Dead," Dr. Stephens declares, her words punching the air. "That is precisely where she would be, dead. Instead of lying safely post-surgery in a hospital bed, comfortable in an induced coma, not a natural one, with a promising likelihood of full recovery. Life, not death."

Jex's face grows paler and paler as the quarrel between the two senior doctors escalates. She is crawling into herself, and has been since Dr. Cohen commenced his yelling session at her. But the words "dead" and "death" and the thoughts of her friend lying in a hospital bed in an induced, post-surgical coma, become too much for her. Without a sound or a whimper she jumps up from her seat and bolts out of the room, so quickly it causes both doctors to stop their words in mid-sentence.

"Jex," Dr. Stephens calls out to her but it is too late. She is down the hallway and into a stairwell before either of the doctors can even open the door.

"Well," Dr. Stephens says, turning back to Dr. Cohen, who seems suddenly meek and unsure. "That's just great. We may never see her in this hospital again. I hope that makes you happy."

Dr. Cohen rubs his forehead with his hand. "That's not what I want at all, Doctor. You know that. She just needs more discipline or she will never …"

"Never what," Dr. Stephens demands. "Succeed? Thrive? Survive? She has a passion for medicine and amazing talents that could exceed both yours and mine if they are just properly…"

"Properly what," Dr. Cohen shoots back. "Coddled? Hugged? She needs to know how to improve…"

"Her friend is nearly dead. Is this the right time to be yelling at screaming at her? Amazing talent or not, she is young and scared and alone."

"I never meant …"

"Oh, Dr. Cohen, you never mean anything you do. Maybe it's time that you grew up a little bit, not her." With that, Dr. Stephens turns on her heel and walks angrily down the hallway. Dr. Cohen begins to call out to her but apparently thinks better of it. Instead, he simply stands in the hallway, watching Dr. Stephens as she turns a corner and disappears.

* * *

It is hard to say how much time has passed since Jex stormed out of the hospital in despair. One hours? Three? Maybe more or maybe less. She wouldn't know if you asked her, her thoughts clouded by panic and shame and uncertainty and fear and sadness; so much sadness. She is curled up in the basement of the public library, trying not to let her tears break into an audible crying. It is a common theme in her life, she thinks to herself, but she's a tough girl. And she is not a frightened girl. But she doesn't feel tough and she doesn't feel not frightened. She only feels despair. Helpless. Hopeless.

"And what, Ms. Blackwell do you think you are doing? Another basement nap on library time?" Ms. Tubman's words pierce the air, jolting Jex out of her thoughts. Jex looks up at her and the look on her face jolts Ms. Tubman every bit as much as her words jolted Jex. She sees tears in Jex's eyes, something she had never seen in the two years since Jex starting working at the library. Jex erratically folds and unfolds a letter sized envelope in her hands, nervously creasing the edges and fingering the handwritten print on its front. She is pale in a way that Ms. Tubman had never seen before. And, when Jex speaks, she speaks with a quiver in her voice that was never there before.

"I'm sorry, Ms. Tubman," Jex says with a complete lack of sarcasm or pretense. "I didn't know where to go."

With a grace and fluidity that she does not often reveal, Ms. Tubman glides down and sits next to Jex; not a common gesture for the normally staid Ms. Tubman.

"What is it, Ms. Blackwell?" All of the disdain and chastising that had always made up Ms. Tubman's personality are gone. There is only sudden and uncompromising compassion. Perhaps it is all that Jex needs at the moment.

In a manner that is completely counter to any element of her personality previously disclosed to Ms. Tubman, Jex jumps into a stream-of-consciousness statement summarizing the last twenty four hours, which started the previous morning with Ms. Tubman stiffly guiding Molly to Jex's secret basement hiding place. She folds and unfolds the envelope with increasing urgency as she speaks. Ms. Tubman does not interrupt a single time. On two occasions, when Jex seemed to be getting emotional with the story, Ms. Tubman gently placed her fingers on Jex's arm, the slightest of touches; it soothes Jex in a way that, if she were to reflect upon the moment later, would have seemed foreign and strange, but endlessly reassuring.

Jex talks about Molly's symptoms and about her crush on the squat kid. She talks about drinking, and how she understood how not drinking could be isolating and difficult for a young kid at a cool party. She talks about tagging with Q and how she hadn't known about Molly's fall and hitting her head; and how if she had thought to ask about that, she would have immediately brought Molly to a hospital. She wonders aloud about whether those few hours would have made it easier for Molly. She talks about how frail and pale Molly looked when she found her in the squat. She talks about the older guy Blake (without dropping his name, no snitch) who didn't want to do anything at the squat at all, thought that Molly was just high or something. She talks about how she insisted, and how another squat girl helped her. She talks about the hours waiting through Molly's surgery, and looking up traumatic brain injuries and induced comas in Kumar & Clark.

And then, for a long time, she talks about Dr. Cohen's diatribe. How it hurts Jex, and how Jex knows, though, that he is right; that she was in over her head. She doesn't cry at all, like in the sniffly, chokey way, but tears well up in her eyes and flow down her cheeks as she talks.

Through it all, Ms. Tubman listens quietly.

"I don't know, Ms. Tubman," Jex says after she gets through the story, with its squats and surgeries; panic and fear. "I think I'm just a fake. I think I'm so smart, but I don't know anything. I just don't know anything. I'm a waster of space."

"Well," sniffs Ms. Tubman haughtily. "I don't know about any of that, but I do know this. You will run into Dr. Cohen types all your life. And even the smart ones, even the brilliant ones, will try to talk you down. It has happened to me my whole life."

Jex sniffles in a way that is quite uncharacteristic. It has a sense of innocence to it that should be commonplace in a sixteen-year-old; but is typically quite absent in Jex. One might even say it was refreshing, if it weren't for the sadness behind the hope in her eyes. "Really?" she asks in a tepid whisper.

"Really," Ms. Tubman confirms, her words an unspoken guarantee. "You are an incredibly bright young person, Jex. There will be plenty of old people like Dr. Cohen that try to tear you down, because you are growing in a way that is foreign and scary to them."

Jex stares at her feet as Ms. Tubman speaks, but it is easily apparent that she is listening carefully to each word. Ms. Tubman continues. "They grew up in a different time and, trust me, the people that were there before didn't think too much of their ways. Because they can't see it. They've worked so hard to make their own way, they forget there are other ways to do things; new ways; better ways."

"Ms. Blackwell," Ms. Tubman sighs. "I know you are not one for trusting. And when I was your age, I certainly trusted no one. Still don't, as a matter of fact." She winks out of the corner of her eye as she says this, and Jex just glimpses the gesture out of the corner of hers. Despite the darkness, Jex can't help but smile.

"But, please, I think I haven't lied to you ever, I'm very sure I haven't. Please trust me on this. You are doing the right thing. You have found your path and you are following it. Take your time. Learn from the things life offers you. They will improve you and you will share the things you learn with many others. You are going to do great things, Ms. Blackwell." She pauses and then continues in a much lower voice, almost out of the side of her mouth. "Don't let these douche bags get you down."

Jex can't help but chuckle and Ms. Tubman chuckles back just slightly, almost a guffaw. Ms. Tubman has said her piece and Jex doesn't respond. The two sit there for a long moment, contemplating. Ms. Tubman, looks down at the envelope that Jex is folding and unfolding. "What do you have there?"

"Oh," Jex says, looking at the well-folded envelope as though seeing it for the first time. "Heh," Jex murmurs in a false laugh. "Well, I've been applying to colleges, mostly because Ms. Gretel over at student counseling is making me. I filled out all the stupid forms but I've been procrastinating the essay. Ms. Gretel has been all up my a … all over me to finish it up. But, I don't know. I just wasn't really able to say anything I thought they wanted to hear."

"Ah," Ms. Tubman says knowingly. "And that's the finished project that you are delaying giving to Ms. Gretel."

"Worse," Jex chuckles. "That time has passed. She texted me, telling me if it's not postmarked by tomorrow, Stanford won't consider me."

"I see. And Stanford is where you want to go to college."

Jex laughs a laugh somewhere between incredulous and defeated. "I don't even think I want to go to college."

Ms. Tubman laughs back the same laugh and then says again, "I see." And then she says, "and I suppose Ms. Gretel told you that if you just sent it in and were accepted, you could decide then whether to go, but if you don't send it in, your decision is made for me."

Jex laughs back. "Yeah," she nods. "Pretty much. But it's not that the decision is made for me, you know. I've made the decision. No one made it for me."

"Yes," Ms. Tubman nods back. "And you're sure it's the right decision, right?"

Jex pauses and then shrugs. "The future … well, the future. I don't know. It doesn't really mean anything to me, so why bother. But . . ."

"But Stanford sounds cool, right?"

'Yeah," Jex laughs quietly. "I guess so." There is a long pause. "It's not for me, though, I want to just tear it up."

"Hmmm," Ms. Tubman says. There is another long pause. Jex folds and unfold the envelope. After more silence, the intercom emits three quiet beeps. Ms. Tubman is being paged.

"Well," she says. "I have to see to that." She stands awkwardly and slowly, straightens her dress. "Thank you for speaking to me, Ms. Blackwell. You are a smart girl and I don't think you need any of my advice. I trust in you to do the right thing, just try to do the right thing for you; not what you think others think is the right thing for you."

"Thank you for listening, Ms. Tubman. I really appreciate it."

"Not at all. And, here," she says, reaching her hand out. "Why don't you let me hold onto that letter for a day, so you don't tear it up or send it out and regret it. You have until close of business tomorrow. I will hold it. If you want to send it out, let me know and I will put it in tomorrow's post. If not …" she just shrugs her shoulders.

Jex pauses for a moment as if about to resist, then lifts the folded envelope to Ms. Tubman, who takes it and quickly pockets it under the folds of her dress.

"Very good, Ms. Blackwell. Have a good day."

"Thanks, Ms. Tubman. Have a good day."

Ms. Tubman walks through the library stacks and up to the administrative offices on the first floor, past the statue of Degas; and the coffee table books by National Geographic; and the little store in the front where they sell old books and cheap knick-knacks. Before she gets to her office, she passes Charlie, an assistant who has been in the library for years. "Charlie," she says, "can you make sure this gets in today's post, walk it over to the post office yourself? I'd much appreciate it." She holds out Jex's envelope.

"Sure, Ms. Tubman. Not a problem." He takes the envelope.

"Thank you, Charlie, you're a dear."

"Not a problem! Have a great day," Charlie replies as he walks down the hallway in a near skip. Ms. Tubman watches Charlie and the envelope walk away. She does not hesitate. She just shrugs to herself, smiles a half smile out of the side of her mouth and continues to her office.

* * *

Jex stands on the corner of Hill and 5th Street, not exactly sure where to go, what to do. The wind is cool on her face. She looks left and then right and then left again. She walks to the bus stop and stands there a while, as though waiting for something, but she doesn't know what she is waiting for. She picks at her fingernail and lights a cigarette. Puffing on the smoke, she looks up and sees a bus driving down the street, headed to the bus stop just a few feet from Jex. It seems familiar and safe to her.

She doesn't feel like driving herself today, anyways. The bus arrives and she gets on, Line 62. She tells herself that she is just going to ride around for a while, listening to music and thinking. Let someone else do the driving for once. But deep down, she knows. Johnny Hobo screams away at her through her ear pods, and she knows. She is going to Reseda.

LITTLE TOY SAXOPHONE

The challenge is clear in Dr. Stephens's voice. "So, Ms. Blackwell," she says with a determined smile. "What are your thoughts on Ms. Awad's condition?"

Dr. Stephens and Jex have returned to the examination room. Ms. Awad is fully dressed and sits on the exam table. Mr. Awad has taken the seat next to her. They all look at Jex expectantly.

Jex doesn't hesitate. Her chin is up. Her voice is firm and full of confidence. "Well, for the ankle, it seems pretty clear that there is some post-traumatic osteoarthritis, I think secondary to moderate osteoporosis in the ankle and related joints."

Dr. Stephens nods her head slightly approvingly. Mr. and Mrs. Amad listen intently as Jex continues.

"There are a few probable root causes, I suspect, mostly the injury she suffered last year where she fractured the ankle. It has been healing slowly, I think, and maybe you are not moving around as much as you used to?" Jex asks this to Ms. Awad, who reluctantly nods her head in agreement.

"And, I don't want to be too personal, but the charts show you have gained a few pounds in the last year or so."

"Yes," Ms. Awad says quietly. She seems to almost blush under her veil.

"We both have gained a few pounds recently," says Mr. Awad, his back straight and rigid, but his tone polite and respectful. "And you are correct, we have not been as active as we used to be."

"I'm not judging," Jex assures them. "You can speak with Dr. Stephens about that stuff later if you want. I'm just breaking down some of the likely causes so that you can have the information and might want to change your lifestyle a little, if you want."

Mr. Awad nods. "Thank you, Ms. Blackwell," he says quietly but firmly. "We appreciate your observations."

"My dear," Ms. Awad retorts, with a sing song in her voice that betrays the smile under her veil. "I do believe Ms. Blackwell is calling us a couple of old lazy bones. We've heard that before, haven't we?"

"No," Jex interrupts quickly, her face turning red. "I'm just setting out the factors, so you know. I would never say that."

"Yes, dear," Mr. Awad says through a thin, knowing smile, as though the two are sharing an intimate private joke to which Jex is not quite privy. "I feel like we have heard that one before. Though perhaps not always so politely." His eyes twinkle but Jex can't help but notice a streak of sadness in them, something that is suddenly clear to Jex has been in his eyes since he entered the room. Jex just sees it now, as he continues. "Well," Mr. Awad smiles, "perhaps it is time we finally take the doctor's orders."

Ms. Awad agrees and murmurs, "Time to take the doctor's orders."

"Remember," Jex emphasizes. "I'm just a hospital volunteer – not a doctor."

"We know," Mr. Awad assures Jex, his voice pensive but friendly. "It is just a little something someone used to say to us."

Jex smiles. "Now," she continues. "About that knee. As I said before, Dr. Stephens may re-conduct some or all of these exams and come to a different diagnosis, but for the knee, it seems clear to me that you have a torn, maybe partially torn, collateral ligament, and also a meniscal tear as a result of degenerative horizontal cleavage in the knee. This is most likely a degenerative thing that happened over time, but was probably, you know, exacerbated by your ankle injury."

"Her knee injury was caused by her ankle injury?" Mr. Awad queries, his brows curled in curiosity.

"Well, not quite," Jex clarifies. "I suspect that Ms. Awad favored her right leg when her left ankle was healing. That caused additional stresses on the leg, including the knee and the joint. This would hasten the degeneration, and could make it happen a lot more quickly than if the ankle hadn't been broken."

"Yes," Ms. Awad says quietly. "I may remember Dr. Stephens warning us that if we don't exercise more, my knees could suffer." You can almost see Ms. Awad's guilty expression as she looks over at Dr. Stephens, who smiles in a way that feigns frustration. Mr. Awad shakes his head slightly and lowers it in slight embarrassment.

Jex doesn't comment, and instead focuses on the diagnosis. "Yeah, so, if you recall, there was a test where I had you lie face up on the exam table. You knee was fully flexed and I rotated your foot a little bit. I created what is called a varus stress at the knee. When I extended the knee, it hurt you a little, and you could hear a click right in the joint. That's pretty solidly a characteristic of a medial meniscus tear. Right here," Jex says as she points to her own knee.

"I see," Ms. Awad says, clearly impressed.

"Yes," Jex says, nodding, before she continues. "And also, I conducted a test where I pulled your tibia while I held my hand on your upper tibia." She demonstrates on herself as the Awads nod in understanding. "I saw significant movement there, especially compared to the other leg, which didn't have any of that movement. In your left leg, the movement was in excess of one and a half centimeters. That indicates an anterior cruciate ligament rupture."

"Oh," Ms. Awad responds. "That doesn't sound good."

"Well," Jex says with assurance. "It's really good that you came to the hospital and saw Dr. Stephens. If there's anybody who can make sure you get the best treatment in the world for your condition, it's Dr. Stephens."

"Thank you, Ms. Blackwell," says Mr. Awad, his eyes still glimmering with that twinkle that lies somewhere between pride and sadness. "We do appreciate your time and your advice."

"Thank you both for giving me this opportunity. I really appreciate it and I know you are going to do great in your recovery, Ms. Awad."

"Thank you, Ms. Blackwell," says Ms. Awad, her voice somehow mirroring the sad, prideful look in Mr. Awad's eyes. "I believe that you are correct in that observation. This time, I believe it is time to recover."

"Thanks, Jex," say Dr. Stephens. "Now," she says, turning to the Awads. "Perhaps it's time to talk a little about next steps."

* * *

An hour later, Jex is sitting alone in the hospital cafeteria, drawing perfect renditions of anatomical joints and ankles in her sketch pad. Steam rises from the cup of tea sitting on the table in front of her. She has ear pods in, listening to "Frank Capra" by Advance Base. There is no place she would rather be, and nothing else she would rather do.

A fan hums above her. The blades clack away in a way that is almost like a pair of maracas knocking. It doesn't seem to bother Jex and she doesn't look up at all. She just sketches away, ligaments and tendons and such. Remarkable accuracy. Her consciousness disappears into the pad and she is disappeared. Disappeared until a finger taps on her shoulder. Jex doesn't jump or flinch at all. She just looks up and behind her to see Dr. Stephens standing there, smiling and with a cup of coffee in her hand. Jex takes off her ear pods and looks up at the doctor.

"Hi, Doctor," she says.

"Hi Jex," Dr. Stephens says through her smile. "Mind if I have a seat?"

"Not at all," Jex says, gesturing to the seat across from her, and Dr. Stephens sits down. She blows into her coffee and cautiously takes a sip.

"So, you did great today," Dr. Stephens states bluntly. "I knew you would be confident and graceful, but you really exceeded expectations."

Jex smiles in a way that is aw-shucks without being either intentional or juvenile. "Thanks," she says. "And thanks for the opportunity. It was a really awesome experience."

The two pause for a second, maybe a few seconds, before Dr. Stephens continues. "You look really good Jex, you do. You could stand to gain a few pounds but you look good."

Jex shrugs back ambivalently. "Whatever."

"You do," Dr. Stephens insists. Then another pause, one of those comedic ones, for timing. "But, do you ever wear anything other than that gray sweatshirt and jeans?"

Jex laughs. "I also have a gray hoodie. Oh, and a black hoodie, too. And one pair of black trousers."

"I guess make-up is out of the question."

Jex looks down her nose at Dr. Stephens. "Really?"

Dr. Stephens chuckles. "Forget I said anything."

"You really have a good relationship with the Awads," Jex says. "That really impressed me."

Dr. Stephens nods. "I've known them for a couple years. I started speaking with them when I had to tell them their son died." She says in a lower tone, turning almost into a whisper. "I stayed in touch."

"That must have been horrible."

"It was truly terrible. I'm encouraged by the fact that they brought him up to you. They are really doing a lot better. For a long time, they couldn't even talk about it. It really was tearing them apart."

"It's good, though, that you have been able to be around to support them. That's a really important thing for a patient to get from a doctor, right?"

Dr. Stephens shrugs. "But how many patients do I do it for? Three? Four? The rest are just nameless and faceless, really. Not when I'm treating them, of course, we give them the best individualized treatment we can. But there's so many patients, and so few doctors, the kind of continuing long-term attention that most of these patients need," she shakes her head, "we just can't give. It's frustrating sometimes."

"Yeah," Jex says, nodding her head. "I can see that. That's lame."

"Yes," Dr. Stephens says with a little chuckle. "It is pretty lame. I don't know the solution. We are just trying to do the best we can."

"Yeah," Jex says again. "You were really amazing in there."

"Jex," Dr. Stephens says, her smile growing wider. "You were the amazing one in there, really. The Awads seem reserved, maybe, but you should see how they usually are. They warmed up to you immediately. That's really very important for a doctor; you have to be able to establish a rapport. Some doctors are never able to do it. You really seem to be a natural."

Jex shakes her head. "I don't know. I was just being me. I feel like a stupid kid."

"Jex, you're anything but stupid. And, unfortunately for someone of your age, with what you've been through and what you've seen, you're anything but a kid. You should spend some more time being a kid."

Jex shrugs again and looks away. "I don't know," she murmurs.

"So, what's next for you," says Dr. Stephens, moving on, changing the subject a little bit. "Summer's here, what's the plan?"

"I'm not sure," says Jex. "I'm just going to take it easy, hang out a little bit. Working at the library, working here. If you ever need anybody to observe or participate in patient exams, let me know," saying the last words with a smile and twinkle in her eyes.

"Understood," Dr. Stephens responds with a wink.

"Other than that, I really don't know," Jex continues. "Try to figure things out?"

"And college?" Dr. Stephens pokes cautiously.

Jex shrugs again. "I don't know. Someday, probably. I just don't know when."

Dr. Stephens nods, but doesn't say anything of substance. She drinks her coffee. Jex drinks her tea. They speak of matters inconsequential; of matters of this and that. Time passes. Conversation, small talk, is enjoyed.

* * *

Jex walks out of the hospital. The sun is bright and shines into her eyes. She pulls her green neon rimmed gas station sunglasses from her bag and puts them on. She walks purposefully to her car, opens the door, turns the key. The engine turns over quickly and roars to life. The light vibration of the wheel feels good in Jex's hands. She smiles and looks out her windshield. The day is growing long but the sun is not quite ready to set. She takes a long swig of water out of a plastic bottle. The cold feels good in her mouth and throat. Even the memory of dryness seems painful. She can't help but smile as the blue sky bleeds lines of pink and yellow and white.

She notices a flyer on her windshield. It's for a protest in downtown LA over the weekend. Anti-poverty, anti-homelessness. She pockets it and plops it into her mental calendar. She rummages in her glove compartment and pulls out a pack of Camel Crushs. She lights one and takes a puff.

The little red Focus with all the bumper stickers pulls out of the parking space and onto Seventh Street, and then turns off onto Grand. Jex taps her fingers on the steering wheel as her favorite Spoonboy song starts to play. The music fills the space around her as she turns onto the freeway and she sings hoarsely along. She is headed home.

Here comes the future and you can't run from it.

Great mistake maker, chronic break taker, a risk taker.

Now it's a year later and I feel the weight of it.

I've got some scars from it, but I don't think on it.

And I've been doing fine.

Ana Gnorisis

Jex hears the resignation and irritation in the nurse's voice and momentarily considers telling him just to fuck off and walk away.

But this is triage and egos have to be left at the door. Jex is used to checking her ego. She grits her teeth and swallows deeply. After a moment, she begins to speak, in a clear, monotone, restrained tone that belies the fevered environment around her.

"Look," she says, her eyes piercing spears right through the nurse. "I know the leg is bad, that's obvious. That's clear. But that's all the triage team looked at. The original tourniquet was shit, but it was the right treatment for that leg, no doubt. But in all that commotion, they looked at the leg and they didn't dig any deeper."

"Yeah," the nurse says, his words doused in sarcasm. "That's what triage is. Hard to see anything that would lead to anything more urgent than the leg. And we have other injured people in this hospital that are more critical than this leg. "This tourniquet," the nurse says, pointing at the careful knots and placement of Jex's handy work, "will do for now, I don't know what the original one was like, but this one is fine."

"Thanks," Jex says without commenting further. "But you say that, but you don't know. Here," Jex says, and pulls Marcus' t-shirt up to his chest, revealing the bruising that marks most of the circumference between Marcus' last rib and upper thigh. She points at the bruising. "There," she jabs with her finger accusingly at the blue and purple blobs speckling Marcus' lower torso. "What about that?"

The nurse blinks and stares at the bruising, his mouth agape just a little bit. Jex continues. "And here," Jex says, gently picking up Marcus' left hand. "I'll just be a second, Marcus," she says to him as she does this. "I'm just going to squeeze your fingertips, just a little bit, ok?"

Marcus murmurs in a way that could not really be called assent, but was probably close enough to consent for the purpose at hand. She squeezes the fingertips. The tips turn white, but when Jex let's go, they do not quickly return to red. In fact, they almost don't turn back to red at all, just an off pink sort of color. "Delayed capillary refill," Jex states with certainty in her voice. "Almost absent for that matter."

"Hypovolemia," the nurse says quietly, not yet reacting to his own diagnosis.

"Yes," Jex says triumphantly. "Hypovelimic shock, for that matter. Stage 3, at least, maybe Stage 4. And that bruising, that's Grey Turner's sign, right?"

The nurse nods up and down in agreement. Jex does not hesitate. "There was a lot of blood on the ground where Marcus was lying, but not enough to take him past Stage 1 or Stage 2 of hypovolemia. But in all the chaos they forgot their basics and they have to remember 'blood on the floor plus four' – because of internal bleeding. When I tested his heart rate he was over a hundred beats a minute – looking at him now, it seems it's only getting worse. Delayed or absent capillary refill; Grey Turner's sign; sweating and confused. Probably in excess of thirty percent blood loss, maybe from retroperitoneal hemorrhage. Like an injury in the abdominal cavity, or something. Shit, why the hell do I keep talking and why are you not moving? There's a real risk of necrosis, right? His organs could be dying right now! What else do I fucking need to convince you this is a high priority critical fucking patient?"

The nurse blinks twice and then he gets it. His flush fills with blood and he is instantly red. "Nothing," he barks. "Let's go." The nurse stands and looks around. "Hey," he barks out to two EMTs who were jogging out of the hospital. They stop in their tracks. "Get that stretcher," the nurse says, pointing at a nearby ambulance. "Get this man prepped and find a doctor. He is T1, repeat T1."

Jex knows this is a serious ranking, Triage-1. Code red, in simple terms – immediate treatment needed. The two EMTs comply, with one speaking into a headphone connected to a walkie-talkie on her belt. Jex breathes a long sigh of relief and sits down next to Marcus as he is loaded onto the stretcher. Eugene, who had been completely stunned into silence watching Jex speak to the nurse, has now recovered enough to place his hand on her shoulder. She looks up and sees his smiling face, framed with the setting of the sun behind him. "You're good, Jex," he says. "Thank you for helping Molly's friend."

Jex looks around through the maddening frenzy around them. "Where is she," she asks.

Eugene points his finger at his truck. "She's chilling in my ride. The whole thing has been hard on her. I don't know what she would have done if you weren't there."

Jex shakes her head as she stands up, looking around at the craze of the crowd. There seems no rhyme or reason, no order or sense to it all.

"What the fuck is happening, right Jex?"

Jex pauses and then shrugs her shoulders. "All that suffering. I feel completely helpless."

Eugene lets out a sarcastic laugh. "Are you serious, Jex? You just saved that kid's life – and you probably saved Molly from having to up her klonopin dosage too much."

Jex smiles and shakes her head again, in a dark cloud already. "I didn't do anything."

Aw, come on, Jex," Eugene protests. "Don't be that way. You know …"

Eugene doesn't have the chance to finish his thought. The nurse has returned from helping to prep Marcus. It is clear he is in charge of this triage effort and the look on his face is a mixture of determination, anger and grief. "Hey," the nurse says loudly, interrupting Eugene in a way that is clear will not be followed by an apology or any other nicety. Eugene – who would typically not take too kindly to such a move – silently moves back. He knows this is not a time to beef about respect. "What's your name," he demands of Jex.

"My name is Jex. Jex Blackwell."

"You have medical training," the nurse says, in a statement not a question.

"No, not really," Jex says, "I'm just an intern at the hospital. I'm not certified or anything, I just help out."

"Well," the nurse says without hesitation. "You'll be helping us right now. This triage is overwhelmed and we need every body that has an inch of medical training. You have your own stethoscope," he says, pointing to the instrument hanging around Jex's neck. "You passed the interview. Come with me, there are two more ambulances about to arrive and I need some help."

Jex gulps but does not falter for even a second. She turns to Eugene and says, "I have to go help. Can you take care of Molly?"

"Yes, of course," Eugene says. "We're going to stick around for awhile. Let me know if you need anything, or a ride home or anything."

Jex pats him on the shoulder. "I think it's going to be a long night. You should take Molly home. I'll be OK. Thanks so much. You're a lifesaver."

Eugene smiles. "Ok, Jex. You have my number if you need anything. You know I'm always around. And I'm really proud of you. You're just incredible."

Jex smiles and the two hug awkwardly. Jex pulls away and points to the truck. "Now go take of Molly. She needs you."

Eugene smiles and says, "we all need somebody."

Jex smiles and pauses as though she is about to speak. Instead, she turns to follow the nurse. Eugene watches her go and, as she walks away, she says over her shoulder, "thanks again, Eugene."

"Thank you, Jex," Eugene shouts back as she disappears into the sea of injured, frightened and alone.

Four hours later, Jex is taking her first break from the rigors of the triage rotation, having deftly ditched, at least for a moment, the annoyingly overworked nurse that recruited her. She has her headphones in, listening to Elvis Depressedly. She smokes a Camel Crush and sips coffee from a Styrofoam cup with one hand, a Snickers bar in the other.

The day has been hectic so far and is nowhere near over. Jex has carried stretchers and wiped foreheads and dispensed of needles and changed plastic gloves too many times to count. She has seen bloodied faces and broken bones, crying eyes and dead bodies. The death toll was thirty-five last she heard, and almost certain to increase, with over a hundred injured. She hasn't taken the time to focus on who did this or why and she really doesn't care; or at least she doesn't take the time to measure whether she cares. She saw some people suffering, and she is trying to ease their pain.

She enjoys her coffee, nicotine and candy without doubting that in another ten minutes, she will be back in the thick of it.

She is looking out into the sky, lost in her thoughts, and so she is startled when she realizes that Dr. Cohen has walked up to her and is, with an odd air of some sort of stoic amusement, trying to get Jex's attention. As Jex takes her ear pods out, it occurs to her that Dr.

Cohen looks almost childlike in his gestures, cheerful almost, in a way that Jex has never seen him before.

"Hi, Dr. Cohen," Jex says with a start and a nervous smile. "I didn't see you here."

"Yes, well I suppose we have all been a bit busy today, haven't we? Not too busy to ingest carcinogens into our bodies though, are we?"

Momentarily forgetting the cigarette in her hand, Jex remembers it and jumps a little. In most other circumstances, this likely would have resulted in quite a talk. Today, Jex thinks on it for a moment and then just shrugs. "Yeah," she says with a stilted smile. "Whoops."

"Yes," Dr. Cohen smiles in return. "Whoops, indeed." He shrugs back and digs out a pack of Davidoffs. "I save these for only certain circumstances," and skillfully lights one with a sleek lighter that looks as though it cost a thousand dollars.

Jex chuckles and can only say, "whoa," before snickering some more and looking down at her shoe as she kicks a small rock.

"Yes, whoa," Dr. Cohen mimics. He leans and whispers conspiratorially. "But please, we mustn't tell Dr. Stephens. I would never hear the end of it."

Jex smiles. "Agreed," she says with a wink. Now the two share a secret. This is not something that Jex would have ever expected. The day is chock full of surreal twists.

Dr. Cohen takes a puff of his cigarette and looks around. "Hell of a day, isn't it?"

Jex nods her head. "Crazy."

Dr. Cohen stretches and allows a thin grin to appear on his face. "I quite hate to say it, but it's exhilarating, isn't it?"

Jex cocks her head. "Exhilarating?"

"Yes, indeed. I resisted admitting it for many years at the beginning of my career. I still don't talk about it in some company. But trauma surgery is exhilarating in a way that nothing else I have ever experienced. I'm a licensed pilot, did you know that?"

"No," Jex says, shaking her head as she watches Dr. Cohen's face intently. He is pure emotion, very much in a way that Jex had never seen in him before. There is a blaze in his eyes that Jex has never seen before.

"Yes, I fly a Glasair with aerobatic capabilities. I built it myself. Really. Everything except the engine. I have over four hundred aerobatic flight hours alone. I've done all sorts of maneuvers – loops, spins, stall turns, Cuban eights. Most things, really. And I'm a high-altitude climber. I summited on Mt. Kilimanjaro. I've even raised three children and managed to stay married for over twenty years," he says with a sardonic smile. "I've pushed my inner resources to the limit in all kinds of ways. Nothing compares to trauma surgery."

Jex nods her head and contemplates that. "You love it," she queries, knowing the answer but wanting to hear more.

"Love it," he says with a chuckle and a pause. "Yes,' he continues after a moment. "I think you can fairly say that I love it. More than anything else I have ever experienced, indeed. When I was a young man, I spent three years teaching math in the Bronx, back when it was really badly impoverished, in very bad shape. Did you know that about me?"

Jex shakes her head.

Dr. Cohen nods, looking out into space as though he is looking back in time. "Those were some of my best memories of my life – like I was really changing something. It's a big reason I decided to go into medicine. Because I felt I could make even more change, help more people, in medicine. The administration and rich old fools make the days slow going, making change, but in trauma medicine – you see change everyday."

The two of them smoke their cigarettes and drink their coffee. "What about you, Jex? I know you aspire to be a doctor. I've seen you with patients. You're a natural. Do you think you might enjoy taking on trauma surgery?"

The statement "You're a natural" knocks around in Jex's head as she considers a response. It is by far the nicest thing that she has ever heard Dr. Cohen say, and it is not lost on her. Despite that distraction, the question is actually an easy one for Jex to answer, as she has been thinking about it all day. She takes a long time to think about it, though, taking a drag and then putting it out on the bottom of her sneaker. She flicks the butt into a garbage can next to her.

"Have you ever read any Shakespeare, Dr. Cohen?"

Dr. Cohen smirks and says, "yes, I believe I am familiar with a play or two of his."

Jex smiles coyly. "I'm sure you are. Well, there's this concept Shakespeare used, it's called a recognition scene. Do you know it? It's actually from the Greeks, ancient greek – they called it anagnorisis. It was one of the first things I remember reading when I was a kid that was really, you know, intense. I had a hard time pronouncing it, anagnorisis. I eventually just did phonetics, and came up with the name Ana Gnorisis, you know Ana and Gnorisis. I even named one of my stuffed bears after it, a red one. Ana Gnorisis the Red Bear. My dad thought I was crazy."

Dr. Cohen smiles. "I am familiar with the concept of recognition scene, or anagnorisis. Such as when Othello realizes it is his own jealousy that led to the killing of Desdemona."

"Right," Jex says gleefully, her eyes on fire. "or in 'The Odyssey,' when Alcinous sends his minstrels to entertain the sad stranger with songs about the Trojan War, and it turns out to be Odysseus."

Dr. Cohen blinks and takes a moment to recall the literature. "Indeed," he says with an approving nod.

"It's like the point in a book when a character moves from ignorance to knowledge, right?"

Dr. Cohen continues to nod, smiling as he speaks. "Indeed," he says again.

"Yeah, that's kind of like how I feel today. Like my eyes were closed and now they're open. Like in *King Lear*, you know? When Gloucester gets his eyes plucked out, and only then can he see how the world goes? That's how today was. I always wanted to be a doctor, you know? I want to help people. Today, something changed. I was ignorant about something, about what helping someone really means, you know? I feel like today opened my eyes to something. Like trauma surgery is what I was meant to do? I didn't really see it until today – and now this is like, you know, my recognition scene."

Dr. Cohen nods his head and contemplates. "Yes. Well," he says with a note of mischief in his tone. "You know most recognition scenes end in tragedy, right?"

Jex smiles and nods. "Yeah, I know." And then she adds, in a tone that is as mischievous as Dr. Cohen's. "But not this one."

"Very good," Dr. Cohen says, a new note of, perhaps, respect, in his voice. "That is quite a complex analysis of Shakespearean and Greek literature, Jex."

She shrugs. "Thanks, Dr. Cohen," Jex says earnestly.

He shakes his head ruefully and looks out into the starry night.

"Maybe something good will come of today."

"Yeah," Jex says, her voice suddenly pensive, those little memories of nights under covers, reading thick collections of Greek mythology suddenly gone.

"Well," Dr. Cohen says, opening up his pack of cigarettes. "One more cancer stick and then back to the battle?"

Jex smiles. "Indeed," she says in a not-too-terrible impression of Dr. Cohen's own affects. He smiles just a little bit and lights Jex's cigarette for her. The two stand silently as they smoke, staring out into the dark galaxy above them.

* * *

The night once speckled with stars is now dark with gray clouds by the time Jex pulls into her driveway. She is exhausted and exhilarated at once. She pulls herself and her bag out of the car and walks from the driveway to the front door of her house. She grabs the mail out of the mailbox and turns the key. She walks in, shuts the door behind her and drops her bag onto the floor.

With just the foyer light on, she rummages through her mail and stops at a thick envelope. The return address is Stanford University. She stares at it for a moment and then walks to the kitchen. She pours herself a cup of water and then, leaving the mail, including the Stanford envelope, on the kitchen counter, walks out to the patio. She lights a cigarette and fiddles with her iPhone so that the music diverts to a small Bluetooth speaker she keeps on the small patio table. She picks a playlist called "evening tunes" and lights a cigarette. She stares up at the sky as Allo Darlin' begins to play, singing about juicy fruit and Joan Didion.

"I saw you in the car park, reading Joan Didion in the dark.

It's easy to see where things begin, it is harder to see where they end. And nothing feels the way it did before, and I am grateful for that."

She smokes one more cigarette and listens to three more songs (by Inky Skulls, King Everything and Mal Blum). She sighs and stands up, stretching a long time, touching her toes and extending her arms as high as they will go. "Erch," she mumbles. She walks to the couch and collapses lazily onto it. Another song by Mal Blum plays as Jex's eyes close shut. The music is like medicine to Jex and it does not take long before she is passed out asleep, a kind of restful sleep that is something almost foreign to Jex.

Jex wakes up three hours later. She looks groggily at her iPhone and sees it is almost three a.m. She has three voicemails, and still laying down she presses play. A moment later the messages play.

12:15 a.m.:"Hi, Jexy, it's Eugene. I'm just calling to see how you're doing, if you made it back from the hospital. What a crazy day. You were really incredible. I'm with Molly at our Aunt's house in Glendale. Give me a call, you should come over breakfast. Everyone wants to see you. Call me soon."

1:15 a.m.: "Hi Jex, it's Dr. Stephens. I heard you and Dr. Cohen had quite a conversation at the hospital today. You must have said something very smart as you seem to have impressed him. He sounds positively giddy, silly old man. Anyways, I am sure it was a tough day, and I would really like to catch up. Please give me a ring when you can. I'd love to talk. Take care, Jex."

2:52 a.m.: "Yo Jex, Q here. I'm on the bus to Venice, downtown is nuts but Imma wanting to do some taggin'. Wanna see you, boo. I'll be under the pier by 4, leaves a couple hours before sunrise – stop by. I wanna see your ass – heard you fucking saved that drummer's life. You the shit, girl. Call me bae. Or just meet me at the pier. Love you."

Jex groggily stands up and walks to the kitchen. She pulls out some coffee beans and her French press. Seven minutes later she is drinking fresh, hot black coffee. She blinks several times and walks to the hallway. She stops in front of the full length mirror in the foyer and stares at herself. She feels a little healthier. The roller coaster ride is long, but she's made it OK so far.

She takes a long, slow sip of coffee and walks back to the kitchen, to the pile of mail on the kitchen counter. Picking up the envelope from Stanford, she lets out a deep sigh, somewhere between confusion and frustration. Placing the coffee mug on the counter, she rips open the envelope without ceremony and pulls out the cover sheet. She is accepted to Stanford University.

Jex rubs her face a long time and then picks up the coffee cup. She takes another sip and rubs her face again. "Shit," she says. She sits down on the cold kitchen floor and does nothing for a long time. Just sits there, thinking.

After a long while, she stands up again, finishes her cup of coffee and pours the rest of the coffee from the French press into the mug. She cleans the spoon she used, and a couple of other dishes that were also in the sink. She picks up the French press, which has no coffee in it anymore, just the grinds collected on the bottom, which Jex stares at for a while.

Jex walks over to Stanford's cover letter and picks it up, along with the thick envelope and its contents of supporting documents, class options, financial aid issues. She walks over to the garbage can, opens it with her foot and drops the cover letter and envelope in unceremoniously. Without a second thought, she takes the French press and empties the coffee grinds into the garbage can, drenching the envelope and cover letter in dark, soggy water.

"Maybe next year," she murmurs, smiling to herself. "I have some other stuff to do first."

Jex grabs her keys and throws her messenger bag over her shoulder. She walks out the front door into the dark night, coffee still in hand. The moon is bright above. Stars twinkle. Her eyes, too. She opens the car door and gets in. She backs up and begins to drive west, towards the ocean. Not to Venice to meet up with Q, though; maybe somewhere up in Malibu. She knows a bridge that no one ever goes to up there, and could use some dope art. Tagging sounds good but, tonight at least, she wants to be alone. She pops in a CD and the music begins to play. She can't help but look again at the stars above her, and the road in front of her. The stars and the road – they seem to go on forever.

ANA GNORISIS: DIAGNOSIS

Appendix

College Application Essay

Applicant: Jex Blackwell

Essay Topic: Discuss an accomplishment or event, formal or informal, that marked your transition from childhood to adulthood within your culture, community, or family.

Essay Title: Jex Blackwell Saves the World.

My name is Jex Blackwell and I am going to save the world. I am going to cure all the sick people, alleviate the pain of the suffering and comfort the dying. I am going to banish cancer and extend life expectancies by a hundred years. AIDS and Zika and Ebola – all will be in our rearview mirror.

OK, my name isn't Jex Blackwell and I probably won't save the world. I was born Debbie Gibson – not the pop diva; just a dumb L.A. kid – a few months before some airplanes hit the Twin Towers in New York. I can't say that tragedy, or any other tragedy, made me want to become a doctor. I only know that I wanted to be a doctor since I can remember. I can't say why. It's just always been there.

Tragedy is a funny word and people use it to mean a lot of things. September 11, that's a good example. Not many people would debate that qualifies as a tragedy. But I don't even remember it happening. I was in diapers at the time. All I know is the endless war ever since – my entire life. That's a tragedy, too.

Some people would say that I have seen my share of personal tragedies. My father died when I was eleven years old. Cancer. My mom died two years later. Drugs. I lived with my uncle for a while; he is nice enough. He is gone now, too. So, last year, I became emancipated. I'm a free girl. I'm all on my own. And even though I'm young, I've lived a lot in these few years. Sometimes in places I wasn't wanted. Sometimes in places I didn't want to be. Sometimes on the Streets. I headed down some scary avenues, literally and metaphorically. I hope I have seen the last of those dark roads. Maybe I have and maybe I haven't. I try not to think much about it.

And since my emancipation – which is a funny word, too, because what is it, really? – I have seen other people's tragedy. I spend a lot of time at the County Hospital in downtown Los Angeles, where I volunteer as an assistant, cleaning and organizing; the grunt work. I see a lot of tragedy there. I spend the rest of my time shelving books for minimum wage at the Central Library not far from the County Hospital. Sometimes, I just walk around downtown late into the evening, thinking. I see a lot of tragedy there, too. Mothers losing children; kids losing parents; families losing their home; all clinging to dignity in the face of blunt tragedy. Not a lot of freedom. Not a lot of emancipated people. A lot of people in pain. A lot of loss. A lot of nameless heroes. Hero is another funny word.

Sophia Jex-Blake is a hero, to me at least. She is a nineteenth century feminist who helped establish the first medical school in Britain that was chartered especially for women. She became the first female doctor in Edinburgh and fought her life not only to ease the pain of those suffering, but also for the rights of women to practice in medicine. These struggles were not easy, I learned from Ms. Jex-Blake's writings. But I learned, too, that in Ms. Jex-Blake's words, "we do well to struggle against that weary powerless feeling, because, given way to, it might overcome all power of energy." Sounds wise enough to me. I pledge to struggle always against that weary powerless feeling. Despite the tragedies. Despite the namelessness of heroes.

Elizabeth Blackwell was the first woman to graduate medical school in the United States. She is another hero of mine, whatever that word means. Maybe someday I will know. Ms. Blackwell devoted her life to learning and to teaching; to healing who she could and showing no fear as a woman in the field of medicine. As to her quest for this knowledge and the skill sets of a doctor, she said: "the idea of winning a doctor's degree gradually assumed the aspect of a great moral struggle, and the moral fight possessed immense attraction for me." This moral fight that Ms. Blackwell describes – any moral fight, really – possesses immense attraction for me.

So, soon after my emancipation – in a dark, dingy, tiny government office near Disney Hall in downtown Los Angeles – for a fifty-dollar fee, a long application form, and a nod from an old white man in a robe, I left Debbie Gibson far behind me. I formally started anew. I became Jex Blackwell, a combination of two heroes; maybe just enough to duct tape together some hope. With that, I am on my quest, a moral fight. I seek any moral fight, as tragic and nameless as it may be. I am a fighter. I am a hero. Some may say I suffer delusions of grandeur. To them, I quote Cervantes' Don Quixote: "obviously you don't know much about adventure."

Now, with the past behind me and the future ahead, Stanford asks me not about my moral fight and not about the struggle against the weary powerless feeling; but, rather, what event marks my transition from "childhood" to "adulthood." Emancipation? Lost family? Changing my name? Disease? Suffering? The Street? Tragedy? Heroism? I must admit, I am not sure what any of these things mean. Maybe I'm not very smart. Maybe I just don't care. I don't know. Am I going to cure all the sick people? Will I alleviate the pain of the suffering? Will I comfort the dying? Am I going to banish cancer? Or Zika? Or Ebola? I don't know.

But in the face of all this tragedy and all this uncertainty, I know I have decided to never stop trying. And maybe, just maybe, that decision marks my transition from childhood to adulthood. You don't think so? "Obviously you don't know much about adventure."

Because my name really is Jex Blackwell. And I really am going to save the world.

ANARCHY ISN'T JUST A FANNY PACK WITH A CIRCLE-A ON IT

By: Bawdy DySmurfia

Anarchy! Anarchy!

Direct action! it's the time!

Anarchy! Anarchy!

Always gaining traction! Crossing every line!

Anarchy! Anarchy!

Moving forward! Never backwards!

Anarchy! Anarchy!

Grooving towards you! Bearing swords!

Because anarchy isn't just a fanny pack

With a Circle-A On it.

Not your Walmart Guy Fawkes mask.

We don't need your poseur scene.

We will tear down those goddamn barricades

And show you what we mean.

Anarchy! Anarchy!

Direct action! it's the time!

Anarchy! Anarchy!

You are jackshit! Stop the lying!

Anarchy! Anarchy!

Moving forward! Never backwards!

Anarchy! Anarchy!

Across the world! Across the world!

Because anarchy isn't just a fanny pack

With a Circle-A On It.

Not your Walmart Guy Fawkes mask.

We don't want your bullshit scene.

We will maneuver through all their defenses.

You will know we really mean it.

Anarchy! Anarchy! Fanny pack! Fanny pack!

Anarchy! Anarchy! Fanny pack! Fanny pack!

Screw your Walmart Guy Fawkes mask.

About P. William Grimm

P. William Grimm is an American writer and filmmaker currently living in London, England. He has previously released two novels, *The Seventh* and *Counselor*, as well as two collections of short stories, *Valencia Street* and *Sick Sense of Hubris*. His short stories have been published online in renowned blogs such as "HTMLGiant" and "Eclectica Magazine." He has also written and directed several short films including the award-winning *Valentine's Day*, as well as *Arrivals --> Departures* and *American Spy in Europe*. Educated at Boston University, Grimm's influences as a writer include Kurt Vonnegut, Joan Didion, Charles Bukowski, Raymond Chandler and Dashiell Hammett. He also digs Encyclopedia Brown and the Three Investigators.

www.ingramcontent.com/pod-product-compliance
Lightning Source LLC
Chambersburg PA
CBHW031945010726

47493CB00007B/2080